Published by Stormy Night Publications and Design, LLC.
Blake, Zoe
Hensley, Alta
Reluctantly His

Digital Cover Graphics: Korey Mae Johnson
Photographer: Emma Jane
Model: David Wills
Original Custom Paperback Illustration: Yozart
Paperback Graphics: Deranged Doctor

INTRODUCING

**The sinfully decadent dream project
of best friends and USA TODAY Bestselling authors,
Zoe Blake and Alta Hensley.**

Alta Hensley, renowned for her hot, dark, and dirty romances, showcases her distinctive blend of alpha heroes, captivating love stories, and scorching eroticism.

Meanwhile, Zoe Blake brings a touch of darkness and glamour to the series, featuring her signature style of possessive billionaires, taboo scenes, and unexpected twists.

Together they combine their storytelling prowess to deliver "Twice the Darkness," promising sordid scandals, hidden secrets, and forbidden desires of New York's jaded high society in their new series,
Gilded Decadence.

RELUCTANTLY HIS

A DARK BILLIONAIRE ROMANCE

GILDED DECADENCE SERIES
BOOK FOUR

ZOE BLAKE

ALTA HENSLEY

THE GILDED DECADENCE SERIES

A seductively dark tale of privilege and passion.

Ripping off the gilded veneer of elite privilege exposes the sordid scandals, dark secrets, and taboo desires of New York's jaded high society. Where the corrupt game is a seductive power struggle of old money, social prestige, and fragile fortunes... only the most ruthless survive.

Ruthlessly His
Book One
#arrangedmarriage

Savagely His
Book Two
#kidnapped/capture

Brutally His
Book Three
#officeromance

Reluctantly His
Book Four
#bodyguard

Unwillingly His
Book Five
#agegap

CHAPTER 1

CHARLOTTE

*W*ithout warning, I was snatched from behind and roughly pulled against a hard male body.

"Where do you think you're going?" growled my father's head of security, like a junkyard dog deprived of a bone.

Still reeling from my father's demand that I now be followed around like a child, the last thing I wanted was to deal with anyone.

With my chin raised and my face averted, I wrenched my shoulder, trying to break the guard dog's tight grasp. It didn't work.

I swallowed past the lump in my throat and responded tightly, "Kindly unhand me, Mr. Taylor. I'd like to leave."

Closing my eyes, I envisioned the *legato* notes of Saint-Saëns' *The Swan* to control my breathing and remain calm. Although I used the technique in cello practice, it had become a necessary tool of survival as a daughter in the Manwarring family.

In this family, I wasn't a beloved daughter or sister.

I was a pawn.

An asset.

No different than a pile of stock certificates to be bought and traded to the highest bidder.

An object.

And apparently, like any object of value, I now needed to be guarded.

His hand shifted to caress the sensitive skin of my inner arm, just under the lace edge of my chiffon puff sleeve. "It's either Sergeant Taylor, Sergeant—or if I'm pulling your hair, Reid—but never Mr. Taylor."

Shocked by the subtle yet intimate gesture and his bold comment, I raised my face to his and gasped at the intensity of his dark gaze.

This was the closest I had ever been to him, to any man really.

Wealthy daughters of billionaire families might as well be displayed behind glass.

Always seen, never touched.

Pretty dolls to be admired for their silent obedience.

Recovering, my tongue flicked out to wet my dry lips. "If you are trying to get a reaction out of me, *Sergeant Taylor*, you are wasting your time."

The constant pressure on generations of Manwarring women, to know their place and never say or do anything to embarrass the family, had turned me into the perfect diamond. Something bright and shiny with no more emotions than a piece of stone.

His head pivoted to scan the empty corridor before he tightened his hold on my arm and swung us in an arc until we were secluded from view in the darkened alcove which housed a tall, bronze sculpture of a naked couple in a sensual embrace.

My heart raced as panic made me light-headed. Or was it his nearness?

Either way, I knew my father was only steps away in his office.

As I was the last remaining *obedient* sibling, it had been made clear to me he would not tolerate even the slightest break in propriety.

Not after what Olivia had done.

And certainly not after the scandal my brother had caused.

Reid braced his forearm over my head. "What's the matter, princess? Are my dirty, lower-class hands too rough for your soft, blue blood skin?"

His comment brought my focus back to the warm, rough sensation of his hands on me. A shiver ran up my spine.

This was wrong. Really wrong.

By breathing intensified.

Princess.

Of course he'd call me a princess. I had heard it all: princess, snow queen, duchess, spoiled bitch. There was no point in complaining or explaining. No one wanted to hear the problems of the poor little rich girl.

Not that I blamed them.

Restrained masculine power radiated off him like heat.

I was used to being surrounded by men with power, but this was different. With those men, their power came from paper. Arbitrary figures plucked from thin air.

Sergeant's power was primal. The kind that came from heavy muscle, an iron will, and the arrogance of knowing you could break a man's neck with your bare hands.

I needed to break free from this man before we were caught together.

Rising on my toes, I strained to look over his shoulder to make sure we weren't observed by the servants. "I won't dignify that with a response. You have no right to cross the line with me. Now move aside."

He leaned in close until his breath warmed my cheek as he chuckled, the sound a dark vibration emanating from deep inside his chest. "If you think this is crossing the line, I can't wait to see your reaction when I—"

My eyes widened as I flattened my palms against his chest and pushed. "Sergeant Taylor, not another word! Let me go!"

Agitation made my voice a high-pitched whisper as I strained to keep it low.

The entire household was on edge after Eddie's kidnapping. The slightest sound of a commotion would bring everyone running.

My cheeks burned at the idea of being found in such a compromising position. To any observer, it would look like we were caught in a lover's embrace.

My father and brother would not have the patience to listen to my excuses. They would assume the worst and lock me in my room until I was thirty.

The small freedoms I currently cherished would be yanked away from me.

Oh, hell.

I really needed to get away from this man. Now.

My fingers splayed across his chest. His skin was so warm beneath the soft, worn fabric of his black t-shirt. I inhaled deeply, and the leather and cardamon scent of his cologne was an unholy aphrodisiac.

This was bad. Really bad.

He didn't budge as his gaze focused on my mouth. "I can't do that."

The breath seized in my lungs. My lips tingled as if he had physically touched them.

Knowing I would deeply regret it, I asked, "Why not?"

The corner of his mouth curled up in a wolfish grin. "Because I'm your new bodyguard."

CHAPTER 2

REID

*M*y objective was simple.

Scare the pretty, pampered princess into running back to daddy and demanding a new bodyguard.

That I had even been approached with this assignment was an insult.

Unfortunately, the Manwarrings weren't used to hearing the word no.

And while I agreed that their precious *commodity* needed to be guarded after recent events, I objected to their insistence that it be *me*.

I had plenty of trained men on my staff who could have taken on the arduous task, but no… they wanted the best.

Only the best for their precious princess.

Fuck my life.

I didn't have time to be a goddamn babysitter.

The Irish mob were not going to just give up their lucrative business interests and territories.

It was only a matter of time before they struck again, and I needed to be ready for it. It wasn't only my job, but my reputation on the line.

If something were to happen on my watch, while I was holding up a wall waiting on princess here to finish shopping or brunching or whatever the fuck she did with her empty days, I would be pissed as hell.

Her chocolate brown eyes blinked up at me.

No, not chocolate, that was probably too common for her.

Her silky, mink brown eyes.

"*You?* They made *you* my bodyguard?"

I pressed the tip of my tongue against the sharp point of one of my canine teeth, the small bite of pain a reminder to control my response.

Stick to the plan.

This is what I wanted.

Still...

My gaze narrowed as I pressed my hips into hers, pushing her more firmly against the wall. "Do you have a problem with that? Is my ten years of advanced military training by the United States Marine Corps not good enough for you?"

Pride. It was just stupid, arrogant pride.

Her lower lip trembled as her big, beautiful eyes misted. "Please. I didn't say that. It's just—"

Cupping her cheek, I ran my thumb over her lip, having an insane impulse to feel the delicate vibrations against my skin. My cock lengthened. Would I feel the same subtle tremble along my shaft?

"Say that again," I ordered.

The skin between her perfectly arched brows wrinkled as she tried to twist her face to the side. "Say what?"

I tightened my grip on her face. "Please. I want to hear you say that word again."

Like the word 'no', I didn't think the word 'please' was in any Manwarring's vocabulary, but it wasn't just that.

With her staring up at me as her hands pressed against my chest, looking vulnerable while desperately trying to hide the fact that my presence intimidated and scared her, the word took on a sensual, erotic meaning. I could just picture her on her knees before me.

Begging me with her gorgeous full lips. *Please, please, please.*
Christ.

My cock hardened further.

Her eyes widened, leaving little doubt she felt the urgent press of my rigid shaft against her abdomen.

Her lips opened. Her hesitant breath caressed my skin as I kept my thumb pressed against her lips. Still, no sound came out.

Suddenly, the single most important thing in my life became getting her to bend to my will, even in this small way. "Say it, princess. Say please."

Beg me.

Her throat contracted as she swallowed. "Please."

Air hissed through my clenched teeth as I pushed the tip of my thumb inside her warm, wet mouth. "Say it again."

Her cool fingers clasped around my wrist as she whimpered.

"Say it again," I repeated more forcefully.

The sweep of her tongue against my thumb almost sent me over the edge as she rasped, "Please."

I leaned my forehead against hers as I pulled her breath into my lungs. My free hand pushed into the soft waves of her hair as I anchored her head within my grasp. I thrust my thumb deeper into her mouth. "Suck it."

Pale pink manicured nails pressed crescents into my wrists as she squirmed within my embrace, trying to dislodge my hand.

It wasn't going to happen.

Although still my plan, my intent had changed.

Over the course of my duties, I had often noticed her.

Watched her.

It would have been impossible not to.

She was just so beautiful, but it was a distant, fragile beauty.

As if she were a porcelain figurine too delicate and expensive to touch.

But now, her warm, soft body was pressed against mine.

Finally.

And I was finding it difficult to keep my baser instincts in check. It was taking all my disciplined training not to flip her around, press her against the wall, and pound into her from behind like a fucking animal.

Especially as I watched those full lips pursed around my thumb as she obediently sucked it.

Fuck me.

This was my boss' precious daughter. His *innocent*, precious daughter.

Men like Lucian Manwarring didn't fool me.

I'd seen it countless times in the upper ranks of the Marines. Officers who were brutally unfeeling and ruthless when it came to the training of the men below them, but who wouldn't hesitate to take a bullet for those same men.

A leader needed to be cold and calculating to protect the unit.

Surviving in the upper echelons of corporate America and among the high society families of New York City was a daily war.

And while the consequences may not be deadly, there were still casualties, like not being the ideal father. I knew that from personal experience, which was why I saw right through Lucian.

I had been hired to guard the protective wall he had built around his daughter... not to tear it down.

Still... I was only a man.

With a guttural moan, I pulled my thumb from her mouth and grasped her jaw, forcing her head back. My lips lowered... stopping barely a breath away from touching her.

Instinctively, I knew if I kissed her... it would be game over.

Her body trembled.

I pressed into her more deeply as my gaze fixated on her closed eyes. The thin skin of her eyelids gave the rapid movement of her eyes beneath them away.

It would be so easy.

Just a taste.

Just a small lick to see if she tasted as sweet as in my fantasies.

The distant murmur of voices, carried as a faint echo down the expansive hallway, broke the spell.

Curling my hands into fists, I launched myself backwards until I was a respectable distance from her.

Charlotte swayed at the sudden loss of my body pushed against her own.

My arm rose, ready to catch her.

Her thick eyelashes fluttered as she opened her eyes. For just the barest of seconds, she stared back at me through an unfocused haze of burgeoning awareness.

Then she slipped behind her father's protective wall.

The color rose on her cheeks as she swiped the back of her hand over her lips as if to wipe the taste of my skin away.

Possessive anger came to life from deep inside my chest. I had to fight the impulse to grab her hair and force her to her knees as I reached for the zipper of my pants, almost overwhelmed by the driving need to imprint my taste, my scent, my mark on her.

With her chin tilted up, she stepped out of the traitorous alcove shadows, back into the glaring light. "Obviously, this is not going to work. I'll ask my father to assign someone else as my bodyguard."

Objective achieved.

My plan had worked.

Which was why what I did next made absolutely no sense.

CHAPTER 3

CHARLOTTE

"*N*ice try, princess. You're stuck with me."

I clutched the pearls at my throat.

To have this man following me around, always standing close by—*watching over me*—would be a disaster. My upbringing had not equipped me with the skills needed to keep a guard dog like Sergeant Reid Taylor on a leash.

I desperately wished that wasn't true. I had plenty of friends who reveled in their feminine power over men, who loved flirting and taunting and keeping them dancing at the end of their fingertips, but I was most definitely not one of them.

Even the very idea has me practically breaking out in hives.

It was a truth universally acknowledged that some women were Elizabeth Bennett and others were her misunderstood and overlooked middle sister, Mary.

Substitute the cello for the piano, and I was the perfect fit. Poor, plain Mary.

And everyone knew, the Marys in this life didn't end up with the handsome and powerful Mr. Darcys.

"Please don't call me princess."

His silver, wolf-like eyes widened, then narrowed as he took a step toward me.

With a hot, humiliating rush of blood to my cheeks and throat, I realized my mistake.

Please.

Oh, hell. I'd said please.

I'd never be able to use that word again. Ever. Without thinking about him… and his… his thumb in my… mouth!

Laughter cut through the tension as a group of servants approached ever closer to where we stood, no doubt heading upstairs to right the bedrooms for the day.

I licked my lips. "Mr. Taylor."

"Reid," he corrected, his gaze on my mouth.

With my hand covering my lips, I mumbled. "*Sergeant Taylor,* you said yourself that you are overqualified for the task. Surely you must realize how unsuitable this arrangement would be for both of us."

His mouth lifted at the corners again in that infuriating wolf-like grin. "I disagree. And don't call me Shirley."

I shook my head, confused. "I didn't call you Shirley. I said *surely.*"

With his hands on his hips, he tilted his head back and laughed. "It's from *Airplane.*"

"Airplane? I'm sorry, I have no idea what you're talking about. I don't have any trips planned."

He glanced past my shoulder as the three women came within view.

Out of the corner of my eye, I caught their curious glances. I wanted to turn and boldly stare them down… but didn't.

With hushed whispers, they pivoted and made their way up the wide marble and mahogany staircase.

Sergeant Taylor kept his face averted, watching them even as he stepped closer to me.

When they were out of view, he turned his full attention back to me. Reaching out, he lifted my chin with his finger. "You're adorable. It's from a movie."

"Oh," I answered lamely, unnerved by his close proximity and the reminder of how boring and awkward I was. *Just call me Mary.*

"Here's what's going to happen. You're going to be a good little girl and go write out your daily schedule for the next week for me. Your father didn't seem to know it."

I resisted the urge to roll my eyes. The very idea of my father taking an interest in my cello lessons and charity events was absurd. My mouth opened to object.

He raised an eyebrow. "*Eh. Eh. Eh.* No objections. Whether you realize it or not, your father is only trying to protect you."

I huffed as I pulled my face out of his grasp. As I waved my hand in front of me, I said, "Fine, but does it have to be *you?*"

My eyes widened as I slapped my hand over my mouth.

Never in my life had I been so forward as to *actually say* what was in my head.

Alarm bells rang in my ears.

I had to get away from this man.

He chuckled. "I don't need to tell you that your father always demands the best." He then leaned in close, his lips almost brushing mine. "And I'm the best, princess."

The long hem of my gown tripped me up as I stumbled backwards in my haste to get away from him. There was no mistaking the sensual, double entendre to his words. "Please... I mean... not please.... I mean..."

Oh, hell.

His hand wrapped around my upper arm again, holding me steady. "Shhh, babygirl. Everything's going to be fine. As long as you obey my rules."

"Rules?"

"Actually just one rule. You never—ever—exit this house without me by your side. Understood?"

Sliding behind the comforting shelter of propriety, I whispered, "It's not appropriate for you to call me babygirl."

"You're absolutely right. It's not appropriate."

His thumb swept over my skin in an intimate, daring caress—deliberately crossing the line.

I shook off his hold and backed up. "I have to go."

"Where?"

My splintered mind scrambled to come up with a lie. "Just upstairs. To my bedroom."

There it was again, that flare of white-hot awareness in the silvery depths of his eyes.

Was *everything* a double entendre with this man?

His hot gaze moved over me. "Perhaps I should accompany you?"

"No!" I cleared my throat. "You said yourself I would only need your services outside the house."

He tilted his head to the side as his hands moved to his hips.

Without volition, my gaze moved over his chest, then lower, catching a glimpse of the rigid bulge in his pants.

Oh. My. God.

He followed my gaze, then grinned. "Actually, my *services* would be available to you at anytime… and anywhere."

Dammmmiiitttt. Another double entendre. It was as if we were sparring with double-edged swords, and I was losing.

My back hit the newel post. "That won't be necessary." I then turned and scurried up the stairs.

He called after me, "Don't forget, princess. Not one foot outside this house without me."

CHAPTER 4

CHARLOTTE

*I*gnoring the suggestive giggles of the servants, I ran past them into my bedroom.

After slamming my door shut, I leaned against it with a hand over my heart.

It took several minutes for my breathing to even out.

What had just happened?

Already, my mind was rebelling against the facts.

No. He did not just almost kiss me.

No. He did not suggest he wanted to take it further.

No. He did not just imply he was remaining my bodyguard because he wanted me.

I closed my eyes as I pressed the back of my head against the hard wood paneled door.

Why couldn't I have thought of some sassy comeback to put him in his place?

I groaned.

I already knew why.

Because I was Mary, not Elizabeth.

I rubbed my neck, missing the comforting weight of my cello

pressing against my shoulder. Whenever I was stressed, sad, or lonely, I reached for my cello.

Crossing past my Colonial-style bed with its obnoxiously girly, frilled lace canopy, I reached for my cello. My fingertips grazed over the cool, smooth surface with reverence.

It was a Stradivarius, one of only eighty made by Antonio Stradivari himself.

It had been a wedding gift from my father to my mother.

The knowledge that my birth had killed the woman he loved had always hung between my father and me like an obsessive fog.

When I first found her beloved instrument in the attic, I had thought that maybe it would bring us closer if I learned to play it.

The memory of the pained expression on his face when, as a child, I *surprised* him with an impromptu concert of *Mary Had a Little Lamb* was forever imprinted on my soul.

As I foolishly beamed up at him, holding my breath, waiting for a kind word, he had stood and silently left the room.

I'd been crushed.

That was the first and last time I had ever played for him.

It was Luc and Olivia who'd convinced me to keep playing. Luc had even swiped my father's credit card to set up online lessons for me.

Every month that passed, I'd expected my father to notice the charge and cancel them.

But he never did.

And while, after I'd graduated from college, he'd adamantly refused to allow me to pursue a professional career in music, he hadn't objected to me joining an informal string quartet who played at children's hospitals, nursing homes, and charity events.

As long as I got to play, I didn't care.

My siblings often came to hear me.

My father never did.

My middle finger ran down the ridged metal D string.

Despite his objections, I had shown just enough courage to continue pursing my love of music and playing. Eventually, he had gotten over it and let me be.

Maybe my father would do the same with this horrible idea of me needing a bodyguard.

I mean, really? Who was going to seriously try and kidnap me?

Marksen had kidnapped Olivia to get back at Luc.

Those horrible criminals had kidnapped Eddie to intimidate Harrison, my new brother-in-law.

No one had any such designs on me. I wasn't the subject of any man's obsession.

Men barely noticed me.

Well, at least most men.

Giving myself a mental shake, I focused. I wouldn't allow myself to act like some silly schoolgirl who naively believed a boy liked her just because he'd tried to steal a kiss. I wasn't living in a stupid *Nancy Drew* novel!

With a huff, I lugged my hard cello case out from under my bed and carefully placed my prized instrument inside.

I had a rehearsal to get to.

I would simply sneak out through the servant's entrance.

Father and Sergeant Taylor would be mad at first, but then they'd probably just shrug their shoulders and assume it was for the best to just leave me be.

Just like Father had with my cello playing all those years ago.

It was a good plan.

This was totally going to work.

It had to.

Lifting my case up onto its wheels, I tiptoed to my door and pressed my ear to it.

I wasn't sure it was possible to hear much through the solid wood, but at least all was quiet.

Just in case, I shifted down to my knees and peeked under the door to see if I spied a pair of heavy black boots.

Nothing.

Cracking the door open, I paused.

Still nothing.

I willed myself to open the door further but remained frozen.

A deep breath calmed my nerves. I didn't have time to hesitate.

One of the members of the quartet had managed to score the Bruno Walter Auditorium at the Library of Performing Arts, and I was due there in forty-five minutes.

If I was going, it had to be now, especially since I wouldn't be able to use a Manwarring driver. To call down for one would just alert Reid.

My stomach clenched at the very thought of him hovering over my practice, making the rest of the members uncomfortable.

I was still new to this group. My family name and wealth had already proved a pretty significant obstacle that I was having trouble overcoming.

After wiping my sweaty palm on my dress, I gripped the handle of my cello case and moved into the hall.

My heart thundered in 5/4 time to the Mission Impossible theme as I checked the corners before scurrying to the back servants' stairs and halls that led away from my third story bedroom to the caterer's kitchen, then out the back door.

I stayed just off the main drive as I made my way to 5th Avenue, refusing to stop and order an Uber until I was sure I was out of sight of the main house and no one had followed me.

I made it to the Performing Arts Library with only ten

minutes to spare, the Mission Impossible theme still playing in my head.

My friend Virginia, Ginnie for short, greeted me as she blew a strawberry-scented cloud of vape smoke in my direction. "Cutting it a little close, aren't you, silver spoon?"

"Just help me with this, debutant darling," I said, using one of our many teasing nicknames for one another. As a fellow High Society daughter, although she hated to admit it, she was my one true friend in the quartet.

She moved down the cement stairs and grabbed the other end of my cello case to help me drag it into the building.

Ginnie was the only daughter of the elite Kristiansens from Bridgeport. Her family was almost worth as much as mine. Although unlike me, she had no problem rebelling against everything they stood for, starting with her multiple piercings and ever-changing brightly colored hair, and ending with preferring Ginnie just to annoy her pretentious parents. "Like the booze," she had said with a wink the day we met as she shook my hand.

"Just to warn you, Ian is having an absolute shit fit over the piece today."

I groaned. We were practicing Dmitri Shostakovich's *String Quartet No. 8*, a notoriously complicated piece.

As she held the door open, she mimicked Ian's nasal voice. "Ladies, we must have a cohesive musical narrative! You are not maintaining clarity and unity through the melody. *Tut. Tut. Tut.*"

Although I was not looking forward to Ian's scolding, the brooding yet frenetic piece suited my mood.

As we made our way into the auditorium, I repeatedly glanced over my shoulder.

Ginnie followed my gaze. "Are you expecting someone?"

I grimaced. "Ask me that in a few minutes."

So far, I had seen no sign of Reid. And since this wasn't our usual rehearsal space, there was no reason to believe he could track me here.

After about five minutes, I finally let myself relax, my eyes sliding closed as I took a relieved breath. I kept my eyes closed and started the breathing exercises that I did before every rehearsal or performance, focusing on the feeling of my own breath filling my lungs and then holding one, two, three, then slowly letting the breath out through my nose.

I took another deep breath in through my mouth, holding one, two, three, then slowly released. I had already memorized the piece that we were working on today. I wasn't sure if the others really cared about being off book, but I preferred it. Not having to focus on the printed sheet music allowed me to feel the music, to experience it the way it was meant to be experienced.

After one final glance over the empty seats, searching for an angry, over six-foot-tall ex-Marine, I decided to focus and start warming up.

The others were busy in the green room grabbing coffees and chatting as they gossiped about this and that.

Taking advantage of being alone on the stage, on a whim I decided to play something I had composed myself. A simple melody that I hadn't played for anyone. I hadn't even given it a name. I wouldn't even say it was my first attempt at composition since I'd never written it down.

It was never intended to be played for anything. It was just the melody that I felt in my soul. Sometimes it was uplifting. It was even hopeful, but more often than not, the sound was melancholic, slow, deep, and lonely.

Whenever I played this piece, it just made me feel in control when so much of my world was utterly devoid of life and choice.

As my bow slid across the final note and I let it drop to my side, barely hanging from my fingertips, a slow clap started around the auditorium.

I opened my eyes to find the other three members of my quartet giving me a standing ovation. I hadn't even heard them come in. A blush colored my cheeks as I waved them off. "Stop. It was nothing. Just something silly I like to play sometimes."

Ginnie took her seat as she picked up her cello. Using her bow to gesture to me, she said, "Knock it off, silver spoon, and take the praise. It was good."

The others agreed as they took their seats. "You should play that for Ian."

I shrugged. "Maybe. One day."

This was what I loved: being surrounded by people who were as passionate as I was about music and who felt it the same way I did as we practiced a difficult piece over and over, getting not just the technical perfection of the notes but the truth behind them.

It was no wonder I lost track of time and the world around me.

It wasn't until a discordant screech of a false note pierced through the auditorium that I looked up.

Reid was there in the center of the aisle among the plush, red velvet audience seats… watching me.

His face was in shadow, but from the way his arms were crossed in front of him, I knew he was mad.

How had he found me so easily?

Ginnie stood. "Hey, buddy, this is a closed rehearsal."

Reid didn't respond.

He just kept his fierce gaze solely on me as he marched down the middle aisle toward the stage.

"Sir," Ian objected far more forcefully than Ginnie as he stepped to the edge of the stage, hands on hips. "I must ask that you depart. You are interrupting our creative process."

Reid didn't even spare him a glance.

When he finally got to the end of the aisle, I thought he would finally break the horrible tension and speak.

Instead, with one powerful jump, he vaulted from the floor straight onto the stage.

Ian staggered back down while Ginnie muttered, "Damn."

Reid's stride hardly broke as he stormed across the stage, not stopping until he was directly in front of me.

Gripping the back of my chair with one hand, he bent down so we were eye-to-eye. There was no mistaking the fury in his intense silver eyes.

"You broke my rule, princess."

CHAPTER 5

REID

"*H*ow did you find me?"

I stared down at her beautiful, upturned face. "Let this be a lesson to you, princess. I'll *always* find you."

I was just following orders.

That was what I was telling myself.

This was just me following orders.

Nothing different than when I was in the Corp.

It had nothing to do with the feel of her skin against my palm or the lingering scent of her vanilla perfume on my t-shirt.

And my fury at learning she had disobeyed me was professional agitation.

Yup, purely professional.

As was my driving desire to pull her over my knee, flip up her skirts, and whip her ass for her impertinent disobedience.

Yup, that was professional too.

Even though I knew deep down that I couldn't—or at least shouldn't—touch her.

She was my boss' daughter.

My boss' innocent daughter.

My charge.

My responsibility.

Mine.

No. Not mine. My job. She was just a job.

A fucking babysitting job.

One that I should have let her go crying to her daddy to get me out of… but not now.

Now, the devil himself couldn't pry me from her side.

"You need to leave." Her words would have been so much more convincing if her voice hadn't shaken, or if she'd actually had the nerve to hold my gaze.

"Do I really need to explain to you the danger you put yourself in with this stunt? It is my job to make sure you don't become a kidnapping target."

I was hired because Lucian was worried about all the socialite kidnappings going on… as if his son wasn't directly responsible for one and indirectly responsible for the other.

Her fingers gripped her cello bow tightly. "Would you please —would you lower your voice? Everyone is staring."

"I don't give a flying fat rat's ass who is staring, Charlotte. Now get your shit and let's go. Now."

There wasn't a doubt in my mind I'd catch hell for speaking to her this way, but at this moment, I didn't give a damn.

The little brat had outmaneuvered me, and it was my own fucking fault for not taking this seriously. I knew better. As in the military, it wasn't my job to question my orders, it was my job to follow them.

I had accepted the job as her bodyguard. There was no excuse for not giving it my full attention.

If something had happened to her under my watch…

Her jaw clenched and tears burned behind her beautiful brown eyes at my harsh tone.

"Fine," she bit out before she slid her chair away from me so she could stand up without actually touching me.

She put her fancy cello into its no-doubt, ridiculously expensive, luxury case, and locked the massive metal latches in place.

A gentleman would have offered to take the case and carry it for her back to the car.

Thankfully, I was not under any such compulsion.

The girl with the purple hair tried to block our path. "You're not leaving, are you, silver spoon?"

Charlotte kept her face lowered. "It's for the best. I don't want to disrupt rehearsal."

The girl turned to the man who'd tried to confront me earlier. "Ian! Are you just going to stand there?"

The man cleared his throat as he fluttered his hand from his chest to his waist, then back to his chest, then onto his hip. "Sir, I think I must strenuously object to this intrusion."

I took two steps toward him, towering over his slim frame. With a nod, I said, "Well, go ahead then. Object. And see what happens."

He blinked several times as he lowered his knees and waved his arms behind him, searching for a chair. As he fell back into one, he cleared his throat again. "On second thought, Ms. Manwarring, you are dismissed for the day."

I bared my teeth. "That's what I thought."

As she passed me, I gripped the back of her neck, squeezing just enough so she knew I could hurt her if I wanted, and marched her out of the auditorium into the empty hallway.

The second the door closed behind us, she shrugged out of my grip and turned on her heel to face me.

"You didn't need to do that," she said, glaring at me like she was trying to exert dominance. I had never had a kitten before, but I imagined they were about as scary as she was.

"Yes, I did. You broke my rule."

"Fuck your rule."

Her eyes widened in surprise as if she had never heard such a foul word come from her own pretty lips.

My gaze narrowed. I had had just about enough of this. "Speak to me like that again, and I'll show you precisely what little brats with foul mouths get."

"I hate you."

She turned on her heel to march out of the building.

Instead, I grabbed her by the back of the neck again and pushed her into an empty room.

Her cello and the case hit the floor, but I didn't care. That case was worth the money her daddy spent on it. Her precious cello would be fine.

She tried to shove past me back into the hallway, but I closed the door behind me, trapping her.

Reaching behind me, I turned the lock on the doorknob. "It's time you and I got a few things straight, princess."

She backed up as she pointed a finger at me. "If you touch me again, I'll scream."

That was all it took for me to snap.

CHAPTER 6

REID

"*And* who's going to stop me?"

I stalked toward her, herding her with my body across the room, as the brief moment of bravado drained from her pretty face to be replaced by a light pink blush.

"You wouldn't dare." Her voice shook as her head swiveled from side to side, searching for an escape.

There was none.

"Let's find out just how much I'll dare, shall we?"

Snatching her around the arm, I dragged her deeper into the room. I kicked a music stand out of the way and sat.

Then I bent her over my knee.

Spanking Lucian Manwarring's daughter was easily the dumbest thing I'd ever contemplating doing in my career. And I was including the time I'd infiltrated a drug cartel compound deep in the Mexican jungle with nothing but a Swiss Army knife and half a pack of matches.

She squirmed as I pulled her long skirt up, crushing it in my fist against her lower back, exposing her cute, round ass that had just enough cheek it would jiggle in a satisfying way when I spanked her. The only thing between me and her untried pussy was a thin scrap of fabric.

She cried out in a strained, soft voice. "I'm sorry, I'll behave. I promise I won't try to sneak out again."

"It's too late for that."

I grabbed the flimsy piece of lace and pulled it over the curve of her ass, making the sides snap. Tucking it in one of my pockets, I caressed her soft skin. Even here she was perfect. Just silky skin covering her delicious curves.

My hips shifted under her to press my lengthening cock against the ridge of her hipbone.

I was almost tempted to lift her up so I could sink my teeth into her ass, marking her with my bite.

"Please," she whimpered again.

"That's it, babygirl. Beg me."

A swift slap to one ass cheek cut off whatever she was about to say. I then followed it with another in quick succession.

I wasn't hitting her hard, not yet. My objective was to warm up her skin first, raise a nice pink flush on her skin before her real punishment began.

When her pale porcelain skin glowed, I knew she was ready for her real punishment.

"Count for me, princess." That was the only warning I gave her before slapping her ass hard enough to leave my handprint emblazoned on her delicate skin.

She jumped and let out a whine. "Please, don't do this!"

"If you don't count, it didn't happen," I ground out, ready to spank her again as I ignored her pleas.

"One." Her breathy voice made my cock even harder.

"What was that, princess?"

"One," she said a little louder, her voice cutting off with a cry as I spanked her again in the exact same place.

"Two," she said before I had to remind her.

Her slight body trembled on my lap.

"Three."

"Four," she counted after each slap.

Her hips had tilted up like she was offering more of her ass to me, and I could just see the glimmer of dampness on her bare pussy lips.

She liked this.

She may not realize it and was probably denying it to herself in her head, but the evidence was clear.

My sheltered, innocent princess liked the rough stuff.

What would she think when she saw my ink or my piercings? Would she be afraid?

She should be.

Or would she be excited?

Everything about her told me she would be terrified at the idea of being with someone like me; someone strong and not afraid to get their hands dirty.

But the way her ass lifted in the air silently begging for more... maybe my first impression hadn't been entirely accurate.

To test my theory, I gave her one final slap, hard enough to make even my callused hand sting.

I expected her to shout out, maybe curse me, or start crying, but instead, her back straightened and her head lifted just enough so she could sink her teeth into her fist to try to silence her needy moan.

When I stood her up to face me, her face was almost as pink as her ass, and tears streaked down her cheeks.

"The next time you disobey me, it won't be five strikes. It will be ten. This was only a warning. Every single time you disobey me, every time you break a rule, I will double your punishment. Do you understand?"

"Yes, sir," she sniffed with her eyes on the ground, like a natural submissive, silently begging me to take care of her.

I brushed away the tears from her face with my thumbs. "Now, since you took your punishment like such a good girl, maybe I should reward you for it. Would you like that, princess?"

I didn't wait for her response. I just swept her off her feet and moved her across the room, setting her bare ass on the cool wood of a nearby table.

"What are you doing?" she asked as I pushed her body back, forcing her to lie down.

"Showing you what happens when you behave for me." I shot her a wink before dropping to my knees and burying my face between her thighs.

I knew her punishment had turned her on a little, but I would have never guessed how wet she had gotten. Her pussy was so sweet.

I lapped up her juices, loving the way her thighs shook around my ears. When I pushed my tongue into her impossibly tight little opening, her muscles clenched around me, covering my lips with more of her cream.

"Oh! Oh, my! Oh!" she breathed with unmistakable innocent astonishment.

The idea that I could possibly be the first man to taste her nearly sent me over the edge.

My hands went from her thighs to her hips as I moved one thumb to rest on her clit, not rubbing, just applying a nice, firm pressure to let her pleasure build. The other hand snaked around to her, no doubt, sore ass. My thumb slid in between her cheeks to press against her asshole.

She jumped as I pressed hard enough for her to really feel it while I fucked her cunt with my tongue.

Her chest rose and fell with her rapid breaths as her hands cupped her covered breasts, then gracefully slid down her body.

Surprisingly, she made the bold move of running her fingers through my hair before she gripped it, pulling me toward her, urging my tongue deeper inside her while her hips started rocking, begging for more friction.

The mental image of her riding my face made my cock painfully hard. It didn't matter. It was worth it just to hear the little moans she couldn't contain behind her lips.

Her thighs closed around my ears as a shiver racked over her body. Her fingers in my hair tightened, and her core clenched around my tongue. "Oh, God. Oh, yes, please. Oh! Oh! Do that again."

Selfishly, I wanted to ruin her for any other man. When she touched her pretty pussy after whoever she married left her unsatisfied, I wanted her to think of me and know that no matter where I was, I owned her.

My thumbs applied more pressure on her ass and clit while moving in slow circles.

And that was all she needed.

Her back bowed off the desk, while her sharp heels dug into my back.

She came undone in my arms.

It had been so long since I was with a woman who got so wet so easily. I was sorely tempted to flip her tiny body over and fuck her right here on this table just to see if I could get her to squirt for me.

But I already knew I had crossed an impossible line.

Fucking her would be one step too far.

I licked her through her orgasm, not stopping until her thighs released my head.

Standing to my full height, I peered down at her.

Charlotte Manwarring, the princess, was laid out on a table, her skirt up around her waist, exposing everything. Her eyes were closed, her cheeks red.

She looked ruined, and it was beautiful.

I couldn't help myself as I leaned over and pressed my lips to hers.

Her kiss was sweet. She melted against my mouth, opening for me.

"Fuck, princess," I said, after reluctantly breaking the kiss.

I was about to lean in and press my lips to hers again when her eyes flew open.

Then her hand slammed across my face.

CHAPTER 7

CHARLOTTE

I needed to get out of here. Now.

After pushing Reid off of me, I stepped out of my shoes long enough to push my skirt back down where it belonged. Hiding behind my hair, I marched straight to the door, trying not to lick my lips to taste the combination of his lips and my shame.

I needed to run somewhere where I could be safe, where I could stop and think and figure out what had happened and process everything.

How could I have let him do that?

I didn't even tell him no.

I didn't even try to stop him.

I let him spank me like an errant child and then... and then... devour me.

Oh, hell. I could barely think it, let alone face the reality of it.

My chest constricted as the weight of humiliation and regret settled on me like an icy, wet blanket.

Wet.

Damn.

Don't. Think. Wet.

Don't ever think about the word wet ever, ever, ever again.

I could still feel the brush of his beard against my inner thighs like some kind of tormenting muscle memory.

Had I really grabbed his hair and pulled him closer as I moaned?

Obviously, I would now need to change my name and leave the country.

Or at the very least, get on my knees and beg my father to assign me a different bodyguard.

I had honestly thought men didn't actually enjoy doing that!

Yet, Reid had seemed so enthusiastic about it. One thing was for certain, he had ruined me for my favorite vibrator. There was no way that mechanical buzzing would now compare to the warm pressure of his tongue.

Halfway to the door… Reid grabbed me.

Spinning me back toward him, he gripped me tight by the back of my neck and locked me to his body with his other hand cupping my sore bottom hard enough to make me cry out.

"You don't get to say when we stop kissing, princess. Only I do."

His words were less spoken than growled as he laced his fingers in my hair and angled my head the way he wanted before he slammed his lips back down on mine.

This kiss wasn't like the first one.

The first one had been gentle, almost seeming like he wanted to explore me, taste me, and know me.

This kiss wasn't about knowing me.

This kiss was about owning me.

He pressed his body against mine as he deepened the kiss, shoving his tongue in my mouth, holding me to him with his hands in my hair, his body pressed against mine, the thick line of his cock pressed into my stomach.

By the time he broke the kiss, my head spun. He then pushed me against the wall, caging me in with his body.

He leaned down and whispered in my ear, "Now, let's get your shit and get you in the fucking car."

Even the gruff way he spoke to me, something about the command in his voice, made my body ache for more of him.

The worst part was I wanted to obey him.

There was something different in his orders from my father's or brother's, something darker and forbidden.

With my face burning from embarrassment and shame, my heart racing, my behind sore, and my core wet and aching, I scurried to the door of the classroom.

As I reached down to grab the handle of my cello case, his large hand covered mine. "I got this."

I pulled on the handle. "It's my cello. I can carry it."

He placed his hand on my waist as he pressed into me from behind. His breath ruffled my hair as he said, "If you don't let go of this handle, I'll bend you forward, flip your skirt back up, and finish what I started."

With a shocked gasp, I released the cello case handle as if it had burned my palm.

Stiffening my spine as I pushed my chin high, I deliberately flipped my hair over my shoulder, catching him in the face. "Fine."

I became annoyed when my impertinent gesture only elicited a chuckle from him. With that, I continued toward the classroom door, unlocked it, and moved to swing it open.

"Open that door and it won't be my hand on your ass, but my belt."

My hands on my hips, I swung around to face him. "So now I'm not allowed to open my own doors?"

He raised an eyebrow as he stepped close. "Are we inside your home?"

I crossed my arms and huffed.

"Answer me."

His barked command made me jump. "No."

He reached around me, brushing my arm and sending a frisson of awareness over my skin. "Then you have your answer."

After checking the empty corridor, he motioned for me to follow him.

"You don't think all this is a tiny bit over-the-top?" I grumbled as I reluctantly appreciated the view of his tight ass in his jeans as I trudged behind him.

What was that saying about bouncing a quarter?

He opened the outer door, swiveled his head from left to right, checking the side street, before allowing me to follow him through. "Depends. Do you think being chained in a basement over several months while your kidnappers send pieces of you back to your father a *tiny bit over-the-top*?"

The image horrified me.

While my father might not have been anyone's idea of father-of-the-year, I knew he loved me, and the very idea of torturing him, and the rest of my family, like that churned my stomach.

He directed me to a massive, shiny black Ford F-150 truck. It was like strolling up to *Optimus Prime*.

"You drive this thing?"

He opened the back passenger door and placed my cello upright in the footwell behind the driver. "Yup."

"In the city?"

After moving to the other side and opening the door, he tilted his head toward the interior. "Yup. Get in."

Like most New Yorkers, I didn't even have a driver's license. I was used to seeing our city streets crammed with yellow cabs, black sedans, and smaller domestic cars... not insanely large pick-up trucks more suited to rolling over small mountains.

There was absolutely no way of entering this thing without literally hauling myself upward in a very unladylike way.

As I surveyed the situation, Reid shifted behind me.

His warm hands spanned my waist.

"Hey!"

"Hush, little girl."

He easily lifted me into the back passenger seat of the truck. Before I could adjust it myself, he yanked on the seatbelt and pulled it across my chest and lap, buckling it.

I bit my lip to keep from letting out a silly, girlish sigh at the protective gesture. After all, I was supposed to be hating having a bodyguard watching over me. Right?

Enveloped in the scent of his cologne, I sat back inside the cool, dark interior as the sounds of the city receded.

When he climbed behind the wheel, I leaned forward as far as the seatbelt would allow. "I don't have to ride in the back as if you were my driver."

Although I'd spent my life in the rear seat being chauffeured around from one destination to another—Father didn't like my sister or I riding the subway because of the possible dangers involved—this was decidedly awkward.

As if the simple division between the front and rear seat was a physical manifestation of the difference in our classes.

Tossing me a sharp look over his shoulder, he started the truck. "I'm not your fucking driver, Lottie. I'm your bodyguard."

I bristled. "I was just trying to be nice. And I didn't say you could call me Lottie."

My name was Charlotte. Full stop. No one, not even my girl-friends, called me Lottie.

His tanned, muscled right arm stretched between the seats as he gripped the passenger seat. There was just a hint of color near the upper shoulder peeking out from his T-shirt sleeve. It appeared to be the bottom half of the U.S. Marine Corp insignia.

"I don't need you to be nice. I need you to be obedient."

A shock of awareness hit my chest.

There it was again. That sexy, domineering, protective vibe that radiated off him like heat.

Leaning to the side, I pulled my cello closer like a shield. "Fine. Well, I need my panties back!"

His large hands grabbed the leather steering wheel as he expertly maneuvered through the cluttered streets. Shifting to the left, he reached into his pocket and pulled out my panties.

Twirling the lacy piece of silk and nonsense around his index finger, he laughed. "You mean these panties?"

With an outraged cry, I lunged for them, but was snapped back by the stupid seatbelt. "Give those to me!"

"Not a chance, princess. These are mine now."

"You're the worst."

He met my gaze in the rearview mirror. "Really? I got the impression earlier I was your best."

My cheeks burned as I smirked. "That's a pretty low bar, considering you're my first."

What I thought would be a snarky comeback turned out to be a terrible admission.

The tires of the truck screeched as he pulled over into an alley.

He got out of the truck and circled around.

Meanwhile, I searched through the tinted windows, my gaze scanning for the threat he must have seen.

My passenger door flew open, and Reid leaned inside, his right arm stretching over my lap as he slipped his left hand around the back of my neck.

"What are you—"

His mouth captured mine, stealing my breath.

38

Once again, he gave no quarter.

When he leaned his head back, my lips were swollen and sensitive from the hard press of his.

He twisted my hair in his grasp. "Don't ever tell a man he's your first in anything, princess. You'll challenge him to become your last in everything."

CHAPTER 8

CHARLOTTE

*T*he entire way back to the house, I kept silent.

Instead, I stared out the window, pretending to be fascinated by whatever was happening on the sidewalks. I wasn't seeing anything. I was counting the seconds until I could be out of this truck and away from him.

The moment that the truck pulled into the portcullis of my father's estate, I opened my own door and ran inside, so agitated, I left my beloved cello behind.

Usually, I would greet the staff by name, maybe even make a little polite chit-chat, but this time, I went straight to my room, unable to even look anyone in the eye.

I locked the door behind me as if that would stop Reid if he wanted to get to me.

With my back pressed against the hardwood, I waited with my eyes closed for him to follow me and try to knock down my door to get to me to finish whatever it was that he had started.

The only thing that followed me was silence.

It took several minutes to realize he wasn't coming, and I

couldn't understand why I felt a sudden disappointment come over my body.

I shook it off and paced around my room, running my fingers through my hair and trying to figure out what I had allowed to happen. I glanced to the side and saw my mother's photo sitting on my desk. The eyes in the photo felt like they were scolding me, like my mother knew what had happened from beyond the grave.

I grabbed the frame and slammed it face down on the desk and continued to pace over the thick Persian carpet that covered the hardwood floors.

The pacing wasn't helping.

It just seemed to make me angrier, making the conflicting emotions and thoughts swirling in my brain spin faster.

So I flung myself on my bed, covering my face with a pillow as I screamed out my frustration into the silk-enclosed feathers.

I screamed again and again, the sound completely muffled by the pillow.

When I finally had released enough energy to calm myself to think clearly, I moved the pillow to the side of the bed. I just lay there, panting from my screams while I tried to decompress.

Reid had embarrassed me. He had made me feel things I had never felt before. Even before he took me into that room, I had been angry.

Yes, that emotion I was familiar with and could label, but there was more, there was something else.

Seen. I felt *seen*.

With my father and brother busy with work and my sister now married and busy with her own business, I often thought it would be days before anyone even noticed if I were missing.

And yet, Reid had noticed.

No.

Don't do this. Don't romanticize this.

42

He was *paid* to notice.

And he was mad because I had disobeyed an order that made his job difficult.

I kicked at the pillow until it fell to the floor. That wasn't entirely fair.

Back at rehearsal, it was obvious he was mad because, at least according to him, I'd put myself in danger, not because I'd made his job difficult.

Then there was what had happened in the classroom.

I leaned to the side and rubbed my ass. Casting a glance at the closed and locked bedroom door, I inched up my skirt and placed my hand over my skin, wondering if it would still feel warm.

Curious, I rose and crossed to my dressing room. Standing before the full-length mirror, I peeked over my shoulder to stare at my bare ass.

I frowned. There was nothing to look at but my pale skin.

Despite the pain of his spanking, there was no lingering mark or redness.

I should be happy. And yet... I was oddly disappointed.

What the hell was wrong with me?

I shouldn't be disappointed that my brute of an unwanted bodyguard *hadn't* left marks on my body.

Turning, I slumped down onto the emerald green with gold piping chaise.

The way he'd manhandled me, the way he'd snapped my underwear from my body. I covered my face at the reminder. Why did he still have my underwear? What was he going to do with it?

Images of him hovering over me, with my lace panties in one of his hands and his other hand on me flashed through my brain. The way he'd touched me, not only in reward but even the punishment.

How he was solely focused on me.

Every time he touched me, I hated it… and liked it.

What did that say about me?

What did it mean that I liked it when a man, specifically this man, grabbed me without thought, exposed my most sensitive flesh, and then had the audacity to touch me in anger?

What did it mean that as he spanked me, I experience more than just pain?

The pain was there absolutely, and it had hurt enough to make me cry, but there had been something else there every time his hand slapped my bottom.

It had reverberated through my body, tightening my core and making my blood heat as my heart raced. My body had responded to his touch with need.

That couldn't have been normal. That couldn't have been right.

Something had to be wrong with me. There really was something in me that was wrong, fundamentally less than the lady I was meant to be.

Why didn't I tell him no?

Why didn't I try to stop him?

What if someone with a key had entered the room?

Everyone had cameras now. If someone had walked in, there would have been pictures of my bare ass on Page Six.

It didn't even occur to me what scandal my actions could have caused until I was back home and safe.

Instead, in the moment, all I could think about was the way his hot tongue felt inside me. The way his dark hair was silky and soft between my fingers, the scrape of his scruff against my inner thigh and the shameful way my body responded to him, demanding more friction.

This was not the way I was raised, but I couldn't even deny it to myself. I liked it, and despite all common sense, I wanted more.

I didn't know when my hand had moved down my body and between my legs, but I pressed my fingers to my clit, where he had pressed his thumb.

The pressure he applied was so much harder than what I could manage. Instead, I closed my eyes and tried to imagine what it would have felt like if his tongue had lapped at my clit instead of penetrating me.

Would he have flicked his tongue over the nerves or sucked them into his hot mouth, pulling at me until I shattered for him?

The faster my fingers moved, the more I thought about Reid and the way he'd touched me. How he so easily demanded pleasure for my body. Pleasure I didn't even know I could feel so intensely.

Then my mind went further, imagining what would have happened if I had let him kiss me. If I hadn't slapped him. If, instead, I let him turn me around and bend me over that desk. Or maybe he would have lifted me in his strong arms and braced me against the wall while he took my innocence.

Would it have hurt the first time he thrust into me? Probably.

All the girls said it hurt the first time, and I think I liked that idea. I liked the idea that the first time he took me would be like the first time he spanked me.

It would hurt, but only for a moment. Then that pain would turn into pleasure that was somehow darker, forbidden, and that made it all the sweeter.

My fingers moved faster over my clit as I thought about how it would feel. Maybe he would be slow and gentle for the first few thrusts, and then as my body got used to it, then he would let go?

Or maybe he would start as brutally as he finished?

My mind conjured images of him thrusting into me from

behind, pulling my hair back and biting my shoulder, pinching my nipples, just adding that edge of pain to sharpen the desire.

I wanted him to take me hard and leave bruises to remind me of the bliss that he would demand from my body.

Darker images flashed through my brain as pressure built in my core, building to another sweet release.

In my head, I saw his hands on my throat, not trying to kill me but to control me. I saw him tying me to a bed and then taking me for hours, twisting me into different positions and claiming me, spanking me, and even pressing his thumb into my behind as he took me.

A sweat broke out over my brow, and I would have sworn I could hear him whispering in my ear. His voice was low and husky as he told me to come for him. I could almost feel his hand slap my ass as he demanded again that I come for him.

My back arched off the chaise, and stars exploded behind my eyes as I came with a silent scream.

And I would have sworn I heard his voice whisper, 'Good girl' in my head.

I caught my breath and stood up, seeing my own reflection in the mirror. My cheeks were bright red, my eyes glassy, and my lips still a swollen dark pink.

I looked ruined and alive.

This wasn't what I was supposed to be. I wasn't supposed to be a woman who fantasized about her guard brutalizing her, taking her hard and fast. I was not supposed to be the kind of girl who derived pleasure from pain.

I was supposed to be a living doll, pretty and silent.

I was born and bred to look good on the right man's arm, raise his children, and further my family's reach.

This was too much. Reid made me want too much.

I had to get rid of him before he destroyed everything.

CHAPTER 9

CHARLOTTE

"*F*ather? Do you have a minute?"

His intense gaze flicked to mine in the mirror before returning to his task. "I'm late for this damn fundraiser to save the pigeons or some such nonsense."

His jaw tightened as he yanked on the end of his incorrectly tied bowtie. "I hate these damn things."

I stepped forward and slipped between him and the mirror. "Let me."

We stood in silence for several moments as I adjusted one end to be a bit longer than the other and flipped it over the other end.

He tilted his head back as I brought it up through the loop.

I studied his face.

Usually, I was so focused on the stern, businessman side of him, or the distant and cold father, that I forgot he was actually a very handsome man.

More than one girlfriend from school had repeatedly referred to him as a "daddy". Although even contemplating that was super creepy, I could see their point.

He was an older, more distinguished version of my brother with his sharp features and imposing height. Despite only being in his mid-forties, his thick hair had hints of silver, giving him a handsome, yet formidable appearance.

No wonder people cowered whenever he entered a boardroom.

He was like a Bond villain without the British accent, especially dressed in a Saville Row bespoke tuxedo.

As I folded the black silk to create a bow shape on the right end, he remarked softly. "Your mother used to do this for me."

A lump formed in my throat. My vision blurred briefly as I focused on my task.

There it was… my mother. The invisible haunting force that would always be between us. Although an arranged society marriage, it had been a love match. They married very young when my mother was barely out of finishing school and when my father was still at university in London.

My brother was a honeymoon baby. Then they had Olivia straight after that. They were a very happy young family.

Until I came along.

I knew it was stupid to blame myself. I was just a baby. It was a hemorrhage during labor. Her excessive bleeding decreased my oxygen. The doctors had to make a choice.

My mother told them to save me.

My father told them to save her.

Barely in his twenties, he had become a widower with two young children and a baby to care for. Except he didn't. He foisted us all off on a succession of nannies and retreated behind an icy wall.

A wall that never thawed.

"Where did you learn to do this?"

I shrugged. "Youtube." The real answer was one of the faceless nannies he had hired over the years.

Unlike in the movies, there had been no gentle bonding with a kind-hearted, matronly woman who treated us like her own.

A nanny position in the illustrious Manwarring family was treated like a dating game. There was one young woman after another who would pretend to be caring for us while outrageously flirting with my father, hoping to be the next Mrs. Manwarring.

The nanny when I was twelve had even gone so far as to sneak into my father's bed naked. Another crashed a party at our house after drugging us with Benadryl instead of watching us and told all the guests she was my father's future fiancé.

He'd ignored them all.

After pinching both folded ends and pulling to change the size of the bow, I stepped back.

My father studied his reflection as he adjusted the bow. "Very impressive, Charlotte."

"Thank you, Father." I took a deep breath as I twisted my fingers in front of me. "Father, about the bodyguard you hired."

He shrugged into his tuxedo jacket. "Reid? Fine man. A former non-commissioned officer in the Marine Corps. Highly skilled."

My cheeks burned. I knew he was referring to Reid's security skills, but I was thinking of his *other* skill. "Yes. Of course. I was wondering if maybe you could assign someone else?"

He turned sharply as his dark brown eyes that so closely matched my own scanned my face. "Has something happened? Was he inappropriate with you?"

I wasn't stupid enough to think this was fatherly concern for a cherished daughter. It was more like examining an expensive car for a scratch in the finish.

I gripped my fingers harder. "Nothing like that. I just think it would be more appropriate to have a woman guarding me, given the intimacy of it."

49

His gaze narrowed. "I hadn't considered that."

Warming up to my argument, I leaned in. "You know how the press likes to make up stories. I would hate for there to be any salacious gossip or some trumped up scandal because someone captured a photo of Reid and me together and made nasty assumptions."

He rubbed his finger under his lower lip as he considered my reasoning.

I knew I had him. I was, after all, my father's daughter, whether he liked it or not, and had inherited his genes for negotiating.

Turning, he selected a Rolex GMT Master II Ice from the spinning watch caddy on top of his valet station. As he latched the watch around his wrist and adjusted his cuffs, I kept silent.

Patiently waiting. A necessary skill when navigating any engagement with my father. And that's what they were—tactical, almost military, engagements, never casual father daughter moments.

Without bothering to face me as he made his way out of the dressing room, he tossed over his shoulders, "Consider it done. This is for the best. It was a waste of resources to have my head of security holding your bags while you shopped anyway."

And there it was again.

Love you too, Dad.

Sigh.

I lingered for several moments after he left.

Checking to make sure there weren't any staff nearby, I kept to the far corner of the room and pushed several wooden hangers to the side to reveal a black dress bag.

Lifting up the zipper, I pulled out a small bit of the champagne cream lace and silk. Rubbing the familiar fabric between my fingertips, I leaned down and inhaled the faint, lingering scent of rose perfume.

My mother's wedding dress.

I'd discovered it as a child one day when I used this place during a game of hide-and-seek.

Since then, I'd had a fantasy of wearing it one day for my own wedding.

A vision of Reid waiting for me at the altar dressed in a tuxedo flashed across my mind. I could even envision a hint of a smile on his stern face as he watched me approach down the aisle in my mother's gown.

A strange sadness settled over me.

Stuffing the bit of dress back into the darkness, I wrenched the zipper back down and shoved the hangers back into place.

I flicked the light off as I left.

Romantic fantasies were stupid.

Besides, it was done.

Reid would no longer be my bodyguard.

CHAPTER 10

REID

*I*f she mouthed off to me one more time, I wouldn't be able to keep my hands off her.

She was one snide look away from being on her knees, choking on my cock, before I... I shook the thought out of my head.

I couldn't think like that while I was on the job. It was a distraction.

I would talk to Lucian in the morning and tell him that he needed to assign someone else—anyone else—to her detail.

If he insisted, I would offer to supervise.

But I could not be left alone with her again, that much was clear.

I had crossed a line today.

Definitely professional, and probably moral and ethical as well.

She was in my charge, my protectee, and my boss' daughter.

I had no fucking business trying to fuck her.

Christ, what had I been thinking?

Stupid question.

I knew exactly what I had been thinking... and doing.

That was the real problem.

She was supposed to be a spoiled brat. A pain in the ass.

Not an endearingly adorable little kitten with tiny claws and a sexy mew.

I should have known better. I'd spent countless hours watching her from afar during Manwarring public events. Always standing to the side, playing the dutiful daughter. Perfectly dressed and behaved.

Like a doll.

But who knew the pretty doll had a moan like a siren and a pussy a man would die for the chance to taste?

Fuck my life.

At least my shift was finally over, and she was in for the night. Before I left her, I'd installed an app on her phone while she was distracted with her thoughts in the truck that would alert me if she left the building.

The fact that I didn't want to leave her... that I'd wanted to follow her into the house and straight up to her bed... was also a problem. A real problem.

After a shower to cool my cock, I headed out to meet an old friend for a much-needed drink. I hadn't seen Hunter for a few weeks. He had been assigned to some need-to-know operation in the Middle East. I wasn't even sure what country he was coming from. Lucky bastard got to see action, real action, and make a real difference. He got to use his training and expertise and get the adrenaline of putting his life on the line for the greater good. I'd be lying if I didn't say I missed that part of my life.

It took me less than an hour to get from work to home and to the bar where Hunter knew enough to have a cold one waiting for me.

"You look like you've seen some... unusual action," Hunter laughed as I downed the entire pint in a single pull.

"Never mind about my gig. What have you been up to?" I asked, needing to change the subject.

"Classified," he said, giving me a shit-eating grin, knowing that not telling me was worse than telling me.

"Asshole," I shot back, signaling the waitress for another round.

She was pretty, curvy in all the right places, and had bright red hair. Under normal circumstances, I would have flirted with her all night.

I would have taken off my leather jacket so she could see my ink, and she would have fawned over them and asked about them. And I would have regaled her with stories of fighting for our country overseas.

Hunter would have backed up the exaggerated stories of death and honor. We never shared real war stories with hook-ups. Those were personal.

We would entertain her and whichever girl Hunter's eyes landed on, and by the end of the night, I would have had her hair wrapped around my fist in the bathroom while she got on her knees to thank me for my service.

Despite the aching weight in my balls and the need to release the stress and frustration of the day, I had no interest in the waitress or any other woman in this bar.

No, my cock ached because of one pampered doll with mink-colored eyes, and I wanted her to be the one to fix it, whether in person or in my mind, while I spent in my hand like a fucking teenage boy.

"So, how have you been?" Hunter asked, eyeing the waitress.

"Same private security bullshit, except this time the protectee is my boss' twenty-something daughter."

He whistled. "Nice. So is daddy's little darling hot?" he asked with an almost predatory smirk.

My fingers curled into a fist as I fought the urge to break the nose of one of my oldest and closest friends.

"Don't speak about her like that," I fumed, throwing him a warning look.

He lifted his hands in surrender. "Damn. Didn't know it was like that."

I took a long swallow of my beer. "It's not like anything. It's strictly professional."

Fucking ironic.

As if pulling her over my lap and spanking her pert, naked ass was the height of dignified professionalism.

He gave me a hard look. "You're not thinking of doing something stupid?"

Too late.

I tossed him an annoyed look as I took out my phone. "Of course not."

He didn't believe a word of the bullshit I was tossing around but changed to a safer topic and began talking about how some green asshole, who thought he was tough shit, had been assigned to the unit, but the second there had been actual gunfire, he'd cried for his mom.

"I'm not speaking figuratively." Hunter laughed as he slapped his hand on the top of my shoulder and leaned in. "He literally cried for his mother. That's what Boot is sending out these days. What happened to the process that took these motherfuckers out of the running? Why wasn't he just sent to the army with the rest of the little bitches?"

Hunter kept talking shit about the newbie, which was fair. We had all gone through it. We had all done our time, made our mark, and earned the right.

And I'm sure if this guy was good enough to get through

basic, then he'd eventually wise up, or he wouldn't and he would find some way to injure himself or invent some mental illness that would get him medically discharged.

To be fair, I was also getting really tired of fuck boys playing Call of Duty for hours and thinking that was enough to make them Marine material, but most of those were weeded out long before they reached my teams.

Out of habit, I checked my phone again and pulled up the tracking app to see where Charlotte was.

It pinged at the exact same location in the house as an hour ago. She hadn't moved. It would have notified me if she left, but I just had to check and make sure.

Hunter nodded toward my screen. "Party girls don't leave the house without their phones, right? They need them to take endless, useless selfies of every drink and duck pout. So she's secure for the night."

"That's the problem. This one isn't like that."

"You're telling me you've managed to land the one daughter of a rich bastard who isn't a pain in the ass, spoiled bitch? Lucky bastard. Sign me up for that cakewalk gig."

I flicked through the reporting history for the evening on the tracking app. No movement. Unease settled in my chest as I answered without looking up. "Party bitches are easier. Predictable. Just follow their social feeds. This one took me almost an hour to find after she snuck off for some damn cello lesson."

He laughed so hard he choked on his beer.

I slammed him on the back.

As he swiped his hand over his mouth, he said, "I'm sorry. Did you just admit that a nothing bit of a girl slipped your net while carrying a fucking cello?"

"Shut the fuck up. I'm serious."

"What's got you on edge with this one? Is there a legitimate threat?"

"The only threat to her safety is me." I ground out. "There have been no stalkers, no letters, no demands, nothing. It's just a babysitting gig."

Since I'd signed an NDA with the involved families regarding her sister's mock kidnapping and her brother-in-law's fiancé's real kidnapping by his own fucking mother, I didn't mention it.

Besides, given the twisted circumstances, I didn't consider those indicative of a possible threat to Charlotte.

And steps were being taken to mitigate the threat of the Irish mob. My sources in the New York Police Department's Organized Crime unit reported the Irish were laying low and licking their wounds, after attracting the extremely dangerous, full attention of DA Harrison Astrid.

So at the moment, there was no cause for real alarm.

"What do you mean you are the only threat?"

"I mean, she pisses me the fuck off. Those gorgeous big brown eyes and the way she tosses her hair, giving tempting hints of her perfume. The way her lips pout when she wants to object, but she bites her tongue, and she practically begs to be spanked..." I stopped and took a sip of my beer to stop myself from saying anything else.

He nodded as he lifted his glass to his mouth. "Right. Right. But there's nothing going on." He then mocked my stern tone as he lowered his brow. "Strictly professional."

My phone lit up with a call from Lucian Manwarring.

Rising from my bar stool, I tossed out a "Fuck you," before I walked outside where it was quieter. "Sir?"

"Change of plans, Reid. Assign Charlotte a female from your staff as a bodyguard."

I gripped the phone harder as I sucked in a breath through my teeth.

Although I had nothing to back it up, I knew there was no way Charlotte had told her father what happened between us earlier.

At least not the intimate details.

But that didn't mean the little brat hadn't run to daddy with a sob story to get me reassigned.

Lucian continued, "So it all works out. I'm sure you have better things to do than babysit."

Everything he was saying was the truth and echoed my own thoughts earlier.

But that was before I'd tasted her...

CHAPTER 11

CHARLOTTE

"*S*urprised to see me, princess?"

I stopped short in the hallway.

Reid stood at the door, wearing black cargo pants and a black turtleneck sweater under a black leather jacket.

"What... what are you doing here? I thought—"

He stepped close.

I backed up, but he caged me in anyway.

He pulled on a lock of my hair, running his fingers down the length. "Nice try."

I bit my lip as I turned my head to the side. "I don't know what you're talking about."

Leaning in, he whispered in my ear, "Yes, you do."

My breath hitched at his nearness.

It was sinister and yet electrifying.

Dangerous.

I swallowed. "My father—"

He stroked the back of my cheek with his knuckles. "Your father agreed with me that only the best should guard his little girl. And as you know from… very personal experience… I'm the best."

Reid then winked as he took the cello case from my hand.

I followed in his wake. "I don't understand. I thought you'd be happy to no longer have to *babysit* me."

We crossed into the portcullis where his massive truck was parked. He opened the passenger door and put my cello inside. "You thought wrong."

I placed my hand on my hip while I gestured with the other. "Why can't one of our drivers take me in the sedan?"

With his hand around my upper arm, he half-dragged me around the back of the truck to the other passenger door. As he swung it open, he said, "Because I like the idea of you riding me."

My eyes widened as a gasp escaped my lips.

He smirked. "My bad. I meant you riding in my truck."

"If you are remaining my bodyguard, there will have to be some professional distance. What happened yesterday can't happen again. Okay? It just can't."

He raised an eyebrow as he crossed his strong forearms over his chest. With a decisive nod, he said, "Agreed."

I shook my head slightly as I frowned. "Agreed?"

So much for the sleepless night I'd spent moving between agitation and fantasy. One second, I was composing a properly regal speech in my head for when I next saw him about obligation and professionalism. The next, I was wondering what it would feel like to have all that heavy, tattooed muscle pressing down on me.

And now… nothing.

Just 'agreed'.

No argument.

No 'fuck my job, you're worth more to me'.

No, 'sorry princess, but I can't stay away from you'.

I ran the tip of my tongue over my teeth as I squared my shoulders. "I mean, fine. I'm glad we are in complete agreement."

Totally fine.

It would have been awkward for both of us moving forward had he declared any such, silly, outrageous, overly attached... super swoon-worthy… sentiments anyway.

"I'm a man of my word, Charlotte."

Before I could respond, he placed his forearm high over my head against the truck.

My back was pressed against the warm metal.

He leaned down until his lips almost touched mine. "As long as you behave like a good girl, I see no reason why I'd have to take you over my knee again."

My mouth opened, but only an outraged squeak emerged.

He chuckled as his hands wrapped around my waist.

I stiffened. "Get your hands off me."

He spun me around. "Relax, princess. Just doing my job, helping you into the truck."

Through clenched teeth, I said, "I can get in on my own."

His chest pressed against my side as his breath tickled my cheek. "Now what fun would there be in that?"

He lifted me inside. His forearm then brushed the tops of my thighs as he buckled me in.

I clenched my legs together. This was bad, really bad.

He couldn't have looked more like the military if he had some type of assault rifle strapped to his back. I hated this.

I didn't have very many friends or people I respected who respected me, but they were all going to be at the Lincoln Center for Performing Arts tonight.

And there was no way I was going to avoid the glances and the questioning looks that would follow me the second he stepped into the room.

I had no interest in fielding those questions.

I would just go in, play, and leave.

If I couldn't get rid of him, I would just have to deal with him and treat him like every other staff my father had hired. No, that wouldn't work. I was always polite to our hardworking staff.

If I was going to keep my distance, I would have to treat Reid like the girls I went to school with treated their staff.

"Fine. You may guard me. For now."

He chuckled. "Thank you for your unneeded permission, princess."

My lips thinned. "I've asked you not to call me that."

He leaned in so close, I could smell the coffee on his breath. "You also asked me to fuck you harder with my tongue."

My mouth opened, then closed. I was not equipped to spar with a man like Reid.

Staring straight ahead as I ignored the furiously heated blush creeping up my neck, I murmured. "I'm going to be late for the performance."

On the drive to the concert, he tried asking me a few questions about what to expect, but it was not my job to keep him informed. It was his job to anticipate and react accordingly.

I hated acting like a spoiled little brat, but maybe if I kept it up, he would simply quit. For the life of me, I couldn't understand why he hadn't just left. Surely this was far below his pay grade.

When we arrived at the Lincoln Center for performing arts, I waited for him to open the door, and then I got out, motioning for him to grab my cello as I started marching off to the hall where I was performing.

It wasn't the main stage, it wasn't even in the main building, but that was fine.

I led Reid to the small outpost building that we were playing at. Most of the building was taken up by the stage and seating, but there were a few dressing rooms in the back where I would go to store my things and take a breath.

I needed to calm my nerves and center myself before my performance.

The hallways I was walking down that led to the dressing rooms were empty as the other performers hadn't arrived yet. Then, someone called my name.

I turned to look in that direction just to see one of the orchestra directors I had worked with previously coming toward me.

Reid stepped between us with his legs spread and his hand on his sidearm in an aggressive stance.

I inwardly groaned. So much for not drawing attention.

"I know him," I said as I stepped around his shielding back.

"Director Hansen," I greeted the elderly gentleman with a bright smile. "How are you?"

"Oh. Well, dear, I'm good, of course. Thank you so much for asking. I'm actually here to see you specifically. I was recently informed of a position that has opened up in the New York Philharmonic. You are the only name that came to mind. I wanted to check with you to see if your situation has changed any."

I gave the man a gentle smile.

He really was so sweet for thinking of me.

I just wished he would stop. This was not the first time he had come to me with a possible job opportunity. But every time he offered me a career that I wasn't even bold enough to dream about, it hurt.

Tonight we were filling in for a last-minute cancellation at a charity concert.

Getting paid for what I loved would be considered a disgrace to my family, but donating my time for a worthy cause was somehow seen as worthwhile.

It didn't matter. At least I got to do what I loved.

"That's very kind of you, Director Hanson. But unfortunately, my situation has not changed, and I am not available to join the Philharmonic. Though I am truly flattered that you thought of me."

"Oh, well." He pushed his wire-frame glasses up higher on the bridge of his nose. "I thought that might be your response, but I had to try. The world should not be deprived of your music."

"The world is deprived of nothing." I smiled. "I'm actually performing tonight with the quartet."

"I know. The second I saw your name on the bill, I bought the tickets. Good luck, my dear. I cannot wait to hear you play again."

"Thank you, Director," I said, giving him a pleasant smile before moving past him to the dressing rooms.

I stopped Reid just before he entered the dressing room with a hand on his chest.

"As you can see, there is no other way in or out of this room. You can stand outside. I will be coming out in approximately fifteen to twenty minutes to go straight to the stage. After that, we will leave and go straight back home, and then you are dismissed."

Without another word, I rudely slammed the door in his face, hating how it made me feel to treat anyone like that.

Standing in front of the mirror, I studied my reflection, really looking to figure out what other people saw when they looked at me.

I didn't have stunning blue eyes. They were dark brown and matched my dark brown hair. I kept my hair in a boring, traditional style, long and wavy, and usually worn loose. Paired with my soft features and my large, almond-shaped eyes, I wondered if people saw a child-like doll when they looked at me.

When I was younger, kids used to tease me by calling me 'precious moments' and saying that I looked like one of those little baby angel statue things. I didn't see it then, but maybe I did now.

Maybe that was why my father, Luc, and even Reid treated me like I was incapable of taking care of myself.

That I was somehow incompetent at being a functioning adult.

Maybe they were right?

I rarely pushed back against my family's dictates. I'd always just done what I was told, but what else could I do?

Ruthlessly, I pushed the thoughts out of my head. I didn't need to deal with those questions right now.

I had a concert to perform. I knew the music front to back. We were doing a selection from *Romeo and Juliet* as composed by Prokofiev.

It was actually some of my favorite pieces, specifically the final song we were slated to play tonight, number thirteen, *Dance of the Knights*.

After a few more deep breaths, I cleared my mind of all the worry, the anxiety, everything that came along with being alive as I rosined my bow.

With every sweep of the rosin along the horsehair, I pushed it all out, leaving no room for anything but the music. It took about fifteen minutes, but as soon as I was centered and connected to the music, it was time to go.

Holding on to that calm feeling with everything I had inside, I stepped out of the dressing room, and almost right into Ginnie, who was arguing with Reid.

"Oh, thank God, there you are," Ginnie fumed. "Your Air Force bodyguard here—"

"Marine," Reid corrected through gritted teeth.

"Same thing," Ginnie said with a dismissive wave, and I had to stifle a laugh, knowing that she was saying it just to piss off Reid. I had to remember that one.

"What can I help you with?" I said to Ginnie.

"Look, the last piece, knight dance or whatever?"

"Yeah, what about it?"

"I can't get some of the flows down, so when the guys are plucking, do you care if I let you take our duet and make it a solo? I mean, if you're not comfortable..." She trailed off like she just thought of that.

"It's fine." I gave her a reassuring smile. "I actually love that part and played it millions of times."

"Oh, thank God. I was going to work on it this weekend, and it just did not happen. You know how it goes when friends call you to go to the club," she said, giving me a megawatt smile.

I didn't.

As the proper, obedient, cello-playing, goody-two-shoes daughter of a billionaire, I didn't get invited for debauched nights out drinking.

It was fine. We all have a role to play in this world. That was mine.

Without saying a word to Reid, we headed toward the stage, both of us carrying our instruments, ready to play our hearts out.

I could feel his eyes on me as we walked down the hallway, his heated gaze boring into the back of my neck. I had to tighten my hands around the fingerboard of my cello to stop myself from reaching back and scratching where he was staring.

When we got onto the stage, despite the lights being pointed straight at us, blinding us to the audience itself, I knew precisely where Reid was.

I could *feel* him.

As we tuned our instruments, I also worked on tuning him out.

I needed to focus.

We weren't the only quartet performing tonight.

We were actually one of the last. I could feel the audience was tired and starting to lose interest. I didn't care.

By our second song, I was lost in the music, and I couldn't feel anything but my bow and the gentle press of my cello between my thighs. When we got to our final song, I closed my eyes and let the music move me.

This piece was meant for the ballet.

It was to be played with a full orchestra with masterful dancers on the stage, commanding attention and conveying the emotion in the piece. We didn't have that. The only thing we had to pull the emotion from the music was our string instruments, and it was all we needed.

As we got to the part that was supposed to be a duet with Ginnie and me, where the music was a softer, comforting embrace, speaking of love and of loss, it was just me. The others plucked their strings, giving me the tempo and the beat as they imitated other instruments in the orchestra, and I was centered.

The music flowed through me. I wasn't looking at the score. I wasn't paying attention to anything around me. I was only feeling what Prokofiev and even Shakespeare himself meant for us to feel during this scene.

Most people when they think of the pain and the anger of *Romeo and Juliet*, think of that final scene, the death of the lovers.

But the wars between the Montagues and the Capulets were real to me.

The clashing of two great families in a way that disregards the individuals of those families had always been a constant in my life.

Whether my family was warring with the Astrids, the DuBois family, or any other number of families at any given time period, I was never kept in the loop. But I was expected to know to whom we were and weren't talking, regardless of how I felt about any of it.

All of that frustration, all of the sorrow, the pain, everything flowed through me into the music.

Finally exhausted and sweating from the bright lights above me, I let out a breath of satisfaction as my bow dropped to my side.

The audience erupted into applause.

I inhaled deeply as I let the blissful emptiness from expending such raw emotion through music flow over me. I had given my all to my music and to the audience, and they were giving back applause, praise, and even gratitude.

We took our bows and made a few comments about the charity we were supporting. Then we made our way off the stage.

A volunteer music intern took my cello and promised to put it in my dressing room, allowing me a few minutes to mingle.

The others were set to celebrate a job well done, but I made my excuses, not wanting to answer Ginnie's burning questions about Reid, and made my way to the back hallway, my intent to sneak out the backstage door for a few cooling, night air breaths, as was my habit.

I made it maybe four steps before a hand wrapped around my upper arm and pulled me into a side green room lounge.

In that moment of post-concert euphoria, I had forgotten about Reid.

Big mistake.

CHAPTER 12

REID

*F*uck the job.

Fuck staying away from her.

A man didn't taste the sweetness of liquid sugar on his tongue, while holding the pure innocence—yet dangerous destructiveness—of fire, and then walk away because of cold, bitter propriety.

Before she could say a word, before she could think of an excuse to push me away, I grabbed the back of Charlotte's head, lacing my fingers in those beautiful brown locks, and pulled her lips to mine.

This wasn't just a kiss, some delicate thing.

I was devouring her, claiming her.

This beautiful siren who had been so breathtakingly stunning on stage. I'd forgotten to breathe. The way she was utterly consumed by the music had transfixed me.

In my life, I'd been fortunate enough to see true beauty.

Sunrise at the Taj Mahal when the golden light bathes the white marble in pastel pinks and oranges. The Iguazu Falls as the water thundered around me while I was surrounded by water crystal rainbows. The simple perfection of a soprano hitting the perfect note at the La Scala Opera House in Milan. Camping outside while watching the night sky light up in vibrant emerald and sapphire from the northern lights.

I'd also borne witness to the most terrible.

Illness wiping out villages, killing the young and the old. Corruption, greed, and evil wreaked on the already impoverished. The pain and hopelessness of famine.

Until I watched Charlotte play, I thought I'd experienced the best and the worst life had to offer.

I was wrong.

Nothing had ever made me feel the way Charlotte did while watching and listening to her play cello.

Despite my intention to keep my hands off her, knowing everything about this was wrong, I couldn't resist.

I had to have her.

I had to taste her again, like somehow kissing her was going to let me experience a fraction of the power she had when she was on that stage.

Her hands went to my shoulders, and I braced myself for her rejection.

"Are you mad?"

I tightened my grip in her hair. "Yes. Fucking insane."

Why deny the truth? A man would have to be crazy to even contemplate what I was planning.

I captured her mouth again as I moved forward, shoving her against the wall, my hips pressing into her stomach, grinding my hardness against her intoxicating softness.

She wrenched her face to the side. Her lips were already swollen, with a hint of red around the pale skin of her cheeks and chin from the harsh scrape of my stubble.

I should feel like an asshole for marking her in such a course and common way, but I didn't.

Her fingernails dug into my shirt. "We shouldn't do this."

That wasn't a no.

And it was all the permission I needed.

I tore at the straps of her black lace gown like an animal, shoving the neckline down and exposing the top curves of her breasts. Pressing my mouth to her creamy skin, I feasted with open mouthed kisses as I grasped the lower hem and wrenched it upwards.

Her cool hand pressed over mine. "Reid, wait."

My fingertips grazed her nipple as I pushed them inside her bra and yanked. When the dusky pink tip was exposed, I latched onto it, sucking so hard, she rose up on her toes.

"Oh! Oh, God."

"That's it, babygirl. Sing for me."

As I reached under her raised hem, I forced her legs open wider by shoving at her ballet slipper-covered right foot with my heavy boot. Then I slipped my hand between her thighs, caressing the warm silk that covered her pussy.

Again, her hand reached down to stop me. "Reid, we can't... someone might—"

The tips of my fingers slipped inside her panties. "I'll shoot the first person who dares open that door," I growled against the curve of her breast.

The thin silk of her panties barely made a sound as I tore them off her and cast them aside.

Placing a hand under her knee, I pushed her leg up as I reached for the zipper of my pants.

In the back of my feverish mind, the more rational side of my brain cautioned that she was relatively innocent. With her sheltered upbringing, I knew for a fact she hadn't had many boyfriends.

And judging by her reaction to my tongue fucking her pussy, none of those dicks had ever gone down on her.

"Have you ever had a pierced cock, princess?" I breathed against her neck, just below her jaw.

Her fingernails dug into my wrist as she tried to hold me back. "A pierced what?"

I ran my teeth along the edge of her jaw. "Cock, baby. A pierced cock."

Gripping my painfully hard shaft, I pulled it out of my pants and slid it between her legs, wetting the head with her cream.

She shoved at my shoulders. "Stop!"

Misunderstanding her reaction, I thrust my hips forward, teasing her clit with the hard ridge of my cock and the smooth metal ring of my piercing. "Easy, baby. I promise you'll like it."

She struggled within my embrace.

I moved my hand from my cock to wrap it around her waist and lifted her off the floor. Swinging around, I laid her on the worn, red velvet sofa which had clearly been a prop from some forgotten opera performance.

The weight of my body pressed her into the soft cushions as I settled between her thighs.

"Get off me!" She cried as she kicked out.

Anger pierced my fog of lust. "What the fuck, Charlotte?"

My cock pushed against her tight entrance. Breathing heavily, I tightly reined in the impulse to just thrust to the hilt. Every cell in my body cried out for the warm solace of her body. For the chance to claim a piece of her spectacular fire for my own.

Tears streamed down her cheeks. "I'm not some low-class whore to be fucked on a dirty couch by some—by some—"

Snatching her wrists, I pinned her arms over her head as I glowered down at her. Surprised I didn't crack a tooth with how viciously I clenched my jaw, I rasped. "By some what? Lowly servant? Go ahead, say it."

She stilled. "That's not what I meant."

My gaze narrowed. "Isn't it? What's the matter, princess? My hands too dirty for your precious, alabaster skin?"

After tucking my cock back inside my pants, I climbed off her as I zipped them up. Running my hand through my hair, I paced several steps away.

It would be beneath me to beg her for sex.

So instead, I turned that anger toward something else that pissed me the fuck off.

"Why the fuck is such a talented woman like you playing on such a tiny, nothing stage?"

Adrenaline still rushed through my veins. Blood still pulsed through my cock. So my words came out like sharp daggers thrown at a wall.

With a sniff, she pushed her dress hem down and swung her feet to the floor. Pushing her tangled hair away from her face, she raised her chin. "Because that's where the charity was being held. And I don't need you judging me."

My arms swung out to my sides as I gave her a condescending bow. "My apologies, *your majesty*, for speaking out of turn." I placed a hand over my heart. "I'll remember my place next time."

Her fingertips swiped under her eyes as she straightened her shoulders. I could practically feel the icy wall she was erecting around herself. The lust drained from her beautiful brown eyes. They went from heavy-lidded and pupils blown wide to cold and distant. "Please, don't put words in my mouth."

My lips twisted in a sneer as I rounded on her. Placing my hands on the back of the sofa, I caged her in. "It wasn't words I wanted to put in your mouth."

She gasped. "You're disgusting."

"And you're a cock-teasing, stuck up bitch."

Her arm struck out to slap me.

My fingers wrapped around her wrist before she made contact. "The first one's free, the second one would cost you more than you're willing to pay."

She wrenched her arm away from my grasp. "Obviously, this entire thing was a mistake. I wouldn't trust you to guard my shoes, let alone me!"

Fuck.

I was thinking with the wrong head and behaving like a fucking teenager by cruelly lashing out.

Rising to my full height, I crossed my arms over my chest. "And you should be playing for the New York Philharmonic. So I guess we're both not living up to our potential."

"Playing in the Philharmonic is not what is expected of me. I have a duty and an obligation to my family, and that comes before everything."

"What the fuck does that mean?"

"It means I'm responsible for helping maintain my family's reputation. The press and public would be brutal if they learned I had taken a paid musician position away from a more deserving candidate. There are certain things that a Manwarring simply cannot do."

"You're wasting your talent," I spit out, knowing she had a point but hating it all the same.

I expected her to cower, to look down at the floor, and she did for a moment, but then she looked back up with her jaw clenched.

"Doesn't that make you a hypocrite?"

"Excuse me? What did you just fucking say to me?" I really was going to beat her ass bright red.

"Shouldn't you be off protecting some small village or whatever the fuck it is you Marines do? Instead, of acting like a useless hired guard dog for my family? Because you are following orders, just like I am."

"My skillset wasn't useless when your sister got kidnapped."

She threw her head back and laughed. "Do you know why Olivia was kidnapped?"

"Do you?"

Her head tilted as her voice took on a condescending lilt. "My sister was kidnapped because Marksen thought my brother was trying to destroy his business, but now they're married and everything is fine, so your skillset isn't needed anymore."

She had a right to know. But it wasn't my place to tell her.

Lucian had made it very clear, he didn't want Charlotte worried about the lingering dangers of the Irish Mob, and I had agreed with him. Even in my rage, I wouldn't shatter her comfortable existence with shadowy terrors.

It was my job to keep those shadows away.

My job.

Fuck my life.

I'd done it again. I'd let my growing feelings for her cloud my focus.

From the jump, I had miscalculated everything.

First, I thought I could scare her into running to daddy to get me reassigned, only to get caught in my own trap the moment I kissed her.

After over a year of watching her from afar, enjoying her sweet beauty and the haunting stillness of her smile, I thought I had her figured out. I thought she was a pretty piece of pink cotton candy fluff.

I never saw her intelligence, her talent, her secret fire.

Until it was too late.

I was already trapped within her flames.

Now, when given the chance for freedom, I'd refused and argued with Lucian to stay on as her guard. Only to once again, have the decision proven disastrous.

"You're still throwing away your talent," I shot back.

Rising with the poise of a queen, she crossed to the door and turned to look at me over her shoulder. "So are you. But sometimes we don't get to choose our own path. It's chosen for us." After swinging open the door, her tone was as cold as ice. "*Sergeant Taylor*, please take me home."

CHAPTER 13

LUCIAN

"*A*re you fucking with me?" I asked as I rubbed my temple.

"No, sir," responded Reid over the phone. "I've reconsidered our previous conversation and believe I'm better served overseeing the security detail while still investigating any future threats."

Yanking on my tie knot, I pulled it over my head before working the buttons of my shirt. "Fine. I'm paying you to make these decisions. Besides, soon it won't be either of our concern."

"What does that mean, sir?"

My office door swung open, and Mary Astrid strolled in with my very flustered secretary following in her wake.

"I'm sorry, Mr. Manwarring. She stormed past me."

I waved the secretary off. Turning to my desk, I said, "I have to go, Reid. Just handle it." I then hit the speaker button, disconnecting the call.

Mary smirked as she sauntered toward me.

Placing her frigid hands on my chest, she deliberately ran her red claws down my skin. "Just like I remember all those years ago."

Instead of just stepping back, I held my ground as I latched my hands around her wrists and pulled her off me. "That night is long in the past. I've told you never to come here."

I'd made it a point to never regret anything I'd done in my life.

Regret was a waste of time.

Decisions were made with the best information in that moment. I was too busy running an empire to muck about second-guessing them. Regardless of how things unfolded.

The one exception to that rule was Mary Astrid.

One drunk, grief-laden night. I played it off as a crap fuck, one of many over the years, but the truth was that Mary was the first and the only woman I'd been with since my wife's death.

I'd tried to move on several times but just didn't.

It was easier to focus on materialistic things that I could rely on, like money.

Damn, I missed Fiona. Why did she have to die so young?

The stab of pain may have dimmed over the decades, but the anger at her loss hadn't.

"Don't be so nasty, Lucian. I'm here to help you."

I raised an eyebrow. "I've seen your version of help, and I'm not interested. If my son learns you're in the building, he'll have you thrown out on your ass."

She adjusted the diamond bracelets on her wrists. "You'd throw out a baroness?"

Crossing behind my desk, I tossed on the fresh shirt I had laid across my chair as I prepared to leave for my polo match upstate. "So you've taken to giving yourself senseless titles now?"

With her son and daughter publicly shunning her for her manipulative actions in their life that almost cost Harrison his wife, our peers were starting to smell blood in the water.

The powerful combined fortunes and influence of the Manwarring, Astrid, and DuBois families had so far kept them at bay, and we'd avoided an unseemly scandal, but that didn't mean it was going unnoticed.

She examined her polished nails. "Not me, darling. Baroness Ophelia Zeigler. She's waiting for me just outside your office."

Instead of meeting her gaze, I moved to the hidden panel which opened to reveal an executive bathroom. There, I unlatched my watch and set it aside as I kicked out of my stiff, Italian leather shoes. "And why is that?"

"I'd heard you've started making inquiries for a suitable match for Charlotte."

Damn the woman.

Apparently, she wasn't ostracized quite as much as I'd assumed. She was like a radioactive cockroach.

Slipping my belt off as I stepped into a change of shoes, I said, "And?"

She lifted one shoulder. "The baroness and I are great friends, and I happen to know she's ready to arrange a similar match for her son, Romney Horace. I thought I could make up for that silly misunderstand with your daughter by helping arrange a match between the two."

Silly misunderstanding. What a quaint term for being the villainess behind a revenge kidnapping.

I grimaced. And who the fuck named their son, Romney Horace?

The damn British.

She leaned against the door jamb to the bathroom and continued, "He'll inherit his father's title one day, making him a baron."

"A bankrupt baron," I quipped.

She waved her hand, making her diamonds rattle, which I

was certain was the point. "Posh, that's just a matter of money. What do people like us care about money?"

We all cared a great deal, and she knew that, but I caught her point.

"Charlotte would be a Baroness," I mused.

Mary stepped forward and put her hands back on my chest. "Exactly, darling."

CHAPTER 14

CHARLOTTE

J'd been summoned to my father's office.

Fear and humiliation added to my already foul mood.

Was it possible he had learned about what happened between Reid and me last night?

Could Reid have told him?

No. Reid might be mad as hell at me, as I was with him, but he wouldn't betray my confidence by tattling to my father about our indiscretion.

Still, my father was a god in my world. The sun which the entire Manwarring family universe revolved around. And as a god, he seemed all-knowing at times.

It was more than possible he had learned of my passionate lapse in judgement from another source.

As much as I dreaded this confrontation, there was no avoiding it.

He would just keep sending servants up to my room with nastier messages until I complied.

My fingertips pressed the cool washcloth to my red, swollen eyes.

Nothing other than an order from my father would have dragged me from the sanctuary of my bedroom today.

Some people took Saturdays off.

For my father, there was no such thing as a day off.

Even on the rare occasion that we went on vacation, he still worked for a full day.

I knew better than to make him wait.

So I headed there immediately, before my breakfast. Despite it being Saturday morning and despite my desolate mood, I dressed as if I was going to go out. I had no plans, but my father saw anything other than perfection as laziness. Laziness was a synonym for failure, and after twenty-four years, I knew failure was not tolerated.

I knocked on the heavy mahogany door and waited for permission to enter, staring at the same beautiful, original wooden door. This door was a symbol for everything in my life that I wasn't able to do. Every single time I disappointed my father, I had to stare at this door first.

Every time my father gave me news that I did not want to hear. When he told me that I was not allowed to work an internship with my sister's magazine, or when he said that I was the family disappointment because I had gone to a party with a few friends and was seen by the paparazzi.

It didn't matter that I hadn't been doing anything. I wasn't even with the girl they had been there to photograph, but I was in the background of a photo that was on page six, and that was enough.

My father preferred this room for all meetings discussing bad news. However, he never gave me any good news. The few times something happened that I would consider good news, I was informed by a member of the staff. Or by an impersonal email.

If Luc heard the news before my father did or before my father had time to pass it on, then he would come to tell me in person, but even that rarely happened.

"Enter," my father's voice boomed from the other side.

I pushed open the heavy door and stepped onto the corner of the ornate Persian rug.

My father sat at his desk, tapping away on his computer, doing whatever needed to be done to be master of the universe while the taxidermy heads of half a dozen predators stared down at me in the same disappointment that my father did, or would whenever he got around to acknowledging my existence.

Ever since I was a child, I had seen those heads as a sign of my ineptitude or my incompetence. To this day I couldn't look at a lion in the zoo without tears burning behind my eyes.

When I was twelve, I invented a little game to keep my mind occupied. I would trace the patterns of the floor with my eyes. Following the intricate floral designs, I liked to try to see if I could find one line in one color that would go from one end of the rug to the other.

So far, I'd never won my game. I honestly didn't think the pattern would allow it, but trying kept my mind focused on anything other than what my father had called me in for.

I had learned very early that stressing about whatever he had brought me in here for wasn't going to do anything but give me a panic attack. Panic attacks, of course, were another sign of weakness and, therefore, another way I was a failure and a disappointment to my family.

I knew it was much better to keep my mind occupied tracing the ins and outs of the floral designs until my father decided I had waited long enough.

I followed the floral patterns, and on my fourth try, I actually found one line that got me about halfway across the carpet.

I didn't think I had ever gotten that far before.

I was actually starting to get a little excited that I might win my game when my father cleared his throat, making me startle and lose my place.

It was for the best.

That was his signal that he was ready to deal with me.

"I have good news for you, Charlotte," Father said as he folded his hands in front of him, giving me his full attention.

This wasn't a good sign. Usually he barely looked up from his computer.

"Yes, sir?"

"I have brokered a deal with the Zeigler family. Have you heard of them before?"

"No, sir."

"They are a titled family from England. They don't have any money, of course. None of those old families do anymore."

There wasn't a question, so I didn't say anything and waited for my father to get to his point. Thankfully, he was always a very busy man, which made him a very blunt man. Very little time for unnecessary details.

"Although the family is dead broke, they have something we do not have, a British title. It doesn't matter how many generations Manwarring Enterprises continues on. We will always be viewed as grubby Paddies. But those stuck-up bastards will be forced to eat their condescension when we have a title in the family. Understand?"

"No, sir."

That was not the response I was expected to give. He just raised an eyebrow at me, so I clarified. "I understand that you want to add legitimacy to our family name, a longer history. I understand the Zeigler family is looking to change their financial status. I just don't understand what that has to do with me."

He spread his arms as he approached me, before cupping my upper arms. "You, my dear, will be the one making this happen by marrying The Honorable Romney Horus Zeigler, a baron living in London."

"Oh." That was the only thing I could think to say.

He actually kissed me on the forehead. "I'm very proud of you, daughter."

Countless cello concerts, school awards, and accolades, and I finally heard the words I'd longed to hear my entire life... and it was for nothing I'd actually accomplished beyond being a daughter of marriage age.

I'd known my father would be looking to marry me off soon, especially with all the recent near-miss scandals with my brother and sister.

I just assumed it would be to someone I had at least met before, even in passing. I had assumed my father would give me the benefit of allowing a potential suitor to court me before informing me that I was to be married. I was in some medieval times nightmare.

"The Zeigler family will be coming to dinner tomorrow night. You will meet your future husband, and you will not embarrass this family. Do I make myself clear?"

"Yes, sir," I answered automatically, still not quite processing the information he was throwing at me.

"I have already asked my secretary to make a copy of the research I have done on the family so you can familiarize yourself with Romney's tastes, habits, likes, and dislikes. I need you to show him that you will be an appropriate wife."

"What if..." I clamped my lips shut. I knew better than to argue.

"What if what?" My father had already returned to his seat and was pressing the space bar to fire up his computer.

The discussion over my future, my chance at happiness, my thoughts on the matter as a whole, was apparently over.

"What if I don't like him? What if he doesn't like me? What if we don't get along? What if he wants to move me to England?" Everything spilled out of my lips before I could stop it.

I had heard of word vomit before, but I had never experienced it.

Anxiety covered my entire body. It was like ants were crawling over my skin. My face was on fire.

"Whether or not you like him is completely irrelevant. You will do what you are told. If he doesn't like you, then you had better figure out a way to fix that and make him like you. And if he wants to move you to England, then you are moving to England. I suggest you pack an umbrella. I hear it rains a lot."

"So that's it? You're just going to barter me off as if I meant nothing more to you than a painting or piece of property."

I didn't know if I had tapped into some kind of weird inner strength or if I was having a mental breakdown.

Probably both.

I'd spent a sleepless night crying into my pillow over Reid.

Everything had happened so quickly last night. The triumph of the concert. Reid's passionate response.

Then our devastating fight.

All night long, I'd gone over every detail of my reaction, imagined all sorts of different outcomes, and yet it all came down to the same end.

The end for us.

The end before there was even a beginning.

No matter how exciting and dangerous and thrilling I may have found Reid, I could not think of a single scenario where I would have thrown away who I was at my very core, to fuck a man I barely knew on an old, dirty couch.

Especially considering it would have been my first time.

I'd long ago given up the girlish notion of some ultra-romantic, special first night with candles and flowers and words of love, but I at least deserved a clean bed, and not some wham-bam-thank-you-ma'am as if I were being paid by the hour.

Being a Manwarring had one terribly arrogant benefit... I knew my worth.

And I knew the power of bitter regret.

At my outburst, my father's fingers stopped moving over his keyboard as he looked at me. The anger and disbelief reflected in his eyes made me wish he'd go back to his computer screen.

Every single time I'd wished that he would actually just stop and look at me when I spoke came crashing down on me. This was a prime example of the phrase 'be careful what you wish for.'

His gaze narrowed. "I have made you a baroness. You will be responsible for elevating our family from a disrespected, tiny Irish village to a county seat in Windermere, England. And you question my motives?"

My fingers twisted in my lap. "I'm twenty-four, father. I deserve to pick the man I marry. Someone I could love, like you loved mother."

The moment I said it, the blood drained from my head so quickly, I almost teetered out of my chair.

He stood from his desk, towering over me even from across the large carpet.

My father was a powerful and intimidating man. It was no wonder no one dared go against him in business.

"Don't you dare bring your mother's memory into this. I'm setting you up to fulfill your duty to this family. Love has nothing to do with it."

I knew I was tempting fate, but this was my future on the line. I stiffened my arms against my ribcage as I whispered, "But didn't you and mother marry for love?"

His fists slammed into the wood top of his desk hard enough to make me jump and stayed there as he leaned forward on his knuckles. "Enough!" he roared.

"I…" I started to say something, my voice shaking, but it didn't matter.

He talked over me.

"No, you don't get to speak right now. You need to listen. I have spent my life working to provide this level of luxury and comfort for you and your siblings. Your sister should have been the one to garner a title in our family, but she went against my wishes and chose another path. So that leaves you. Your siblings selfishly married for love and did not improve our standing. You will not do the same. Is that understood?"

"But I…" The tears burned at the back of my eyes, and a lump formed in my throat, making it difficult to swallow.

"You will do what is required of you, without any further argument. This marriage and your children will make our family a part of the aristocracy. I will not allow your childish notions of romance to interfere with that. I know what is best for you."

"Yes, sir. But…"

"You are dismissed," he said, retaking his seat and focusing on his computer.

And that was it, the end of the conversation.

He would hear nothing else.

The choice had been made.

I was to marry a man I had never met, and there wasn't a single thing I could do to stop it.

CHAPTER 15

REID

"*D*id you hear Miss Charlotte's going to be a baroness?"

"No! Spill!"

Two of the upstairs maids were gossiping in the corner as they stocked their baskets with cleaning supplies.

"I overheard them shouting at one another in Mr. Manwarring's office. He's marrying her off to a British baron. And she was all like—it's my life, and I'll do what I want, you can't make me!"

"She didn't! To Mr. Manwarring? Can you imagine?"

The first one nudged her with her shoulder and giggled. "I can imagine him getting all growly and domineering as he made me obey."

The second one giggled. "You're terrible."

"Like you haven't thought about it. The man's a freaking *daddy*. I'd fuck that man sideways if he looked twice at me."

"Who would you rather be, the new Mrs. Manwarring or a baroness?"

"That's a tough one. One is dirty hot sex and gobs of money, the other is an English title and people bowing and curtsying to you."

Then at once, they both said, "Hello, *Daddy*."

After their laughter abated, the one shook her head as she reached over the other for a stack of white rags. "All the same. I like Miss Charlotte well enough, but can you imagine being so spoiled you'd turn down marrying a freaking British lord?"

The one sighed. "She's literally living a freaking Downton Abbey episode, even if the man winds up being pasty and boring in bed."

"True."

I'd been sitting in the Manwarring kitchen, drinking a cup of coffee.

Having gotten shit for sleep, the caffeine was badly needed.

With my expression neutral, I waited until they'd left the room.

Then calmly stood… and hurled my mug against the exposed brick wall. Shattered pieces of white porcelain littered the coffee-stained floor.

My phone lit up.

LUCIAN MANWARRING

Change of plans.

Need you to run point coordinating security with Zeigler's head of security.

They will be taking over some duties regarding Charlotte.

AND THERE IT WAS.

God fucking dammit.

My body hummed with the conquering instinct to just march upstairs, snatch Charlotte to me, and claim her for my own.

It was an unhinged, ludicrous idea.

And I didn't give a shit.

This wasn't just about being cockblocked by her last night, although I was hardly accustomed to such occurrences from a woman.

She had been right to stop me.

What the fuck had I been thinking?

She wasn't some bar-fly whore to be fucked against a bathroom wall.

Although the green room sofa wasn't quite that bad, it was far below how a woman of Charlotte's caliber should be treated.

She wasn't just any woman.

Not Charlotte. She didn't just fall at my feet. She demanded my attention, my infatuation. Then she decided how far we went. No other woman had ever had that power over me, and I couldn't say I liked it, but I did respect it.

And this had nothing to do with blue blood versus blue collar or her being an heiress.

This was about her. And her only.

And the deference I should have shown her sweet demeanor, intelligence, and talent.

At least, that was what I had been contemplating earlier while drinking my morning coffee, waiting for Charlotte to emerge from her bedroom.

Things had changed.

The anger I'd experienced last night was nothing compared to the pure rage coursing through my blood now.

I should have been relieved. I knew that was what I had initially asked for. That I was never cut out to be her babysitter, regardless of whether the threat was real or not.

But I didn't want to see her marry some privileged prick, either.

I stared at my phone in disbelief.

It didn't make sense.

Why wouldn't she tell me? Why would she have kissed me the way she did if she was supposed to marry someone else? Why would she let my hands explore her body if she was meant to belong to someone else?

Was this the real reason she'd stopped me last night? Her dalliance with the help had gone too far for the bride-to-be.

This was the brutal reminder I needed about who exactly Charlotte Manwarring was.

She wasn't a sweet, simple girl. She wasn't even just a talented musician. She was a member of an elite class, a born and bred frigid bitch that used the people around her without any regard to who or what they wanted or needed.

My fingers curled into a fist.

As with any man with a military background, I wasn't suited for introspection, mulling over questions with no answers.

Action brought answers.

I marched upstairs, looking for her.

CHAPTER 16

REID

*I*t didn't take me long to figure out where she was.

I just had to follow the angelic, sorrowful sounds of her cello.

I burst into a beautiful octagon room in the far north tower of the mansion.

In the middle of the intricate white, black, and grey marble mosaic floor, under the soft light of a massive crystal chandelier, Charlotte sat with her cello.

The longer she played, the more I was transfixed by the music and could feel my anger and my indignation slipping. I needed to hold on to it like a weapon.

"Is it true?" I demanded as I shattered her solitude by marching into the secluded space.

"Yes," she said as she placed her bow across the nearest side table, put her cello in the upright stand, and then rose. "It's true."

"How long have you known?"

"I was informed this morning." She didn't look at me when she spoke, just picked a spot on the floor and stared at the fancy patterns.

I stalked toward her. "Look me in the eyes, Charlotte."

She shifted backwards with my approach as her large, glistening chocolate brown eyes stared up at me. As if she were a woodland creature staring down the barrel of a damn gun. I hated the fear, vulnerability, and sadness I saw reflected in their depths as much as my anger fed on it.

"This morning? Bullshit. Do you love him? Does he know you like fucking the help?" I clenched my teeth together as I spoke to keep myself from shouting at her.

"That's not fair," she fired back as she continued to move around the intimate space, hugging the walls. "I've never even met him."

Enough of the cat and mouse game. I snatched her by the arm and pressed her against the wall, pinning my forearm over her head. "Then why are you going through with it?"

"Because I have to!" she screamed, and she shoved against my chest and rushed past me, her voice on the edge of hysteria.

I followed closely behind her. "Why the fuck for?"

She threw her arms wide. "Because that's my obligation," she said before closing her fist and pounding it against the center of her chest. "It's my responsibility."

I grabbed her upper arms and yanked her to me. "Fuck that, princess. You can lie to yourself, but don't you dare lie to me," I bit out as my gaze focused on her lips, the need to shut her beautiful mouth strong.

"It isn't bullshit." She struggled in my embrace. "It's family."

"Fuck your family." I slammed my mouth down on hers, forcing my tongue past her lips, I showed her everything I was too angry to say. The kiss was bittersweet.

She broke free. "No. You see me as some privileged little rich girl, but that privilege comes with a price. And that price is my obedience. My freedom. I have rules that I have to obey. Just like you do."

I ran my hand through my hair as I paced away before turning on her again. "That's a fucking excuse, like a lie a little princess tells herself to make herself feel better. The truth is, if you didn't want to marry him, you wouldn't."

Her fingers curled into claws as she raised them to the sides of her head as if she were about to pull out her hair in a rage. "How do you not understand this? There are decisions in my life that are not mine to make. I am given orders and rules and there is no choice for me but to follow them. You were a Marine. You should know what that's like."

I threw my arm wide. "It's not the same. I was answering the call of a higher purpose. A fucking sacred duty to protect my country. You're throwing your life away to chase some impossible childish dream of pleasing your daddy."

If she had spent any time at all thinking about people other than herself and pleasing her father, she would know I knew the difference.

Her cheeks flamed with indignation as her hands curled into fists. "How dare you say such a thing to me."

"What's the matter, princess? Don't like hearing you're only doing this to finally make your father proud, while he turns around and sells you to the highest fucking bidder?"

She launched herself at me, pounding on my chest with her small fists. "Fuck you! I don't owe you an explanation!"

Letting her take her frustrations out on me, I raged back, "The hell you don't. I've had my tongue in your pussy."

Tossing her tangled curls out of her face, her chest rose and fell with her heavy, agitated breath. "That doesn't mean you suddenly own me! You're just a..."

My eyebrow rose as I sensed blood in the water. "I'm just the what, Charlotte? A lowly bodyguard? The fucking help? Beneath you?"

Her eyes widened as she sensed the rising tension in the room. "I didn't say that."

I pushed her backwards as I moved forward. "So what was all this? Were you just slumming it before you settled down as the dutiful bride? Was I just some wild fling, a taste of danger before you forced yourself to accept some pasty limp dick inbred aristocrat between your thighs?"

The longer I talked, the more my irrational rage took over.

Just the idea of my sweet girl opening her legs for another man nearly sent me over the edge. I wanted to tear my shirt and beat my naked chest with my fists as I yelled to the skies, *she's mine, and only mine, back the fuck off!*

She pressed her palms over her ears as she stumbled backward. "Stop! Stop saying such things."

My hands wrapped around her wrists as I wrenched her arms down. "The truth hurts."

Her body weight tilted back, trying to break my grasp. *"You pursued me!* You were the one always dragging me into dark corners!"

"I was just playing the part, princess. Isn't that what you wanted? The Neanderthal bodyguard manhandling you into submission."

She gasped.

I pressed my advantage. "Forcing past your feeble resistance to get you to admit you like being treated like my whore."

Her head shook violently. "No. That's not true."

"You're lying. I bet your sweet pussy is wet right now just thinking about what I'm capable of doing."

"Get out! Leave now!"

"Not a chance. Not until I earn my salary. After all, you might as well get your money's worth."

"I hate you."

I reached for the buckle on my belt. "That's the tragic part, princess. You don't hate me. You hate yourself."

Her eyes filled with tears. "What do you want from me?"

"Get on your knees."

"What?" she asked, her eyes wide.

"You want to follow orders, then get on your goddamn knees." I put my hand around the back of her neck and pressed her down. "And suck my cock."

"You can't be serious," she said, gasping as she stumbled to the floor. "You're really going to make me do this?"

I gave her a cruel smile. "Don't act like you don't want this, princess. But it's your choice. However, if you don't, I'll tell your father what his daughter does in the dark after her recitals. Do you think your new husband would like to know how wet your pussy gets when you're spanked?"

"Blackmail? Really?" she said, looking up at me with disbelief in her eyes. "Isn't that beneath you?"

And if her lips hadn't looked so soft and inviting, I might have relented, knowing I was only trying to hurt her as she had hurt me. "The only thing I want beneath me is *you*, but for now, having you on your knees with my cock down your throat will do."

I reached for my belt buckle. "Now be a good girl and open your mouth."

She clenched her jaw as she stared up at me, hatred in her eyes.

When I took my cock out, she stared at it for a moment biting her bottom lip.

I loved the way she looked at it, a mix of admiration and more than a little fear.

My piercing had that effect. It was a surprising benefit to the metal cock ring I'd gotten on a dare, fresh off my first mission.

Sadly, I didn't have all fucking day to just let her stare at it. I wasn't even going to give her time to explore it.

She was just going to swallow it.

"You know what to do, princess," I said, grabbing a fistful of her hair and pulling her face toward my cock. "Just like any other cock you've sucked, just bigger, harder, and pierced."

She opened her mouth and tentatively stuck out her tongue to taste the tip, flicking it over the head of my cock, tasting the pre-come and the ring.

Even that little lick was enough to send a shock of pleasure to the base of my spine.

"More," I demanded, tightening my grip on her hair.

She looked up at me, beautiful brown eyes wide with a mix of righteous anger and lust. She opened her mouth and wrapped her lips around the head of my cock and slowly sucked, flicking the tip of her tongue across.

I tilted my head back and let a moan slide through my lips, and that seemed to be all the encouragement she needed. She inched down, taking more and more of me until she had managed to actually press her nose to the flat of my stomach.

No one had ever been able to take that much of me before.

I hated to admit it, but I was impressed.

Even while knowing she was driven by spite to do so.

When she got to the base, she didn't move. She continued to suck while she choked herself on my length. The way her throat constricted around my shaft made me see stars.

With more care than I felt, I drew out of her mouth and then pushed back in, making sure I didn't hurt her too much.

She braced herself by putting her hands on my thighs.

I was fine with that until she started digging her nails into the muscle.

Charlotte wanted to feel like she was actually the one in

charge. Like she was the one who controlled my pleasure and my pain.

It was cute.

"Dig those claws into my thighs, kitten. I like it," I said with a growl.

With both of my hands gripping her hair tight, I thrust into her mouth harder, pushing even further back into her throat.

I praised as I breathed heavily, "That's right, suck my cock nice and deep."

I stared down at her, prostrate at my feet. As always with this, the power dynamic shifted.

Her eyes were closed as her hand slowly moved between her thighs to her core. Fuck, this woman would be the death of me.

All sugar and spice, and everything filthy and tight. Her mouth. Her pussy. And now, just like with my punishment spanking, she was getting off by having my cock forced past her tight lips.

With a frustrated growl, I pulled my cock out of her mouth.

"Did I say you could touch yourself?"

"No."

"No, what?" I said, pulling her hair just hard enough to make her wince.

"No, sir," she said, practically panting with her pupils blown wide and her lips wet and swollen.

"That's right. When you are on your knees for me, you are mine. I decide when or if you get pleasure. Now open." I tapped my cock on her bottom lip a few times before shoving it back into her mouth.

This time, I held her head still as I fucked her mouth. Her cheeks hallowed around me, giving me the most perfect friction.

I tossed my head back again as the pressure in my balls grew, and that familiar tingling started at the base of my cock.

"Swallow every drop," I promised as I started to fill her mouth with my seed.

I came so hard I was lightheaded as I pulled my still-hard cock from her lips. She swallowed everything except for a single line that spilled down her chin.

"Bad girl," I said, scooping the come from her chin and forcing my thumb into her mouth for her to suck.

The moment she did, my control snapped.

Wrenching her to her feet by her hair, I flipped her around and pressed her cheek against the nearest wall.

Fisting her dress, I pulled the skirt up over her hip before tearing her panties off.

I gave her pert ass several smacks.

She cried out as she clawed at the expensive, hand-painted wallpaper.

Caressing her warmed up skin with my palm, I pushed my hand between her thighs.

If this was ending, it wasn't over until I had absolute proof of her beautiful submissive response to sucking my cock.

She was wet, as I knew she'd be.

Using my two middle fingers, I teased her clit, applying rapid, steady pressure as I rubbed the sensitive nub over and over again.

Charlotte rose on her toes as her head fell back on my shoulder.

Strung as tight as her bow, it didn't take long for her to come undone in my arms.

Before she even had a chance to recover...

Before the blush was gone from the spanking, I'd just given her asscheek...

I tucked my cock in my pants and walked out of the door, slamming it behind me without saying a word.

Charlotte cried out the moment the door closed.

I rubbed at the painful, empty feeling in my chest as I left her to her tears.

CHAPTER 17

CHARLOTTE

I was dead inside.

As I surveyed the crowd of guests milling about the stunning entrance hall, the oppressive cold weight of my decision enveloped me like a dark storm cloud.

It was a nasty joke how perspective changed everything.

My whole life I'd resented being treated like a precious doll to be admired and flattered from a distance but not treated as if I had any emotions or opinion or intelligence. I thought then that it was a death-like existence.

Until now.

I realized that then, I had been frozen, existing in a suspended cocoon of ice until the right person came along to thaw me out.

Until Reid came along with all his fire and energy.

But I had frozen the flame. Killing it.

Killing any chance I had at an exciting life filled with experiences that tested my limits.

Killing any chance of freedom.

And all for what?

My father's love? His acceptance? To finally have him no longer look at me as the child who ruined his life? To have him be proud of me?

What a fool I was.

Blinking back tears, knowing I was only torturing myself, I surveyed the sea of faces, searching for him.

He wasn't there.

My heart fell.

"Ah, here she is now," my father announced to our guests as I walked down the intricate curved stairway. "You have to excuse her lateness," he continued with a sharp edge to his voice. "Bridal nerves."

I plastered a pleasant smile on my lips, playing my part in this new farce of a life I'd chosen.

My father had asked me to time my grand entrance, orchestrating it so my new fiancé and his mother would be standing in the entrance hall with the perfect view of me coming down the stairs in my *Oscar de la Renta* hollyhocks threadwork tulle gown.

I hated it. Hated that it screamed innocent virgin and whore at the same time.

The perfect packaging for selling off an heiress for the low, low price of a British title.

Don't worry, groom.

Your bride will be a virgin at the altar and a whore in the bedroom... the perfect wife.

My *Cadolle* nude satin corset was so tight, I could barely breathe.

My ribs ached, but it supposedly was worth the sacrifice for a silhouette that was practically sinful.

I lifted the diaphanous folds of tulle so I didn't trip down the stairs as I descended. The underskirt was a micro mini but covered with yards and yards of soft, delicate tulle with stitched flowers so the outline of my legs was concealed yet visible.

It probably cost a fortune, but it made me feel so cheap.

My father had even asked that I wear my hair loose in waves to give me the appearance of youth and vitality.

As if at twenty-four, I was already past my expiration date.

Still, this was what was expected of me, so I put on the show that my father deemed necessary. I made my way down the stairs, stopped next to my father, and greeted our guests.

"Please excuse my tardiness," I said, playing off my father's earlier words. "It's not a habit, I assure you." I smiled politely, meeting my soon-to-be mother-in-law's eyes and casting them back on the floor.

"Yes, well I'm not sure if I believe that. I hear many American girls are less than punctual," sniffed Baroness Zeigler.

The older woman, maybe in her late seventies, wore a modest black cocktail dress that was the epitome of ageless and refined. Her silver hair was twisted into a chic chignon at the nape of her neck to show off her stunning earrings that an untrained eye would assume were diamonds, but I knew they were glass.

They didn't sparkle right.

Her lips twisted in disappointment as she looked me over, and the longer she looked down her nose at me, assessing me, finding my every flaw, the more I wanted to turn and run screaming back to my bedroom.

Mary Astrid waved her hand over my form. "Don't worry. I'm sure that's something you can train out of her with enough time."

Train out of me?

As if I were some show pony lacking discipline?

And what the hell was Mary Astrid doing here anyway? Had Lucy and Amelia seen her?

I pressed my lips together and forced a smile before my gaze moved to the man standing next to her.

"Allow me to introduce my son, The Honorable Romney Horace Zeigler, the future baron."

The cocktail party conversation din evaporated. Like birds spooked out of the trees, there was silence as the guests averted their faces but still strained to eavesdrop.

"It's a pleasure to meet you," I whispered dutifully, as I took my first real look at the man I was expected to spend the rest of my life with. Over the last few days, while I was cloistered in my room, avoiding any sight of Reid, I had refused to open my computer and Google his name, knowing if I did so, I might lose my nerve.

He was handsome enough, tall, and a little on the thin side, with sunken ashy cheeks that gave him the impression of chiseled cheekbones and a small mouth that twisted into a condescending smirk.

I hoped it was a way of covering his nerves, but I doubted it.

"The pleasure is all mine," my fiancé said, the sincerity not reaching his eyes as he took my hand and brought it to his cold lips so he could kiss the back.

His hands were also cold.

Everything about the man seemed cold and damp, like the weather from his home country.

Reid was always so warm.

The second he touched me, my stomach flipped as bile rose in the back of my throat.

I feigned a blush, and my father led us all into the formal dining room that had been set using the finest china we owned.

Luc was already there with a drink in one hand and the other at the small of his wife's back. They were laughing at something Marksen had said while Olivia adjusted his tuxedo collar.

I so longed to join them, but as the center of the attention, I was still on stage.

Playing my part.

Always playing my part.

I stood back while my father made the introductions and waited for the signal to sit.

I was sat of course, with my fiancé on one side and, thankfully, Amelia on the other.

I really did love my sister-in-law. She was just so much fun. She also understood the struggle of what it meant to be a woman in our class and having to learn how to balance what she wanted with what was expected of her. I admired her courage. There was no way I would ever manage to summon the bravery to go against my father's wishes the way she had gone against her mother.

According to Luc, there was a lot more to the story, but I had yet to hear everything.

I leaned over. "No offense, but what the hell is your mother doing here?" I whispered behind my hand.

Amelia let out a long, frustrated sigh. "Don't get me started. That woman has no shame. She's set herself up as some kind of attaché to the baroness. It's absolute pandering."

My brow furrowed as I watched the two older women lean over the silent, elderly baron as if he wasn't even there while they chatted animatedly.

I was ready to settle into what I had hoped would be a barely tolerable evening when Reid entered and took his place standing by the door.

Directly across from where I was sitting.

CHAPTER 18

CHARLOTTE

*M*y cheeks warmed as he settled his fierce gaze squarely on me.

Thank God the surrounding guests were too stuck up and self-involved to notice.

In a desperate moment, I half expected him to leap over the table, grab me, and run out of the room like a wild animal wrestling its next meal from the rest of the pack.

Luc shot him a questioning look but didn't say anything.

Placing my napkin on my lap, I glanced over at my father, but he was busy trying to engage my future husband in a conversation about recent investments.

How was it possible that the world's most enigmatic, dangerous man had just strolled into the room, giving off waves of heated anger, and I was the only one to pick up on it?

The answer was simple.

Because all that heated anger was only directed at *me*.

Erotic visions of our last time together warmed my face even further.

The raw sexuality of it. The passion mixed with anger. My own willing submission to his firm hand.

My breath hitched.

I should have hated him for what he made me do that day.

I should have hated him for blackmailing me by forcing me on my knees like a common whore.

I should have hated him for making me come and then deserting me.

But I didn't. I didn't hate him for any of those things. I hated him because he made me feel something I didn't know was possible.

Every time he and I were alone together, he made me feel *more.*

More energized. More aware. More emotional. *More alive!*

He showed me things about myself that I would have never known were possible.

Like my attraction to domineering, controlling, Neanderthal-ish, manhandling bodyguards.

What did that say about me?

That I liked it when he spanked me like an errant child.

I never knew an orgasm could feel the way it did, and I had no idea that men put rings in their cocks. I had so many questions, but the one that kept popping up in my head over and over and over was...

What would it feel like inside me?

I pushed those thoughts from my head and focused on the man who was by my side.

He and my father were talking about expanding Manwarring Inc. into London.

Romney had several ideas that even I knew weren't financially sound, but my father rather strangely let him keep talking as if he were making sense. Usually, my father would have humiliated the man for stupidly opening his mouth and wasting his time by now. I'd literally seen him make other men cry at events like this.

And yet with Romney, he was feeding the man's ego by appearing to consider his ludicrous, misguided financial ideas.

Olivia and Luc shot each other dubious looks. They knew far more about business than I did, but it seemed like my instinct was correct.

It was obvious why the Zeiglers were destitute.

Grand ideas and schemes were not the same as financial literacy.

Dinner dragged on, course after course of nothing but the men speaking and the women sitting in silence.

Amelia and Olivia occasionally whispered to each other about how boring and awfully tiresome this dinner was.

Amelia tried drawing me in, but my soon-to-be mother-in-law stared daggers at me every time I dared to open my mouth.

Crap. Was this a glimpse into my future?

Would I be expected to nod and agree as pure nonsense dribbled out of my husband's mouth?

Surely not. Surely he would appreciate a wife who was a true partner, who had intelligent opinions of her own. Right?

It didn't really matter if I was involved in the conversation or not. My focus was on trying not to look at Reid, because I knew he was still staring at me. I could feel the weight of his gaze. The weight of his judgement.

He openly stared while I wasn't brave enough to even look in his direction.

Not with the way that woman kept giving me disparaging glances.

I knew immediately she disapproved of me, and if I dared to look at Reid, she would instantly know absolutely everything and would have no problems calling this marriage off immediately.

Somewhere between the second and third course, there was a natural lull in the conversation, and Luc took the opportunity to brag about Amelia's art school to our guests.

He was always doing that.

I was pretty sure it was to show off his wife and her accomplishments. He always beamed with pride when she talked about her beloved art school.

What I wouldn't give for someone to be that proud of me.

"It's actually going wonderfully. In fact, I've been meaning to ask you…" She turned to face me. "We're having a charity event in the next few weeks. The kids are doing some exciting things with digital media. Specifically in projecting color and matching it to music and using fans for wind and some other really cool things. They want to run an experiment for the next showcase."

"Oh?" I put my fork down. I hadn't eaten much and had mostly just moved my food around on the plate. "What kind of experiment?"

I was genuinely interested and happy for the opportunity to join the conversation for the first time all night.

"Well, they're playing around with all of the senses. And for music initially, they were just going to download something and play it. But one of the kids saw you perform at the charity event a few days ago."

My gaze flashed to Reid.

The corner of his mouth lifted as he raised an eyebrow in a knowing, arrogant smirk.

Damn the man.

Amelia continued, breaking my impossibly erotic thoughts about Reid spreading my legs and settling between them as he lowered the zipper to his pants. "They wondered if you would be willing to help them. They said something about the song you ended with. She wasn't sure what the song was, but she said it sounded like oxblood and anger, then teal and sorrow. Whatever that means," she laughed.

I knew exactly what the student meant. Amelia would too when she heard the piece.

"It sounded like teal?" The baroness laughed. "What a preposterous, imbecilic thing to say. Who describes music with colors?"

The coppery tang of blood pricked my tastebuds as I literally bit my tongue to keep myself from firing back that she was the imbecile to stifle a child's creative description with her rigid conceptions.

Clearing my throat, I choose instead to pretend I hadn't heard the mocking indignation as I asked, "What exactly would I have to do?"

"Just show up and play. They are working really hard to give the audience a full sensory experience, and they thought that having you play live and putting you in the middle of a stage with the colors swirling around you would take their project to the—"

Romney interrupted Amelia as if she weren't even speaking. "What instrument do you play?"

The cologne he was wearing was far too strong and smelt like rubbing alcohol and baby powder.

Resisting the urge to exchange an astonished glance with Amelia, I politely responded, trying not to breathe too deeply, "Like most musicians, I can play several string instruments as well as piano. But I prefer the dark, somber tones of the cello. It's my passion."

"Oh God." He made a face, scrunching his nose like he finally got a whiff of his own fragrance. "I hate the cello. Such a depressing instrument."

I hadn't expected him to love my playing, or even really listen, but for something that was so important to me to be dismissed without a single thought or any hesitation stung.

Reid stepped forward, fists raised.

Luc sprung from his seat to intercept him. "Reid, old boy, I just remembered that I... left my car running and need your help."

As Luc hustled a clearly pissed off Reid out of the room, the baroness pushed the knife in further.

"I always thought it sounded like screeching, dying cats," his mother added, making my father scowl.

He wiped his lips on his napkin before tossing it to the side of his plate with perhaps more force than was necessary. "Then you've obviously been listening to inferior musicians. My Charlotte playing is enchanting. She's a master of her craft. The concert Amelia is referring to was some of her best work."

Enchanting?

Master of my craft?

Wait... did he just imply he was at the charity concert the other night?

Listening to me play?

I stared at my father with undisguised confusion and wonder.

Had I been too harsh on my father? Had he secretly been watching me perform all these years?

The baroness snorted. "With all due respect, Lucian. Britain enjoys the finest musicians in the world. I doubt your daughter's amateurish, American plucking compares."

Italy, Austria, Germany, France, Russia, the United States—all countries with finer reputations for generations of exceptional musicians compared to Britain. And what was with her using the word American like a disparaging descriptor?

Romney lifted his glass as he chuckled. "Now, Mother, leave the poor girl alone."

Finally. Maybe there was hope for our marriage yet.

After taking a loud sip of his wine, he continued, "It's not like she'll continue to play after we are married." He placed his hand over mine and squeezed. The gesture painfully constricted my fingers, my rings crushing into the sensitive sides. "She'll be too busy doing her duty and giving me sons."

The air seized in my lungs as my spine stiffened.

In horror, my gaze swung to the empty doorway where Luc and Reid had disappeared not seconds earlier.

I then looked over at the grayish glow of Romney's skin. Did he know how dangerously close he'd probably just come to having his ass handed to him, if not by Reid, then definitely by my brother?

"Enough of that talk." Ever the smooth businessman, my father steered the conversation back to business.

I leaned over to Amelia and whispered, "Give me the details, and if I'm able, I will absolutely help."

"Thank you," she mouthed.

The rest of the evening was just as brutally painful.

My father had flown in some celebrity chef for the evening, but the food was nothing more than dust and sand in my mouth.

My thoughts ping-ponged between anger and confusion, knowing that for the rest of my life, I would never be able to get Reid out of my head, while also being utterly devastated that my one solace, my cello, had been dismissed as a boorish, amateur hobby by my fiancé and his mother.

I wondered if he would even allow me to continue to play for charity events, or would he think it pulled too much time away from me being treated like a freaking broodmare?

After dessert, it was time for the women to retire to one of the formal sitting rooms for a glass of sherry and small talk while the men went to the parlor for cigars, cognac, and shop talk.

Olivia and Amelia could see the hard time I'd been having at dinner.

Of course, I knew they didn't understand why, but my sister

and sister-in-law were at least courteous enough to keep the baroness entertained with questions about London, their favorite places to go shopping, and other frivolous things.

I should have known enough to participate in the conversation. To contribute in some small way. But I couldn't be bothered.

Amelia's mother may have been what Luc called a shrew, but she'd taught Amelia how to interact with aristocracy.

Olivia was well versed in London shopping because of her magazine.

I, on the other hand, could speak for hours about Vivaldi, but when it came to clothes, shoes, or gossip, I was lost.

Even if my mind hadn't been occupied mainly by Reid, who had returned to his post near the entrance, a permanent scowl on his face.

I was so far out of my depth, the only thing I could do was listen politely, sip my sherry, and try not to rub the spot on my shoulder where my cello would usually rest.

After what felt like years, the baroness rose to leave.

Looking down her nose at me, her upper lip curled as she turned to Mary Astrid. "You misled me regarding her breeding and decorum, but hopefully with some vigorous training, she won't be a total loss."

Misled her? So I had Mary Astrid's meddling to thank for this.

Mary nodded as she slipped her arm through her friend's, after giving a long-suffering sigh. "At least you have a chance with her. I'm afraid my own daughter is a hopeless disappointment to me."

My mouth dropped open, ready to defend Amelia if not myself.

Amelia placed her hand on my right knee as Olivia placed hers on my left.

Amelia leaned in. "Don't. Trust me. It's not worth it."

My lips thinned as I nodded.

Again, I wondered if this was my life now. Subsisting on swallowed words.

With their departure, the rest of the guests moved to join the men.

The parlor was empty.

Except for me... and Reid.

Swallowing my pride, I rose and ran my sweaty palms over my voluptuous tulle skirt before crossing the room. Clearing my throat, I whispered, "Sergeant Taylor, may I have a word?"

I had no idea what I wanted to say to him, only that I needed to say something.

After a long pause, he finally spoke. "No." He then turned and walked out of the room.

It took more strength than I knew I possessed to not just crumple to the floor and cry.

CHAPTER 19

REID

I could murder the slimy bastard and make it look like an accident.

Or I could kidnap, then murder him, burying the body where no one would ever find it, depriving his disgusting mother of the solace of finding his body.

Even better, I could snap the bastard's neck in broad daylight while he was standing next to his mummy dearest, and disappear into the crowd before his body even hit the ground.

No. That was too easy.

I'd get far more satisfaction puncturing a vein and watching the blood and life slowly drain from the man's eyes as he writhed around on a filthy, warehouse floor.

What was I thinking?

None of these plans were practical.

If I murdered the piece of shit, her father would just find another one.

No. What I needed to do was kidnap Charlotte.

Drag her away to some isolated shack on a beach on the

other side of the world, where I would fuck her senseless until her belly swelled with my child.

Then there would be nothing her father could do to separate us.

Curling my hands around my steering wheel, I let out a howl of rage as I rattled the wheel with my grip.

There wasn't a chance in hell I would do any of that for the simple reason that it would upset and embarrass Charlotte.

Charlotte.

My sweet babygirl.

My sweet, innocent martyr to her family name.

I knew all about the hard pull of responsibility when it came to the family legacy. I'd resisted a similar pull several years ago, but it had cost me dearly. I hadn't spoken to my own father, or anyone in my family, for close to a decade.

She was right about one thing. Freedom had a steep price.

I went to a bar to drown my frustration in a few drinks, but my rage did not abate.

How dare they disrespect my princess like that?

They took that beautiful angel and made her feel worthless.

After several drinks and turning down a few women, I left my truck in the parking lot and walked back to the estate, hoping the cold air would sober me up.

* * *

I HAD BEEN JUST drunk enough to actually consider doing this, and now I was sober enough to pull it off.

In only a few moments, I went from being outside to standing at Charlotte's bedroom door. Being the head of security and knowing all the guards and alarm codes had their benefits.

It was well after 2:00 a.m. and she was curled up in bed asleep, like an adorable little kitten.

This was wrong. Her bedroom should be sacred, somewhere that no one could enter, let alone a drunk man with a massive chip on his shoulder, and a raging pierced hard-on.

"Princess, wake up," I said, stumbling into her room.

"Reid?" she asked, blinking several times and clearing the sleep from her eyes.

"Shhh," I said as I took off my shirt, throwing it to the side and then kicking off my boots. "We don't want to wake anyone up."

"No one else has a room in this wing anymore." She sat up, pressing the thick down comforter to her body. I couldn't see much. The light in the room came from some ambient city light outdoors, but mostly the full moon. "What are you doing here?"

"What I should have done days ago," I said, unbuckling my pants and letting them fall to the ground.

Her eyes met mine, and I stood up straight, letting her take in all of me.

Slowly, her gaze trailed over my body, taking in all of my tattoos, the muscles from years of training, the scars, and the piercing on my already hard cock.

"Reid, this isn't right."

I leaned my knee against the bed and captured her face in my hands. "You don't think I know that? You don't think this all started as some bullshit plan to get you to run complaining to your father?"

"Well, it worked. I did! I kept up my side of your plan. You're the one who told my father no."

My thumbs caressed her cheeks. "Yes, you did—you beautiful, stubborn sweet pain in the ass. I was the bastard who went and fucked things up by falling for you. Fucking hard."

She tried to look away, but I tightened my grip. "Please, don't feed me some line. I get enough false flattery from the world because of my family name."

I slowly shook my head. "It's not some damn line, baby. For years, I watched from the sidelines as you were paraded through one event after another. I thought it was all an act. I figured there was no way you could be as sweet and innocent as that shy smile of yours hinted. That you had to be a spoiled brat behind the scenes. And I was right."

Her mouth opened on a gasp. "Hey! I'm not that spoiled. I mean, sure, I'm used to certain levels of luxury, but I've always been grateful and—"

I laughed as I kissed the tip of her nose. "I was wrong because you were even sweeter, kinder and more beautiful than I imagined. And when you play the cello, it's like the best of humanity is calling out to me, past all the ugly memories of war-torn devastation."

Her cool hand came up to cup my cheek. "Oh, Reid."

I turned my head and kissed the center of her palm. "Ignore me. I'm rambling because I'm a little drunk, but that doesn't mean what I'm saying isn't true."

She bit her lip. "This isn't fair. You shouldn't be saying such things to me. It's… it's too late."

"I don't believe that. Tell me you don't want me, princess," I said, the name not coming out with its usual venom. At some point, 'princess' had gone from an insult to a term of endearment. "Tell me to get dressed and leave and never come back."

"I can't," she breathed, still staring at my cock.

She wanted me as much as I wanted her. Even though a sober voice screamed in the back of my mind that I was making a selfish, brutish mistake that would only hurt her in the end, I didn't care. I was beyond caring. Tonight was my breaking point.

"Good girl," I said as I climbed further onto the bed and sealed my mouth over hers.

For a long moment, I just kissed her, loving how her body melted against mine, her fingers going to my shoulder and pulling me in closer as I devoured her lips. She tasted so sweet. She was so soft under my fingers.

Without breaking the kiss, I pulled the duvet down and climbed beneath the covers with her. She was so warm, the bed so comfortable and inviting, I never wanted to leave. I would have been perfectly content spending the rest of my life in that bed, between her thighs.

She was wearing a gorgeous light pink nightgown trimmed in black lace.

It was expensive and beautiful... up until the moment I ripped it from her body.

I had seen enough of her to know she was stunning, but nothing could have prepared me for the body she kept hidden under all those old-fashioned prim and proper dresses.

The dress she had on earlier showed off her curves, but in an unnatural, stiff way that clearly had made her uncomfortable.

The clothes she usually wore were conservative, lady-like, almost dainty. They managed to conceal a body that looked like it would have been better suited to a super model.

"Fuck, princess," I said, looking down at her before sweeping my hands from her shoulders to her full breasts. "God, I can't wait to bury my cock inside you."

I let out a territorial growl before kissing down her neck to her ample chest.

"You can't," she said.

"Yes, I can," I said between flicks of my tongue over her nipples. I loved the way she responded to me, little goose bumps pebbling her taut skin. "I'm going to fuck you so hard and for so long, I won't stop until you come on my cock. Twice."

My hand moved between us to caress her pussy. "Tonight, I'm going to make sure you see God before I fill your sweet little cunt with my seed."

She arched under me, her hands on my shoulders and her

hips subtly grinding against me, begging me to get her ready for me.

"No, you can't. We can't... do this."

"Excuse me?" I said, looking down at her as I braced my forearms on either side of her head. "Don't you dare deny me again. Not now. Not after what I witnessed tonight."

"It's not about that. I've just never..." Her words trailed off.

"You've never what, princess? Been with a guy like me? Don't worry, baby, I'll make sure you're wet enough to take my cock."

"I've never been with anybody," she blurted out with a gasp as my lips circled her nipple.

"What did you just say?" I sat up so I could see her face in the moonlight that spilled through the gauzy curtains covering her bay windows.

"I've never been with anyone. I... I want to, I want to be with you, but I can't be shamed like that on my wedding night." Her eyes started to fill with tears while hot rage swirled in my gut.

"Are you saying that pompous ass, the one who was sitting at that fucking table, that man who's never known a day's work in his fucking life, will be the only one to ever be inside you?"

The entitled prick was going to get my girl's innocence, and it had me seeing red.

She didn't say anything.

She just nodded with her eyes lowered.

"I don't accept that." I rolled off of her and grabbed her by the back of the neck, pulling her across my body with her beautiful ass in the air.

"Tell me you want him," I said. "Tell me that you're okay with him being the only man to ever truly fuck you."

"I'm okay with it," she said, and I slapped her ass hard enough that she buried her face in the comforter over my shoulder to muffle the scream.

My hand went between her thighs to her wet pussy, and she instantly angled her hips, giving me a better angle.

"Tell me the truth," I said, rubbing her clit, making her so much wetter for me.

"No."

I took my hand from her clit and I spanked her ass again, leaving a large red handprint on her perfect ivory skin.

"Tell me you don't want me," I said, rubbing her clit in tight little circles, making her thighs tremble.

"I don't want you."

The second the words passed her traitorous lips, I slapped her ass again for lying to me. Over and over, I rubbed her clit until she was shaking, and then I spanked her ass some more when she lied to me.

I kept it up, edging her each time until her entire behind was hot to the touch, bright red, and her pussy was hot and swollen.

My cock was so hard, I wouldn't be able to take it much longer.

"Stop lying," I said through gritted teeth.

"Fine, I want you. I want to be with you. I want to know what it feels like for you to..."

The silly girl couldn't even say it.

"What it feels like for me to what?" I was taunting her now, but every second I saw her, knowing she was with someone else was torture for me.

"To make love to me, but I can't. I want it, but I cannot be shamed on my wedding night. Please understand."

I didn't want to understand.

The last thing I wanted to do was have to understand how because of the job I had chosen, because I had chosen to do something worthwhile with my life, that I wasn't good enough for her.

"I don't make love, princess. I am not a boy you read about in your silly little sweet romances. I am a man. I fuck, and I want to fuck you. I want to bury my cock inside of you and fuck you until you're screaming my name and will never forget who owns you. I want you to live the rest of your privileged, empty life knowing only one man will ever take you in the way you crave."

"Reid, please. I can't," she whimpered, and I broke.

With an angry growl, I grabbed her by her hips and turned her around so she was kneeling on the bed, straddling me reverse cowgirl. God, I would have loved to watch her ass bounce in this position. I bet she would ride me like a thoroughbred.

I slid my body down so my face was between her thighs and then pushed her hips down to meet my lips. She tasted like the sweetest honey.

With one hand on the small of her back, forcing her to stay still, my other hand reached up for her head and made her bend down so she could start sucking my cock.

If I wasn't going to get to fuck this perfect pussy tonight, I was at least going to taste how sweet it was.

I was going to make her come on my face so that every time he touched her, she would think of me.

It didn't matter who she was married to or who got access to this body or anything else.

She would know that this pussy would always belong to me.

And to drive that point home, if I couldn't fill her with my cum, she sure as fuck was going to swallow it.

I was ready to hold her head by her hair and eat her pussy like a man possessed while fucking up into her throat until she passed out.

But I didn't have to.

She took control in the sexiest way possible, instantly sucking my cock, from base to tip, moving in fast, fluid motions while grinding her pussy against my face.

My girl liked it when I worked her up. She liked it when I spanked her round little ass.

And she loved it when I fucking manhandled her.

That arrogant prick would never have her like this.

I took comfort in knowing that no one else would ever experience Charlotte so free and wild. No one would know how primal my girl got in the sack when she needed to come.

When her thighs trembled, I took over.

Holding her hips, moving her at the same pace that she was before, but with more friction, I thrust up into her mouth, meeting her halfway over and over, loving the feeling of her choking a little bit every single time I hit the back of her throat.

She was mine.

To my complete horror, I came first, unloading everything into her mouth as she latched on harder, sucking me dry.

Tasting my come must have been enough because as soon as she started swallowing, she came. Her back arched harder, and she moaned around my still-coming cock, sending the most amazing vibrations up my shaft.

Her pussy throbbed against my mouth, releasing more of that creamy nectar.

I held her to me, letting her ride out her orgasm while she drained me.

Finally, she fell over on her side.

For the first time in my life, I wanted to take a girl and hold her, wrap her in my arms, and keep her safe and warm in bed while we slept. I wanted to be her protector, her savior, and her everything.

Her bodyguard.

But that could not happen.

I might have been the only man in the world that would ever make her come like that, but she wasn't really mine.

Not in the way that I wanted her to be.

I stood up and grabbed my clothes, ignoring the chill that ran over my skin. I was not able to even look at her. If I saw her lying there completely naked, hair a mess, her body still glowing, I wouldn't be strong enough to walk away.

For my sanity, this had to end.

"Reid?" Her voice was sweet, almost like a question.

"You have my apologies," I rasped. "This was a one-time thing. From now on, our relationship will be entirely professional."

I kept my voice cold and distant as I got dressed, still not strong enough to look at her.

"Oh…" That was all she could say, but it was enough.

I left before I did something stupid, like turn around and kiss her again.

CHAPTER 20

CHARLOTTE

I stayed in my room for the next three days.

I knew Reid was still on duty, and I just couldn't face him.

There was no way I could look him in the eyes and not cry.

He didn't get to see my pain.

He didn't get to see how much he had hurt me.

He'd known I was innocent. He'd known I had never been touched by another man, and he still pushed past my limits and made me feel the most amazing hot passion, just to leave me cold and alone afterward.

Sergeant Reid Taylor did not deserve my tears.

Shame and heartbreak filled me every single time I thought about what I had done.

About how something had come over me in such a way that I hadn't even known what to expect. And instead of controlling myself, I had given in to it. I'd followed my instincts, and I didn't know if what I had done was considered good or normal.

What kind of woman grinds down on a man's face like that?

What kind of a man holds a woman's hips and encourages

her to do that, to feel something so amazing, and then just leaves without so much as looking at her?

I was so embarrassed and so heartbroken over the way he'd callously left.

As if I didn't matter, though I guess I really didn't.

Men like Reid had to have women tripping over themselves to get his attention left and right. What would he want with a silly, spoiled rich girl like me?

Who had no real skills other than playing an instrument that apparently sounded like cats dying.

No one came to check on me.

One of the maids left food for me a few times, but my father didn't say anything or send a maid to ask if I needed a doctor.

Nothing until three days had passed.

I was called down first thing in the morning of the third day.

I got showered and dressed as I was supposed to, strictly on autopilot, and went to wait in his office. This time, he actually didn't make me wait too long. I barely had time to trace a single pattern in the Persian rug.

"Your engagement party is tonight. I've already had a dress delivered. You are to be ready and presentable at seven. The engagement party will start promptly at eight at the Waldorf Astoria. The baroness has taken on the responsibility of planning everything. So there is nothing for you to worry yourself with."

"Yes, sir," I said, not looking up from the carpet.

It was fine. I had no interest in planning any type of celebration.

"Good. I suggest you go do some research on the British aristocracy so you don't make a fool of yourself tonight."

"Yes, sir," I responded, still on autopilot.

"The other night, her son was taken by you, but his mother was less than impressed. Thankfully, he seems to have his mother in line, somewhat. But you would do well to ingratiate yourself with her. She is how you will be introduced to London society, and I need those business contacts. The current baron is too old and broken to be of any use to us. Fortunately, your husband will have the title, probably soon, but he is a fool. A fool I can control, but make no mistake, your duty is still to this family first."

It was terrifying how smoothly he had my fiancé's father in the grave and my future husband under his thumb.

"Yes, sir."

"You are to be on your fiancé's arm the entire night at his side. And you had better show more wit and intelligence and good breeding than you did at the dinner party. I was able to cover your lack of attention as simply nerves. I won't be able to do that again."

"Yes, sir," I said again, still staring at the Persian rug.

He placed a hand under my chin to raise my gaze to his. "Cheer up, Charlotte. Soon you will have a beautiful home of your own, a title, and perhaps a few babies to care for. Your husband will barely be a daily consideration. Trust me, I know what these aristocrat types are like."

"If you say so, Father."

"I do. You needed this. Whether you want to admit it to yourself or not. Your life was going nowhere. You needed a push out of the nest. I'm doing this for your own good."

I swallowed as tears pricked the back of my eyes.

He wasn't wrong. For so long, I'd blamed my father for the stagnant, stifling life I'd been leading, when in reality, I'd been happily playing along. Like a bird singing in a cage.

It was so much easier to blame him than to look inward.

Was it really fair to only blame him for this marriage when I had been basically sleepwalking through my own damn life?

Was it fair to blame Reid for waking me up?

It seemed I was blaming everyone but myself.

If I were now in this awful position, then it was just possible that I had only myself to blame.

"I understand, Father."

"Good. You're dismissed."

I turned on my heel and left his office, passing Reid as I left.

He didn't so much as look at me as I walked past.

It was like a knife slicing into my heart.

His anger and hatred were so much easier to deal with than his indifference.

I went back up to my room to find the dress had already been laid out.

The dress was similar to the one I had worn before, except instead of black with pink flowers, it was white and the waist on the corset was transparent. This one did have a full and opaque skirt but a slit that went almost to my hip.

I hated it.

But my engagement party wasn't really about me. It was more of a trial run to see how I would act on this man's arm. How I would look and if I could rise to the occasion.

As if failure were an option.

* * *

THE BALLROOM WAS BEAUTIFULLY LAID out.

I had been to several events in this ballroom. The Waldorf Astoria did have one of the most amazing ballrooms in the city. I tried to take comfort in the fact that most women would have killed to have their engagement party here.

I stood in the middle of the room, making polite chitchat with people I barely knew, accepting their congratulations and well wishes as I was waiting for my fiancé.

Reid was there, standing in the corner in a three-piece tuxedo, looking like sin.

Jealous rage boiled in my gut as I watched several women and even a few men take notice of how he looked more like James Bond than a bodyguard.

My fiancé arrived about an hour late, reeking of gin and vermouth.

"You look lovely, darling," he slurred, not really looking at me.

"Thank you," I said automatically. "You do look dashing in that suit."

What I had wanted to say was a biting comment about his mother's view on punctuality, but I didn't. There would be no point.

"Of course I do. Now do your job and start introducing me to the right people," he groused before grabbing my arm a little too forcefully and dragging me across the room to where Harrison was talking with my brother.

"Harrison." I smiled sweetly. "Have you met my fiancé?"

"No, I haven't." He offered a hand to Romney.

"May I present the Honorable Romney Zeigler. Romney, this is Harrison Astrid, District Attorney to the State of New York, and Amelia's older brother."

While the men shook, Romney shot me a quick quizzical look.

Being the well-trained lady that I was, I pretended to turn and look at something behind him while I quietly whispered in his ear. "Amelia is Luc's wife. She was at the dinner the other day."

He nodded and said something about Amelia's school, and the men started chatting.

I took half a step back, still on Romney's arm but giving the men a little space to talk for a few moments while I took stock of the others in attendance that I needed to introduce Romney to.

"Actually, Charlotte," Harrison said, pulling me back into the conversation. "I'd love your opinion."

"Oh?"

"Luc and I are on a charity board who want to raise money with an opera performance of *Lohengrin.*"

I sucked air through my teeth. "Oh my!"

Luc placed his dirty glass on a passing tray and snatched a glass of champagne for both of us, handing me one of the delicate crystal flutes. "Exactly! The battle-ax head of the board won't shut up about the epic romance, handily ignoring all the nasty bits."

Romney chortled as he drained his own glass, then took my untouched one from my hand and drained that as well. "Yeah. I mean who wants to sit through a Chinese opera anyway. Lo Hang Gin," he laughed. "What a stupid name. Stupid Asians."

I placed a hand on his upper arm. "Actually, it's a German opera by Wagner. The problem is the composer's difficult personal views, so he's rather controversial."

If I had been paying more attention, I wouldn't have made such a stupid mistake.

"Excuse us for a moment. I see someone we need to speak with," Romney said through thinned lips while taking my arm, digging his manicured nails into the soft skin of my elbow.

I had to rush to keep up with his long stride while smiling to anyone we passed, so it didn't appear as though he were dragging me out of the room.

By the time we reached the double doors at the other side of the ballroom, I was a little winded and my feet were killing me.

I didn't care how fashionable they were, *Louboutins* were a form of medieval torture and should be banned under the Geneva Convention.

We left the ballroom, and he dragged me further down the hallway until we got to a private conference room, still beautifully decorated, but clearly meant for business rather than pleasure.

He pushed me over the threshold and had barely slammed the door before screaming, "How dare you?"

His cheeks turned red, and spittle flew out of his mouth.

I flinched at the grotesque display.

"What did I do?" I asked, not sure how he'd become so mad so fast.

"You will never correct me again. I don't care if we're in public, or we are alone in my bed and you're sucking my cock like the paid-for whore you are. I own you. Understand, *wife*?"

Shocked by the crudeness of his words, I stumbled backward, easing toward the exit and safety... Then something inside of me snapped.

Enough.

It had taken years of hiding behind a polite, doll mask, but I'd finally had enough.

Maybe it was Reid's influence. Maybe I was just finally coming into my own.

Crossing my arms over my chest, my gaze narrowed. "You have that the other way around. You're not paying for me. My family is buying your father's shriveled up, useless, dusty old title. *I own you!*"

"You stupid American bitch."

The back of his hand slammed across my face, hard enough to throw me to the floor.

CHAPTER 21

REID

The solid hotel door splintered off its hinges under the weight of my boot.

Charlotte was on the floor in a pile of wedding-white tulle, looking like a broken doll.

Romney rubbed his fist as he straightened his shoulders. "How dare you enter this room without permission. I'll have you fired."

Ignoring him, I crossed to Charlotte.

Gently placing my hands on her waist, I lifted her to her feet. Cupping her cheek, I ran my thumb over the emerging bruise as I brushed away a tear.

She wrapped her hands around my wrist. "You should go," she whispered. "He means it. He'll get you fired from your job."

My brow furrowed. "Protecting you isn't my job, babygirl. It's my purpose in life."

"Get your hands off my wife."

His wife?

Nevermind that Charlotte was not officially his wife yet.

That this piece of shit excuse for a man would make any claim on my woman had me seeing red.

I kissed Charlotte on the forehead. "Go find your brother or father. Romney and I are going to have a little chat."

She shook her head as she urgently whispered, "I can't. I need to smooth this over before anyone finds out. Don't worry. I'll convince him not to get you fired."

Romney placed his hands on his hips. "If you don't leave this instant, I will call up my security team and have you thrown out with the trash."

I didn't even bother turning in his direction. I would deal with him soon enough. "Baby, I don't give a flying fat rat's ass about my damn job. Now, do as you're told."

There was no profit in having her witness what I was about to do.

Romney huffed as he directed his next comment to Charlotte. "Look at you, throwing yourself at the help like a common trollop. My mother will hear about this."

Fuck, I was going to enjoy beating this man bloody.

I turned as I shrugged out of my tuxedo jacket. "Thanks for that. It's been at least two weeks since I've hit someone."

Romney blanched as the thin skin of his throat contracted. "I'm not afraid of you."

My eyebrow raised as I rolled up my sleeves while slowly stalking him into a far corner of the room. "The human body has countless fear markers. Your paler than normal skin is the blood rushing to your hands and feet."

Romney stretched out his fingers before him.

I continued, "Your pupils are dilated, allowing your brain to hyper-focus on the threat before you. Your heartbeat is elevated, pumping more oxygen into your muscles."

With a nod of my head, I gestured toward his hands. "Your hands are trembling. That's from the surge in adrenaline."

Without warning, my arm snapped out as I grabbed his throat.

My fingers squeezed as I lifted him up against the wall until his feet were dangling in the air, kicking. "It's all part of your fight-or-flight response, and you have no idea how badly I want you to be stupid enough to fight."

I barely registered his feet hitting my shins. His pale face pinkened as his thin lips turned blue. A high-pitched shriek pierced the room as he called out, "Help! Help me! He's going to kill me!"

He had struck Charlotte. My Charlotte.

While I wasn't stupid enough to kill the man, I would make sure he left this room on a fucking stretcher. He needed to know how it felt to have someone bigger than him, stronger than him, hit him in the face.

I savored the fear in his eyes as I lifted my hand and pulled it back slowly.

I hadn't even hit him yet, and he was crying, his fingers trying in vain to pry my other hand from his throat as he stared at the fist I had cocked back. "Not the face! Not the face!"

Jesus Christ, what a piece of shit.

My fist slammed into his face with punishing force.

His cry of fear turned into a scream of shock and pain.

The blood spraying from his nose to stain his crisp white, way-overpriced shirt was satisfying, but not enough.

I didn't give him a moment to recover. I didn't even leave enough time for the pain to fully register before I hit him again with the same intensity in the exact same place.

Each hit was more and more satisfying, but it was still not enough.

He'd dared to touch Charlotte, my princess.

I didn't give a fuck what her father had planned... she was mine.

If Lucian Manwarring thought his family had connections, he hadn't met mine yet.

I'd go toe-to-toe with him any day, even if it meant reconnecting with my own, estranged father. Charlotte was worth it.

Romney wasn't good enough for her. No mortal man would be, not even me.

But at least I was willing to spend my life fighting to deserve her.

Unlike this bastard, who seemed to think he deserved her simply because of his title.

How could he?

This flaccid little runt couldn't take care of her. He couldn't even take care of himself.

This was the man her father thought could protect Charlotte against the Irish mob?

The more I thought about it, the harder I punched over and over, hitting his face, then moving down to work his body, hitting his kidneys a few times hard enough that I was sure he would be pissing blood for the foreseeable future.

"Reid," a soft voice started to cut through my haze of rage.

I kept punching even after he went limp in my arms and stopped making the piggish squealing sounds.

"Reid," the voice came again. "Reid, please."

The second her delicate, perfect little hand landed on my shoulder, the fog of rage lifted, and my tunnel vision vanished, allowing me to drop the useless man at my feet.

He made a vague gurgling sound that told me he wasn't dead.

It was really a shame.

I looked over at Charlotte, a bright red mark blooming on her cheek, and I wanted to kick him all over again, but she pulled on my arm.

"Reid, you need to leave now. I'm sure someone called the

police. You need to go. They are going to fire you for this. I can't stop them, but I don't want them to arrest you."

Her concern for me was adorable.

Giving the pile of cloth and blood that was Romney a final kick, I grabbed my tuxedo jacket as I reached for her hand. "Let's go."

She stared down at the blood smeared across the knuckles of my outstretched hand. "I can't go with you. I have guests to deal with, and I have to figure out how to deal with this, and I..."

I wiped my hand on my pants, not wanting to get any blood on her beautiful white dress or porcelain skin. Really, I didn't want her tainted by any part of that man.

Then I wrapped my arm around her waist and pulled her against my chest. I cut her off with a searing kiss, knowing it was the only way to shut her up and keep her from spiraling out of control.

"Please..." She looked up at me, her eyes blown wide.

I loved that I affected her as much as she affected me.

Reaching into my pocket, I took out my phone and snapped a photo of her bruised cheek.

I fired off a text to her father.

REID: *Your future son-in-law's handywork.*

Lucian: Where is he? I'll kill him.

Reid: Mostly taken care of. Just follow the blood. I'm getting Charlotte out of here.

Lucian: Go. I'll handle things here.

LIFTING my phone to show her the screen, I said, "There. Your father knows he hit you, and I've dealt with him. Let him handle the fallout. Right now, I need to get you out of here."

Her eyes were still wide as she pressed the back of her thin fingers to her cheek, no doubt trying to cool the burning ache and stem the swelling.

She didn't move, just looked at me and then down at the slumped-over, unconscious form of the lesser man.

We didn't have time for this.

I grabbed her. "Princess, this is not a request. It's an order."

She nodded but didn't move.

So I grabbed her and threw her over my shoulder.

CHAPTER 22

REID

*T*he hallway was fortunately still clear.

"Reid! Put me down this instant!"

"Hush, babygirl. I'm working."

Her small hands pressed against my back as she tried to leverage herself up. "This is preposterous. You have to let me go explain to my father."

With a closed fist, I punched the button for the back service elevators. "Your father knows all he needs to know right now."

Careful of her head, I ducked as I entered the elevator before hitting the lower ground level button for the kitchens. Having swept the building before the event, I knew of multiple escape routes.

Finally, I lowered her to her feet and placed her before me. Grasping her chin, I tilted her head back. "You're going to be a good girl for me and follow quickly and quietly."

"But—"

I placed a finger over her lips. "Emphasis on quietly."

Her lips moved against my finger with her frustrated sigh. "This is crazy. I can't just leave."

The corner of my mouth lifted as I winked. "Technically, you're not leaving. You're being kidnapped."

The key to not getting stopped was to stare straight ahead, not make eye contact, and walk with a determined purpose.

In less than ten minutes, I had Charlotte in my truck. I wasn't taking her to the safe house or even back to the Manwarring estate.

I was taking her home.

Charlotte was silent the entire trip.

Even when I pulled into the underground parking garage of my building.

It wasn't until I opened her door and helped her out that she started asking questions.

"Where are we?"

"I am taking you to my apartment, where it is safe, and you can be alone and unbothered for a bit," I said, taking her hand and leading her to the elevator.

"Where are we?" she asked again as the shock began to settle in.

Her body pressed against mine as I wrapped my arm around her shoulders and held her close.

When we got to my apartment, I opened the door to the simple one bed, one bath, with a small kitchenette space. Truth was, I didn't need a large space because I spent little time cooped up here. At least it was clean.

Fortunately, the curtains were all closed, not that it would have made a difference. But if they were open, she would have seen the bare brick of the building next to this one not less than a foot away. Far from the sweeping views of Central Park she was used to from her own large bay bedroom windows.

"This is where you live?" she asked, walking around, looking at my Ikea furniture and bare tabletops.

146

"Yes, when I am in the city. This is where I call home. I'm not here very much, but it's good enough."

"Okay…"

I could see the wheels spinning in her head, and for some reason I refused to put my finger on, I wanted her to feel at home here, too. I wanted her to like it.

"I like it. It's cozy," she said, sitting on the very edge of the sofa, her ankles crossed demurely under her as if she were preparing to be served afternoon tea during a friendly visit, instead of sitting before me in a blood, splattered mock wedding gown.

She really was a lady. A sweet, innocent girl that had been far too sheltered for far too long.

"You want to tell me what happened" I asked as I tossed my tuxedo jacket over a chair and pulled on my bowtie.

She played with the tulle fabric folds in her lap. "Not much to tell. I said something that made him angry. So he slapped me."

I inhaled slowly through my nose as the rage rose again in my blood.

Maybe I should have killed the bastard.

Unbuttoning my cuffs before pulling the tail of my shirt out of my pants, I asked, "What'd you say that set him off so badly?"

She looked up at me through a shock of tangled curls, her neat chignon from earlier hanging lopsided and adorably ruined.

When she told me what she'd said, I threw my head back and laughed. "That's my girl."

Her smile faded. "Yes, but that's the problem, Reid. I'm not your girl. I made a promise to my family."

"That's bullshit."

"That is my life," she corrected. "It's an ugly reality of my station. I don't get the luxury of making my own choices."

I watched a single tear slip down her reddened and slightly swollen cheek, and it broke something deep inside of me.

"Fuck that. Choose something different. Your father didn't arrange Luc's marriage. He sure as shit didn't arrange Olivia's. They made a choice. You can make your own."

"No, I can't. Luc and Olivia aren't useless like I am. They have skills they can use to survive in the real world. I have nothing. No life skills, nothing I can use as a trade."

"Your music," I insisted, and she laughed.

"Do you know how much a professional cellist makes? I wouldn't even be able to afford a cute apartment like this one. I will have nothing, and I will be cut off from everyone I know."

"So?"

"So!" She stood up, and her hand went to her shoulder as she rubbed the little spot where her shoulder met her neck. The same spot where her cello rested when she played.

The exact spot that made her body light up when I kissed her there.

"You want to hear me say it? Fine. I'm not brave enough to make that choice. I'm not brave enough to leave my family and all the money and all the safety of privilege behind."

I marched across the room and pulled her into my arms. "Have it your way, princess. You don't like choices, then I won't give you one."

I then kissed her with everything I had, and she kissed me back just as hungrily.

Sweeping her off her feet, I carried her into my bedroom and laid her on the only piece of furniture I'd spent time and money picking out.

My bed.

Charlotte was a lot of firsts for me.

The first woman I ever caught feelings for, the first woman to talk back to me, and it made my dick throb instead of turning me off.

She was the first woman I had ever spanked, and the first woman I had ever craved.

She was also the first woman I had brought back to my apartment and laid across my bed.

My bed was private.

It was a level of intimacy I had never wanted before having her here.

Having my princess in my bed felt right.

"Reid? What are you doing?" she asked as I reached underneath her for the zipper to her dress and peeled it off of her body, wanting to burn it when I saw the red lines on her ribs from the corset-style top.

"I'm going to show you how a real man treats his woman," I answered before I placed kisses on the tops of her breasts.

Her hands slid into my hair, holding on while I worked my way down her body, stopping first at her breasts, licking and sucking her nipples until they were tight little peaks. And when her breathing became faster, I kissed each of the red lines left by the dress over her ribs.

She was panting as I moved to the flat of her stomach and then to her slick, needy little cunt.

There was no reason to waste any time teasing her more.

That could come in round two or three.

I wasn't patient enough to wait.

My tongue dove between her folds, licking up her sweet essence before concentrating on her tight little bundle of nerves. It had occurred to me to work her up slowly, but I really was just out of patience, and I needed her now.

Needed to claim her as my own.

I needed her ready for my cock that was so hard it fucking hurt.

Nothing short of an intervention from God himself would stop me from taking her tonight.

It didn't matter if her father, her brother, or the entire world disagreed.

She was mine.

Mine for now and for always.

And no one was taking her from me.

She came on my tongue like the good girl she was.

I reached between us and unzipped my tuxedo pants, letting my cock spring free.

When I knew her body was relaxed, her pussy wet and desperate for more, I kissed my way back up her body until I reached her lips.

While she returned my kiss, I lined my body up with hers.

Her breath hitched as I pushed inside her, slowly letting her body adjust to my shaft before sliding in to the hilt.

"Oh, God." she gasped.

"God has nothing to do with this," I whispered in her ear. "You belong to me now."

CHAPTER 23

CHARLOTTE

"You're mine now," he all but growled in my ear as he thrust inside me, taking my innocence.

The second he pushed inside me, it hurt.

But he was gentle and slow and distracted me with soul shattering, possessive kisses while he stilled and let my body adjust to the new fullness of his intrusion.

It was so much all at once.

I felt scared and shaken up from before but also safe in his arms.

A strange desperation took hold of me. Desperation for something... more. The feeling confused me because I didn't know what I wanted.

This wasn't right. I wasn't supposed to do things like this.

Good girls didn't go home with their bodyguards and fuck them.

They certainly didn't let their bodyguards spank them. And they definitely didn't let them lick their pussies. They also absolutely did not drop to their knees to suck their guard's cock either.

Good girls didn't do any of that, but I reveled in it.

Perhaps, just perhaps... I had the potential to be a bad girl—a very bad, disobedient girl— after all.

Just like I'd reveled in it every night secretly under my covers when I touched myself thinking of Reid, I was reveling in his touch now.

And when he called me a good girl, I melted for him every single time.

I didn't have a choice. I fell under his spell, letting his touch, his kiss, and his claim pull me in.

If this meant I was a disappointment to my family, I couldn't bring myself to care.

I hadn't asked for this, but I wanted it.

"Reid, please," I shamelessly begged.

"God, princess," he grunted before slowly pulling out of me and thrusting back in.

The twinge of pain was gone, replaced by a darker need.

Something primal.

The way he called me princess made my stomach clench. He didn't say it like he had before. It wasn't meant to belittle or mock me. He said it with a touch of awe—as though for him, I was his princess. Not a weak girl who was clueless, but a prize who needed to be cherished and kept safe.

"Reid, please," I begged again. I didn't know what I needed, but I needed something, and I knew he was the only one who could give it to me.

"You're going to take my cock nice and hard now, babygirl," he growled.

I almost came apart just hearing those words whispered in my ear. "Yes, please. I want to..."

"You want to what?" He pulled out again, leaving me feeling cold and empty.

"I want to be your good girl. Please give me everything. Show me how to be good for you."

"Fuck," he swore, but it sounded more like a prayer as he thrust forward.

This time, he didn't stop. He kept going, thrusting in harder and faster each time.

As the pressure in my core built, I needed more. So much more.

I wrapped my arms around his back, with my legs hooked around his hips, holding on with everything I had while his slow, even thrusts became harder.

Yet, I still needed more.

"Fuck," Reid roared as he pulled away from me.

"What happened? What did I do?" I asked, sitting up suddenly, feeling empty and alone.

He didn't answer me.

He just grabbed my head with both hands and pulled my lips to his.

He pulled me closer, and I moved to get on top of him, but he broke the kiss and turned me around, then bent me over.

"Get on your hands and knees, baby. I need to fuck you harder."

I did as he said and buried my face into the pillow so he couldn't see the heat rising from my chest to my face. I felt so exposed in this position. I could feel his eyes take in all of me. His hands ghosted up my thighs to my ass, where he spread my cheeks a little.

"I was the first one in this perfect, sweet little cunt. I will be the first to take this perfect ass too, but not tonight."

I didn't even know what that meant, but he placed a kiss on the base of my spine and sent shivers running up my back. He licked a quick stripe from my clit to my opening and then up higher, all the way to my spine. My breath caught at the strange sensation.

That didn't feel primal. It felt sinful in the best way possible, but it wasn't what I needed at that moment.

"Reid, please." I still had no idea what I was begging for.

"Don't worry, princess. I have you." He pressed his cock to my opening and slid in with one long, fluid motion.

This position was so much better.

It put all the pressure in the places inside of me that just felt magical. He didn't wait for me to adjust. He pushed inside me over and over in a way that was brutal and almost violent.

His body bent over mine while I pushed up my hips and spread my knees to give him an even deeper angle. A move he rewarded, reaching in between my legs and strumming my clit with his fingers.

My head spun as I tried to process that he was saying something. I didn't answer him fast enough, and his hand slammed down on my ass.

"Are you going to be my good girl and come on my cock, or do you need to be punished first?" He gave me another warning smack on my ass.

"I want to be your..." My words trailed off when he lowered my head and chest to the bed, flattening everything but my hips that were tilted at a more severe angle, putting just a little pressure on my lower back.

"Say it," he demanded, and I realized the best part of this position.

I wasn't facing him.

I could close my eyes and pretend I was someone else, someone who could give in to the carnal pleasure without the weight of her obligations. I could close my eyes and be anyone else who could freely enjoy Reid and give him everything she was.

I gave in to the fantasy. "I want to be your good girl."

"What was that? Whose good girl do you want to be?" he asked, spanking me again.

His voice sounded a little off, like he had been running a marathon, and I loved it. He was losing himself in this as much as I was, and I needed it.

"Who do you belong to?" he barked, the slight pain adding to the immense pleasure.

"You," I cried as I plummeted over the edge and screamed. "I'm yours!"

"You're damn right, you're mine."

He continued to fuck me as I rode out my incredibly strong orgasm, until with a shout, he filled me with his hot come.

Reid lay on the bed next to me and pulled me in his arms so my back was pressed to his front, and he kissed my shoulders as my eyelids became too heavy to keep open.

* * *

I WOKE up hours later with his hands roaming my body, his lips pressed to the sensitive spot on my shoulder.

"Charlotte," he whispered.

I didn't dare answer him, in case speaking broke whatever spell we were under. Instead, I turned in his arms so I was facing him and pulled his face down to mine.

This time, when he took me, he was soft, gentle, and sweet.

His lips stayed on mine, and my legs wrapped around him while he pushed inside me deep and slow. It was different than before. This wasn't a claiming. He wasn't telling me he owned my innocence.

He was showing me affection, and it made my heart ache, and tears burned my eyes.

This was what I wanted my wedding night to be. This was the dream that I had been too afraid to even ponder.

I wanted a man who could take me with passion and wild abandon in one moment but in the next make love with a sweet, gentle disposition.

Reid was the best of both worlds, and I wanted him.

Only him.

I didn't want to be with anyone else.

I didn't want to be forced to marry someone through family obligations, who couldn't make me feel the way Reid did.

"Don't cry, Charlotte. Just stay here in this moment with me." He kissed me again, and I did as I was told.

I stayed in that moment with Reid, letting him show me all the things I didn't know I was capable of feeling.

The third time I woke up, the digital clock on the side of the bed said 2:00 a.m., and I knew I needed to go home. I carefully slipped out of bed and gathered my things.

"The bathroom is right there," Reid murmured sleepily, pointing behind him. "That is the only door you are allowed to go through right now."

"What?"

Reid sat up and yawned. "If you need the restroom, it's right there. If not, get your ass back in this bed."

"I need to get home."

"You really don't." He gave me a deadpan look.

"But my father."

"We will deal with all of that in the morning. Get back in bed."

"But I need to…"

"You need to get your ass back in this bed and go to sleep where I know you are safe."

"If I don't?" I asked, raising an eyebrow as I dropped my dress and shoes back on the floor, knowing I was standing in front of him completely naked in a shaft of moonlight.

His dark gaze raked over my bare flesh, leaving a trail of heat over my skin.

"If I have to get out of this bed and drag you back here, then so be it. But I will be spanking that ass a cherry red before I tie you to the headboard. Then, who knows if I will ever let you go. I might just leave you naked and bound, ready to be fucked whenever the mood strikes me."

In a rare moment of brazenness, I asked, "Is that supposed to entice me to get back in the bed or make a break for it?"

He launched out of the bed, stark naked, straight for me.

A high-pitched scream of excitement escaped my lips as I scurried away from his grasp.

I ran into the living room, and he had me inside his arms in five seconds.

He picked me up and carried me back into his room.

Just being in his strong arms made me feel safe, his skin warm against mine.

I liked the feeling of our skin-to-skin contact more than I would have thought.

It made me realize how touch-starved I had been my whole life.

I pushed that thought out of my head and added it to everything else that had to be dealt with tomorrow.

As if reading my thoughts, Reid growled, "Tomorrow, we will deal with the rest of the world, but tonight, you're mine and only mine."

A somber chill entered my chest, knowing tonight would be all we had.

Tomorrow, the dream ended and reality would return with a terrible vengeance.

CHAPTER 24

REID

"**G**ood morning." Charlotte walked out of my bedroom, looking like a gift from God. Her hair was a mess, there were little smudges of mascara under her eyes, and her lips were swollen, slightly bruised from my kiss.

She looked freshly fucked and somehow more comfortable in her own skin. More importantly, she looked more comfortable in nothing but one of my white undershirts.

I stared at her for a moment, just taking her in, wondering who I would have to kill to make sure this was the sight I was greeted with every morning.

Suddenly, I understood what Hunter had meant when he'd griped about settling down in one place. I could just see living my life here in the city, doing private security, or maybe back in Texas, spending my days working on the family ranch.

My evenings would be spent listening to her play at home just for me and in front of crowds at the Philharmonic. Then every night would be spent burying my cock in her tight little body until she became swollen with my baby.

"Good morning, princess. How did you sleep?" I asked, shaking myself out of my daydream stupor.

"I don't think I have ever slept that good in my life," she admitted with a blush coloring the tops of her cheeks. "But I did wake up a little sore."

"That is to be expected." I nodded and shook out a few ibuprofens from a bottle I kept in the kitchen cabinet right next to the coffee. It made it easy to find when I was hungover. "Have a seat. I'm making breakfast."

"Okay," she said and sat on the bar stool on the other side of the counter, where I placed her cup of coffee made with the flavored creamers I knew she liked.

I had woken up a few hours ago and decided that when my princess rose, she would have a breakfast worthy of her, and we would discuss what it would mean for her to be mine.

I'd ordered the groceries and had them delivered about twenty minutes ago.

She would still have rules to follow, but now they were much more strict.

I would still be with her every moment until the threat on her life was dealt with, but now there would be much fewer clothes involved when we were in this apartment.

"What's for breakfast?" she asked.

"Protein." I flipped the bacon that was sizzling in the pan and put a few pieces of Dave's Killer Bread into the toaster. "How do you like your eggs?"

"However you make them." The way her smile lit up her face made my chest ache, and I leaned in to kiss her, not being able to resist her pull.

"That was not what I asked you, little girl. Tell me how you like your eggs."

"Scrambled with cheese."

"Good girl." I kissed her again.

She watched me as I moved around the kitchen, her eyes never leaving my hands as I worked to prepare our meal.

"Do you like to cook?" I asked.

"I don't know. I was never allowed to learn."

Jesus fuck. She really had no life skills.

"Come here," I ordered.

I moved her in between my arms and handed her the fork to beat the eggs. I stood behind her, whispering the directions in her ear with my hands on her hips.

God, I was so tempted to say fuck the eggs, and put her on the counter and eat her for breakfast.

I was about to do just that when she bounced on her toes, so excited she didn't even notice her ass rubbing against my hard cock. She had poured the eggs into the hot frying pan that I had cooked the bacon in and had already poured out the excess grease.

Charlotte was excited the eggs were cooking. I would let her have this for now, and I would have my second breakfast soon enough.

We ate in silence. The eggs were overcooked, but I didn't care. She was happy and safe. That was enough for now.

"So, I should get going soon. My father will want to discuss what happened at the party last night."

"You don't have to go back there." I struggled to keep my tone light and even.

"I do. I live there. I have to face my father and figure out what is going to happen after... everything."

"Nothing is going to happen. You are going to stay right where you are. You're mine now."

"I'm not yours. That isn't how that works." Her eyes went to the ground, but her lips were in a firm line.

"That is exactly how that works, by your own admission. I fucked you last night, claiming you as mine." I moved to stand

161

directly in front of her and tilted her chin up so she could see how serious I was. "And you liked it. Admit it."

"I…" Her voice cracked, and I was not having it.

I grabbed a handful of her hair and yanked it back, forcing her head up.

Leaning in really close, I whispered in her ear, "Admit it. I brought you back here and made you my little pet, and you fucking loved every minute. You loved the way I ate your little cunt, almost as much as you loved the feeling of my cock buried deep inside of you. I bet you even loved the feeling of my come dripping from your cunt as I held you last night."

"I…" She still couldn't make a full sentence.

"You want to go back to your father so he can sell you off to some asshole who hits you and will never be able to make you feel the way I do?"

"Reid, please. Don't make this harder than it already is."

"No, I don't think so, princess. The only thing you beg for is my cock. You sure as fuck won't beg me to watch you marry some prick who doesn't deserve you. You belong here, with me, in my bed, bouncing on my cock."

"It's not that simple," she whispered.

"It is that simple," I barked, losing my temper.

After everything I had done for her, risking my career, the only thing I gave a fuck about was her. I put her in my bed, something I had never done with any woman before. I fucking made her breakfast, and I still wasn't enough for her.

"It isn't, please understand." Tears filled her eyes.

"Here is what I understand, princess," I spat the word, making it an insult again. "If you want to go back into that den of vipers, you will be going with my come leaking from your pussy. This is mine." I grabbed her bare pussy, finding it already wet for me. "This will only ever be mine. It doesn't matter who you spread your pretty little legs for. I was here first, and we both know that no one will ever make you feel the way I can."

"Reid, please," she said again, but it was different this time.

Her voice was breathy, her pupils were wide, and her pussy was hot and wet on my fingers.

She wanted to be claimed by me.

Her body craved me, her heart wanted me, but her silly little brain refused to catch the fuck up.

I ripped my shirt off her, threw it somewhere behind me, turned her around, and bent her over the kitchen counter.

"Is this what you want, princess? Just a good old-fashioned hard fuck from the stableboy? Far be it from me to deny such a spoiled little brat."

I slammed into her, not giving a fuck how sore she was or if she was ready for me.

I didn't really need to worry about the last part. Her cunt was dripping wet and greedily took me in, clenching around me like a hot velvet glove.

The scream she let out was pure animalistic need. She knew she needed this, she needed me to remind her who she belonged to, and if she kept on her bullshit about obeying her father over me, I was going to make her call me 'daddy.'

I should be the only man she obeyed. I was the only one who really gave a fuck about her needs or her safety.

I could only imagine what would have happened to her if I hadn't been there last night, and that pissed me off even more, so I took my anger and frustration out on her pussy.

She came apart on my cock, but I didn't let up, I didn't stop to give her a moment to recover. Considerations like that were only for good girls, not little brats who tried to deny what was rightfully mine.

"Oh, God," she panted, as I fucked into her harder, pushing her past her limits.

She screamed out another orgasm, this time her pussy contracting around me and her come splashing out around my cock, coating my hips and running trails down my thighs.

She could squirt.

If she saw reason, then I would have fun exploring that later.

"Oh, God!" she screamed again, trying to bury her face in her arms.

"God has nothing to do with this, princess."

I slapped her ass cheek before spitting on her asshole and rubbing my spit in with my thumb before sinking one then two fingers in, claiming all of her.

Charlotte took it. She took everything I gave her and even lifted on her tiptoes to give me better access. She could take everything I gave her, and she still couldn't see she was made for me.

That ended now.

With my free hand, I grabbed her hair and yanked her head up so she could see the mirror across the room.

"Do you see that?" I growled, still slamming into her. "Do you see how desperate you look when I fuck you? How beautifully feral? Do you think your fiancé can make you feel this? Do you think anyone else can fuck you, own you like I can?"

She stared in the mirror, looking at herself, taking it all in. I wondered what she saw.

I saw a man taking what was his.

Claiming his woman and showing her why no one else would ever be able to compare.

She probably saw herself slumming, sowing her wild oats before settling down in a comfortable life of mindless monotony, broken only by her husband beating her.

The anger burned in my veins and made my cock throb.

I hated her for it.

I hated her for making me feel like I wasn't good enough when I was the only one who was.

"Do you know what you look like right now?" I said, letting my anger turn my voice cruel.

She shook her head, and her thighs started trembling again. She was going to rocket into her third orgasm, and I was going to make sure she knew exactly what this feeling was like.

"You look like a greedy little slut. A needy whore who will never be satisfied by a 'suitable husband.' You are letting yourself be whored out for a title and a life of disappointing sex. How does it feel knowing that the only way you will ever be able to come is by fucking the help?"

Her eyes were wide and full of tears when I bit the sensitive spot on her shoulder, twisted my fingers in her ass, and changed the angle of my thrust to hit her g-spot, making her come with a scream and my cruel words in her head.

I came right after she did, filling her with my cum and holding her down on my cock until I had emptied everything inside of her.

She was still shaking when I pulled out and moved away from her.

I didn't even so much as look at her as I washed my hands and then started moving dishes to the sink to be taken care of later.

"Go put your dress back on. Do not clean yourself up. Do not put on your panties," I ordered.

She didn't say anything, just left to find her things.

When she came back out, her hair was straightened, her makeup cleaned off, her dress in place, and her shoes on. If I didn't know better, I would say nothing had happened last night.

"Panties?" I asked, needing to know if she'd followed directions.

She held out a scrap of white lace that I took from her and

put in my pocket. I had never kept souvenirs from women before, but I had never been with anyone like Charlotte.

"Did you clean my come from your body?"

Her cheeks turned bright red again, but she shook her head no.

"Let me see."

She lifted her dress and showed me her glistening thighs that were still wet with the mixture of our cum.

I nodded before changing my pants and grabbing a shirt and my keys.

"Then let's go return you to your father and abusive fiancé," I said.

She flinched at my words and looked like she wanted to say something, but I didn't want to hear it.

We pulled up to the back servants' entrance to the house, by the loading dock where the kitchen accepted deliveries.

After helping her out of the truck, I caged her in between my body and the open door. "This is your last chance, princess. Come back with me. Be mine. Leave all of this behind. There is nothing in that house that I can't give you. Nothing."

"I can't," was all she said without meeting my gaze.

CHAPTER 25

CHARLOTTE

"*I* can't marry him," I said into the phone the second Luc picked up.

I sat in my bedroom, looking out at the treetops of Central Park.

The first thing I should have done when I got home was take a shower, but I didn't want to wash Reid off of me yet.

I wanted to be able to still smell him on my skin to help give me the courage for what I needed to do.

"What do you mean you can't marry him?" Luc asked.

"I mean, I can't marry the man father wants me to marry." My voice faltered a little, but I pulled my stomach in and sat straighter to help my words sound as strong as I needed them to.

"Father said that you wanted this?"

I didn't bother to hide the laugh that escaped my lips. "Do you really think Father asked what I wanted? Do you think what I wanted mattered to him at all? Father wants a title in the family. That was the only want that was considered in this match."

There was a pause on the other end of the line for a moment and then a sigh of disappointment.

"You're right," he said, and I could just picture Luc in my mind standing and pacing around the room like a caged animal trying to figure a way out of the situation I was putting him in by telling him what I wanted. "But I thought you agreed to the marriage."

I knew he would try to help, especially after being with Amelia had changed him.

He used to be exactly like our father. Only his ambitions and the family money mattered.

Then Amelia was literally forced into his life.

Before Luc met my sister-in-law, he wouldn't have helped me. Now, he was the only chance I had. I just prayed Amelia's influence was enough.

"I went along with it because I thought it was what was expected of me. I was doing what I thought I had to."

"Does this have something to do with what happened last night?"

Suddenly, it felt like my heart was in my throat, and a cold sweat broke out over my back. Did Luc know what happened between Reid and me last night? Had Reid told him? How else could he possibly know?

"I..."

How did I admit to my brother that, yes, Reid had made love to me over and over and then taken me hard this morning, and I knew that the only way I could ever be happy or even content was in Reid's arms?

How could I admit out loud to my brother that Reid made me feel seen, heard, and protected, as well as all the carnal pleasures he had shown me were possible?

Being in Reid's arms made me forget everything else. The

only other thing that had ever consumed me so completely was my cello.

"Reid told me one series of events, but Zeigler had a very different story. Could you clarify which one is true?"

"What did Reid tell you?" I asked, trying not to let the relief show in my voice.

There was no reason to hint to Luc at what really happened.

"Reid said that Zeigler got mad at you and hit you. Then he hit Zeigler repeatedly. Zeigler's story is a little different. He said that you and he had an intimate moment, nothing too untoward for an engaged couple, and Reid, in a jealous fit of rage, attacked him. Then kidnapped you."

What did it say about the events of last night that I honestly forgot that he had hit me?

My fingers went to my cheek, pressing down, and it was still a little sore, but nothing compared to the ache between my thighs.

"Zeigler didn't like that I corrected him, especially not in front of you and Harrison. He informed me that I was never allowed to correct him in public, said some very crude things about what my role as his wife would be, and then he struck me."

"He actually hit you?"

"He backhanded me across the face, hard enough that my cheek swelled, and I still have a little bruising. Nothing that concealer won't cover now, but last night, there was no way to hide it. Reid escorted me out of the party at my request so I didn't have to explain what happened."

"So then Reid didn't attack..." Luc's voice got scary quiet.

I knew he was angry.

The cold, quiet kind of anger which meant he was planning revenge. The only other time I heard him like this was when Olivia was taken by Marksen.

He saw what Zeigler had done to me as an attack on the family.

I was still a Manwarring, and I was his sister.

A soft, soothing warmth spread in my chest.

My brother really did care about me.

"Reid defended me. I won't lie. It was brutal, but Luc, I don't know how far Zeigler would have gone. He was very angry, and if Reid hadn't been there... I don't know what would have happened. Please don't make me marry a man like that."

"Father is already taking care of it. He's been on the phone all morning threatening fire and brimstone to keep it out of the media. But this won't be the end of it. He's already talking about arranging another marriage to help you weather the storm. Sort of a bait and switch."

"I think I have an idea to keep me safe from any more of father's matchmaking. But right now, I have to get ready. I have a charity event this afternoon."

"Well then, break a leg," Luc said with a hollow-sounding laugh.

I knew that laugh. I had heard it before. It was his business laugh. The one he had when someone said something funny, or he was trying to be charming, but behind that laugh, he was already making his next move.

I really did have a charity event to go to this afternoon. I was excited to play, but there was something far more important I needed to do there.

I needed to talk to Ginnie.

I took my time in my large marble bathtub, letting the hot water soothe away the aches and pains as it washed away Reid's touch.

I hated that the expensive soaps I used would completely remove any sign of him from my skin. The thought of Reid marking my body in a way that couldn't just be washed away made my core clench.

I lay back in the tub, sinking all the way down into the steaming water, closed my eyes, and relived last night. I had been so caught up in the feelings, the cravings, and the urgency, I hadn't really appreciated what he was doing to me.

There wasn't time to process any of it.

So I took far longer than I needed to and reveled in everything.

Even the anger as he took me this morning.

How he hated bringing me back.

There was something powerful in that.

His need to mark me with his seed, to have me walk back into my father's house with Reid's come still drying on my thighs, made me feel... not dirty, but different.

Like I had a secret.

I knew I was changing and on the precipice of something great, even if no one else knew. A new chapter in my life was beginning, and I belonged to someone who wanted me for me, not for what my father could provide.

And frankly, after finally being brave enough to stand up for myself, I deserved the luxurious bubble bath.

I couldn't wait to see Reid again. I wanted to show him that I could be his good girl and I would fight to be his.

Actions spoke louder than words, and I needed to show him how I wanted to be his.

I thought about telling him my plan when he dropped me off, but he was already so angry, and I couldn't risk disappointing him if I wasn't strong enough to go through with it. I couldn't bear the idea of disappointing him.

It didn't matter anymore.

He was escorting me to the charity gala, and on the way there, I would explain everything. Then I would play my heart out for this event, talk to Ginnie, and figure out what my next moves were.

Covering the bruises on my face took far longer than I had planned. And by the time I was ready to go to the event, I was running about five minutes late.

I ran downstairs, my cello in hand ready to meet Reid at the front door.

I couldn't wait to tell him about my plan.

I wanted to see that look in his eyes, the one that said, 'You are mine, and I am proud of you.' He was going to call me his 'good girl' and whisper dirty things in my ear, and then after the charity, he would take me back to his place and reward me for being so brave. But he wasn't there.

Instead, waiting for me was a different man, dressed similarly to how Reid did in solid black, with his sidearm barely covered by his jacket.

"Ms. Manwarring," he greeted me with a friendly smile. "My name is Hunter. I will be escorting you tonight."

"Where is Reid?" The abruptness of my question was rude, but I didn't care.

Hunter rubbed the back of his neck while looking behind me, above me, and to the side. Anywhere but my face.

"He had something come up and asked me to fill in."

He was lying to me. I could see it in his face.

He was lying, and he didn't want to be.

Which meant he was covering for Reid, who just didn't want to be here.

My heart, which was so full of hope and excitement just a few seconds ago, deflated.

Tears stung behind my eyes, and my stomach clenched.

I wanted to run back to my room and throw up, then cry.

I wanted to call him and demand to know why.

But I was a Manwarring, and I had an obligation.

I gave Hunter a gracious smile and prayed he didn't look too closely, or he would see the pain behind it.

"Okay, well. Then we should be off," I said.

Hunter nodded and offered to take my cello case as we walked to the car.

I tried to be strong, but one single thought kept circling over and over in my mind, making me want to crumple.

If I was his, why would he entrust my safety to someone else?

There may not have been a threat against me, but I wasn't enough of a fool to assume that Zeigler would take the insult of our broken engagement lying down.

I doubted he would come at me directly, but why didn't Reid care enough to protect me himself?

CHAPTER 26

ROMNEY

"*H*ere, take these."

The sunlight burned my eyes after I lifted the cloth ice bag from my black eye.

My mother stood before me, holding out her hand. She dropped two white tablets onto my palm.

"What are they?"

"*Paracetamol,*" she answered as she handed me a glass of water.

I frowned. "Aspirin. Christ, Mummy. We're in New York. You could spit and find a drug dealer."

She moved to the breakfast sideboard to prepare her usual breakfast, a tall glass of ruby Red Grapefruit juice with *Pimms.* "Don't be vulgar," she chastised as she added ice to her drink.

I threw the ice bag across the room as I marched to the same sideboard to pour myself a gin. "I'm in pain. I need something stronger."

She flounced onto the sofa in the lounge between our penthouse bedrooms. Arranging her diaphanous caftan around her, she said, "Stop it. You're a Zeigler. Start behaving like one."

I cast her a dark look over my shoulder. "I am behaving like one. I agreed to marry that simpering bitch, didn't I?"

"And look what a mess you've made of it."

I rounded on her. "I made of it? It's not my bloody fault. How was I supposed to know she was fucking her gorilla of a bodyguard? You're the one who set me up with a whore who's fucking the help."

"Don't be stupid, Romney. All high society women fuck the help. The blood of British aristocrats would be water thin if it wasn't reinforced with peasant stock every few generations."

I grimaced. "Now who's being vulgar, Mummy?"

She leaned forward. "We need to fix this. We need to—"

A knock on the hotel suite door gave us both pause.

I raised a finger to my lips as we both held our breath.

While we had told anyone of influence we were staying at the Ritz-Carlton while we remodeled our family home, the truth was that we had been kicked out of it by the banks. Ever since, we had been practically squatters at the Ritz, avoiding the general manager as he tried to collect on our painfully overdue bill.

Another knock.

My father emerged from the bedroom. "What the devil is that racket?"

My mother rose and placed a retraining hand on his arm. "Stop talking, Chiswell. We don't want them to know we're here."

I rolled my eyes. Why couldn't the old bastard die already and give me the title?

Then a high-pitched grating voice came through the door. "It's meeeeeeeee, darrrlllinnng."

My mother cracked open the door and hustled Mary Astrid inside, then surveyed the empty hallway before slamming it shut and putting the chain across. "So how bad is it?"

Mary hooked her arm through my mother's and strolled into the suite as if she owned it. With dramatic flair, she placed her hand on her chest. "Well, because it's you, darling, I've called in favors all over town and have kept the worst of the story out of the papers. As far as anyone knows, there was a security breach that ended the happy event early."

"Christ." I retrieved the ice bag and moved to the sofa. Throwing my legs up on the cushions, I placed the bag over my eyes again.

There wasn't a doubt in my mind that if there was nothing in the press, it was Lucian Manwarring's influence, not Mary Astrid's.

Mary helped herself to a heaping portion of scrambled eggs and several sausages. As she piled the food onto her plate, she continued to speak, "But we need to act fast, darling, because rumors are already swirling."

The ice in mummy's glass rattled with her agitation. "What do you recommend we do?"

"The best way to avoid a scandal is to change the narrative. Give everyone something else to talk about, of course."

I rolled my eyes, then immediately regretted it as a sharp pain exploded in my head. I groused, "Excellent. Remind me. Did that work well for you when your notorious affair and bastard DA son came to light?"

My mother waved her hand in my direction. "Romney, behave."

Mary Astrid narrowed her gaze. "As a matter of fact it did. After all, I still have plenty of money."

Touché.

My father ignored the entire debacle by burying his nose in the New York Times. As if this entire fucking mess wasn't his fault. Damn useless man, investing the entire Zeigler family fortune in a ridiculous Ponzi scheme.

Mary Astrid licked her fingers after eating a greasy sausage. "Don't worry. I have a plan. Romney, how good are your acting skills?"

CHAPTER 27

CHARLOTTE

"*Hey*, Charlotte! Ready to Rock Bach on a Boat?"

I smiled as Ginnie greeted me with the silly name of the charity fundraiser.

Dressed in a beautiful black dress paired with combat boots and an incredibly dark smoky eye, she strutted over to me. I loved how she could always pull off the most daring looks that would seem ridiculous on most people but were always edgy and flawless on her.

"In a moment," I said, eyeing Hunter, who, after setting my cello on its stand, had made himself scarce.

He was currently standing on the edge of the stage, keeping an eye on the crowd. Watching me, but also giving me my space and privacy.

He was doing precisely what he should have been, the same way Reid was supposed to but never did.

It made me hate Hunter a little more. It wasn't fair or deserved, but it was what it was.

"Can I ask you a few personal questions?" I asked Ginnie, lowering my voice.

"You can ask, but I can't promise I will answer." She shrugged and sat on the metal folding chair, crossing one leg over the other. Her massive combat boot looked like it was going to slip off her dainty leg any second.

"How did you do it? Was it worth it? How hard was it to survive? Would you do it again?" The words tumbled through my lips, and I couldn't seem to stop.

"Do what exactly?"

"I know who you are," I said. "I know you come from a family like mine, and you gave it all up, and I want to know why and if it was worth it," I said, slumping down in my own chair.

"Oh, that." Ginnie's eyes widened with understanding. "No, it wasn't easy. It was the hardest thing I ever had to do. Not everyone who comes from money, especially not the kind of money my family has, would survive that kind of lifestyle change. Sometimes, I still miss the life I led, but I wouldn't change it for the world."

"What do you mean?" I asked.

"Look, I don't know your specific situation, so I'm not going to tell you what to do. It's a huge decision, and the only way you can live with the decision you make is if you are the one who makes it. I can tell you that if you give it up, it will be hard in ways you don't even know. You will have to learn how to budget your money and fend for yourself. That means having a job, or sometimes two, learning to cook, getting your own apartment, and you will even have to shop and probably clip coupons. Also, I hope you like ibuprofen and potatoes. Both will become a staple in your life."

"Is it worth it?" I asked, needing someone to tell me what I already knew in my heart.

"It is if you love what you are gaining more than what you are giving up. If the love of your life is Birken bags, then no. And no judgment. There are some things I didn't know I would miss as much as I do. But if you love something more than anything else, and that is what you are giving it up for, then yes."

"What was that important to you?" I shouldn't have pried, but I couldn't help it.

"My music. Not just this." She motioned around the room. "Don't get me wrong. I love classical music, but my passion is playing cello in my metal band. It makes me feel things that I didn't know people could feel. The music moved me, and my family didn't understand it. They gave me a choice, and I decided I could try living without the money, but I couldn't live without the music."

She had put words to exactly how I felt about Reid.

If he would still have me, I would give it all up for him.

I didn't know what he made as a security guard, but between that and what I could potentially make from the Philharmonic, if they would still have me, I was sure we could scrape by.

If he would still have me.

"We can talk more about this later if you want," Ginnie said as she picked up her cello.

"I'm in a bit of mood, can we change up the set?" I asked, taking my seat and picking up my cello.

Her darkly-lined eyes lit up with mischief. "What were you thinking?"

"*Champagne Problems* by Taylor Swift."

Her head tilted to one side. "Ah, this is starting to make sense. Let me guess, the bodyguard?"

"How did you know?"

"Please. The man is a walking sex god."

We hadn't rehearsed it, but we played off each other, switching between who played the melodies and who harmonized seamlessly.

I sang the song's heartbreaking and very meaningful lyrics in my head as I closed my eyes and played.

By the end of the song, a small group of people who had moved to watch us play started clapping.

I swiped at the tears in my eyes and played it off as adjusting my eye makeup.

We then launched straight into another song, creating a playlist that had both classical pieces and a few pop songs for the next hour.

The yacht we were on was well on its way to giving the guests the perfect view of the Manhattan skyline at sunset, which we could only view through the windows of an interior lounge. The damp evening air was dangerous for our expensive instruments.

"I need a breather and a drink," Ginnie said. "Let's take fifteen and head out onto the deck for some fresh air."

"Sounds perfect."

After letting Hunter know that I would be stepping below for a moment, we carried our cellos to the small stateroom we had been assigned as a green room. They were too valuable to leave on their stands out in the open among the drinking crowd.

I couldn't wait for this event to be over so I could head straight back to Reid's apartment and tell him the news. I wanted to see his face when I told him I was going to stand up to my father and refuse to marry Romney. That I wanted to be with him and only him.

Already I could imagine the cozy mornings making him breakfast before I headed out to work. Trips to local flea markets on the weekend to find fun, kitchy items to decorate the apartment with. Wearing jeans and an old sweater as I headed out to my job as a clerk in some small, beloved neighborhood music store.

It was all going to be so wonderfully *normal*.

There were butterflies in my stomach. I was like a kid about to set off on a grand adventure filled with new experiences and challenges.

As I emerged from the warren of small hallways below, a very pinched British accent said behind me, "Charlotte, darling. I need to speak with you."

My spine stiffened as I turned around to face my former fiancé.

"What are you doing here?" I asked, taking in the kaleido-scope of colors on his face that was poorly disguised by makeup. Even if he had properly applied the concealer, it wouldn't have done anything for the swelling. Or for the bandage across his nose.

His gaze hardened as his left cheek twitched. "I came to speak with you and apologize for the misunderstanding last evening."

My natural instinct was to cower and then do whatever he said.

But I wasn't his. I wasn't a dog my father bred and trained to sell off for breeding.

I belonged to Reid. Only Reid.

I wanted to make him proud, so I wasn't going to give this asshole the satisfaction.

"Misunderstanding? Here we call it assault."

"Whatever. It's in the past. Come, let me show off my beau-tiful fiancée and show the world the rumors from last night's party are just that." He took my arm and pulled me toward him. "Silly rumors. We shall put them to bed, and soon we will be wed and…"

"Are you insane?" I yanked my hand out of his grip. "We're not getting married."

"You are making a scene." His voice lowered and his eyes darted around as if people were watching him.

I searched over his shoulder for Hunter. "Let go of me now, or I really will make a scene, and then I will have my guard throw you overboard. It's a cold night. I don't know if you will make it all the way back to shore." I bared my teeth as I spoke, trying to channel Reid and his command over every situation.

I may not have had the fortitude to be him when it came to my father, but I wasn't about to let this man walk all over me.

Romney started as his shoulders hitched high over his ears. His gaze shifted around us, searching the crowd. "If that gorilla comes anywhere near me again, I'll have him arrested for attempted murder."

His threat chilled my rebellious ardor. It wouldn't serve to gain my freedom by having Reid's taken away. To diffuse the situation, I lied. "That bodyguard has been let go, but that doesn't mean I'm not still guarded. I suggest you walk away."

"Come with me now." He grabbed my arm again, this time hard enough to hurt. "This marriage is happening if I have to whip you all the way up to the fucking altar."

"Let go of me." I tried to pull my arm away, but he squeezed tighter. Any tighter and he'd break my arm. "I am not going to marry you. The engagement is off."

"You don't get to make that call," he seethed as he dragged me to a more secluded point on the deck.

I dug my heels in, not wanting to move. "If you don't let go, I will scream!"

Before he could respond, there were several loud gunshots, then a booming voice, "Ladies and gentlemen, this is a robbery."

CHAPTER 28

CHARLOTTE

*M*y eyes widened as I lowered my body and moved closer to the wall.

A thousand thoughts clashed around my mind.

Where is Hunter?

Is Ginnie safe?

Reid.

Reid.

Reid.

It was too cruel that the moment I decided to actually start living by telling a man I loved him, I would be gunned down in a vicious robbery.

At least we weren't with the main guests...

While people screamed and cried out, the gunmen corralled them at the bow. Several of the ski-masked men held out open black backpacks as they demanded jewelry, phones, and wallets.

This was all so very strange.

What kind of thieves robbed a yacht full of people? It seemed like an incredibly chaotic and foolish thing to do. There were countless places to hide. It required a boat as a getaway vehicle, which was not guaranteed since someone could sound the alarm before they even reached the harbor.

So odd.

I surveyed the situation from a side deck on the starboard side, slightly out of view, as I desperately searched the assembled crowd for Ginnie's familiar face. I didn't see her. Hopefully she was safe below deck.

Safe for now.

Oh, why had I left my cellphone in my cello bag?

As I hunched against the wall, straining to hear the demands of the robbers, Romney straightened to his full height and cleared his throat.

I snatched at his sleeve. "Get down, Romney."

Instead, he wrapped his hand around my wrist and wrenched me away from my meager shelter. He then marched down the hall, toward the men with guns.

I yanked on my arm. "What are you doing? Romney? What are you—"

As we came within view of everyone, Romney cleared his throat again. "Here now. I demand you cease this nonsense immediately."

A wave of nausea forced bile into the back of my throat as the dark, beady eyes of all five gunmen trained on us.

Through fear-clenched teeth, I whispered, "Shut up," as I tried to twist my wrist out of his grasp.

Romney looked down at me. In a loud voice clearly meant to be heard over the tense din of the party guests, he said, "Do not fear, my darling bride. I will keep you safe from these ruffians."

Ruffians?

Is he serious?

One of the masked men stepped forward. "Oh really, tough guy?"

He reached a black gloved hand out to me and snatched the

diamond and platinum tennis necklace from around my neck. He then held it aloft. "What are you going to do about it?"

Romney threw off his jacket. "How dare you touch my bride! Now you'll pay."

What is happening?

Why does this feel like a bad soap opera?

Romney surged forward and attempted to seize the man's gun by the barrel.

They struggled.

As I stared, dumfounded, a strong arm wrapped around my waist and wrenched me backwards.

My heart soared. Reid.

I turned to see the stern continence of Hunter, his associate. "Get behind me."

While incredibly grateful that he was here to protect me, there was still a part of me that was disappointed it wasn't Reid, as ludicrous as that idea might have been, since Reid would have no way of knowing I was in danger right now.

With his body as a shield and using Romney as a distraction, Hunter backed away as his hand hovered over his sidearm.

Before we got out of earshot, I heard Romney whine. "You're supposed to give me the gun!"

What the fuck?

* * *

JUST AS WE neared the stairwell to the lower deck, one of the gunmen spotted us.

He raised his gun. "Hey, you two! Stop!"

Just then Romney, showing courage I didn't think he was capable of, stepped in front to block us. Placing his hands on his hips, he puffed out his chest. "Don't worry, Charlotte Manwarring. I, *The Honorable* Romney Horace Zeigler, future *The Right*

Honorable Lord Zeigler, heir to the Zeigler barony, will protect you."

The man fired, clipping Romney on the upper arm.

He bent over, clutching his shoulder. When he pulled his hand back and saw blood, he screamed. "Blood! That's real blood! Are those real bullets?"

The man fired again.

Hunter turned and blocked the fire as he hustled me down the narrow stairwell.

Unfortunately, Romney followed us.

Hunter kicked open the door to a small supply closet and pushed me inside.

Again, unfortunately, Romney squeezed in next to me.

After giving him an assessing once-over glare, Hunter turned to me and said in an urgent tone. "Stay still and silent. I'll be back."

I reached out to grab his shirt. "Ginnie. You have to find my friend."

He nodded. "I'll do my best. Remember. Silent."

The closest was thrown into darkness the moment he slammed the door.

A second later, Romney flipped on the light switch. "Who is he to be giving us orders?"

I flipped the switch off and rasped, "He's my..." I stopped.

I didn't want to say bodyguard. Bodyguard was such an intimate term. That was Reid's job. And only his. "He's my security detail. Now be quiet."

He flipped the switch back on. "I don't take orders from you or him. We have to get back up to the deck where the guests can see us."

I turned the light off. "Why on earth would we need the other guests to see us?"

He flipped it on. "Because they need to see me rescuing you!"

In my shock, I forgot to turn the light back off. I stared at him with wide eyes. "What have you done?"

He leaned his head down into his chest, giving him a double chin. "What? Me? Huh? What? Nothing."

I grabbed his shirt front and shook him. "What did you do? Did you hire those men?"

He flung my arms off. "Stop asking questions."

I pressed my hand to my forehead. "Oh my God! Romney you have to stop this! Now. You have to go call this off before someone gets hurt."

Twisting his torso, he pointed to his arm. "I *did* get hurt."

I scoffed. "It's barely a scratch."

Just then, there was an exchange of gunfire just outside our door.

I crossed my arms over my chest as I hunched down, curling into a fetal position.

All I could think about was Reid's big strong body and his large arms and his hard muscled chest as I desperately wished I was in the safe shelter of his embrace in his bed right now.

The door to the closet swung open.

My hope that it was Hunter to tell us it was all clear was dashed.

It was two of the gunmen. "Here he is!"

Romney raised his arms and waved his hands. "I'm going to tell my mummy about this. You're not following the script!"

I gasped. "You did hire these men!"

At least there was a positive aspect to that. If these men were just hired actors, they couldn't be that much of a threat. Right?

Maybe the bullet that hit Romney was a fluke. I'd heard before that even blanks could be dangerous. Maybe it was a stunt gone wrong?

The gunman pointed what looked like a very real gun at me.

"You shut your face." Then he pointed to Romney. "And you, your money wire didn't clear."

Romney's eyes widened, right before he snatched me before him as a human shield. "She's an heiress! Her father is loaded. Billions!"

Through clenched teeth, I said, "We are so not getting married."

The gunman dragged us both into the hallway.

And that was when I saw him... Hunter lying face down in a pool of blood.

Terror nearly strangled the oxygen from my lungs.

Romney may have hired them, but these were definitely not actors.

They were a real threat, and I was in real mortal danger.

CHAPTER 29

REID

*H*unter: *SOS three, maybe four armed masked assailants. I've been shot. They've taken Charlotte and her douchey fiancé hostage as well as every other guest on the ship.*

I stared at the text message Hunter had just sent me.

There was no fucking way that some bougie charity event was being robbed. Almost every person at that event should have their own private security around the perimeter.

Reid: *Are you fucking with me?*

I sent the replying text and kicked back on my couch, lifting my feet on the table and laying my head on the pillow she had slept on last night.

It still smelled like her.

Like Earl gray tea, mandarin oranges, and flowers. She smelled soft, feminine, and refined.

Sitting on my couch and smelling the pillow she slept on was a new low for me.

I used to torment and beat the shit out of men who did pussy shit like this, but now I got it.

Not that I would ever admit that to anyone, ever.

Hunter: *No. I don't know if anyone has gotten the word out. The assailants have taken all of the cell phones.*

It was not the first time Hunter had played this prank on me.

When he'd tried to fight me on why I wanted him to take the job, I knew, I just knew he would pull this kind of shit.

Some half-assed way to make me see her again and face my feelings. I was not the kind of man who did shit like that. You would never catch me sitting at home watching *The Notebook* and crying over true love or whatever it was men like that cried over.

She was just a girl.

I'd had her and now she was gone.

She'd had her little dalliance with the 'bad boy'. She'd made it clear that was all it was, so I took my pound of flesh by fucking her like I would every other girl and took her home.

It was over. Hunter needed to accept that because I sure as fuck had.

Reid: *Then how do you have yours?*

Hunter: *Because after I was shot, I played dead while they picked up your fucking girlfriend and her future husband. I lay still in a puddle of my own god damned blood just so I could text you as I was bleeding out.*

Reid: *How badly are you injured?*

I sent the text as I ran around my apartment, getting my shoes and coat on.

God, I was so fucking stupid.

Yeah, I was mad at Charlotte, but there was no excuse for her to be without protection.

I thought Hunter would be enough, but clearly, I was wrong.

Now she was stuck at an event with her asshole fiancé to keep her safe.

Jesus, she would be better off with the assailants.

Hunter: *Two GSWs. Non-fatal areas, losing blood.*

Reid: *Okay what hotel are you at?*

He dropped a pin for his location, but it couldn't have been right. It was in the middle of the ocean. I stared at my phone in disbelief for a second before I rolled my eyes.

Reid: *So you are fucking with me. That wasn't fucking funny, asshole.*

Hunter: *The charity event was moved to a yacht.*

A yacht changed everything.

It meant that Hunter was probably the only paid security because most people thought being isolated would make them safe.

Clearly, it didn't. It made them a more vulnerable target.

On my way, I texted back as I ran down to the basement, ignoring my car and instead grabbing my Kawasaki Ninja motorcycle, a gift from a grateful Japanese businessman after I had helped pull him and his daughter from a questionable situation some years ago. This little beauty maxed out around 200 mph, and strictly speaking, was not street-legal.

I checked my phone one more time to see if there was an essential update from Hunter, but there wasn't. He wasn't able to get a better view of the assailants without being spotted. So, he had no idea what was happening on the deck.

I was going in blind, but I did not give a fuck.

These assholes had stuck a gun in my girl's face.

No one did something like that and got to live to brag about it.

If the rest of this day was going to go the way I was pretty sure it was, breaking every traffic law in the state of New York didn't even scratch the surface of the shit that I was about to get into.

Throwing the helmet to the side, I hopped on the bike and checked my phone one last time for any updates. Then I looked at the map for the fastest route to get to the harbor.

According to the GPS, it would take me about thirty minutes

to get there. That was thirty minutes far too long. I pulled out of the parking garage, revved the engine a few times to make sure it was good and warm, and took off.

I didn't remember most of the trip getting to the harbor.

There were definitely a few times I avoided traffic by hopping on the sidewalk, making people dive out of my way. There was also a strong possibility I may have clipped a little old lady. I'm sure she was fine. I was even more sure I didn't give a fuck.

Two cops tried to pull me over, but they just simply couldn't keep up with my speed.

I doubted any of them were even able to get my license number, and if they did, fuck it.

I would deal with whatever bullshit they threw at me once I knew Charlotte was safe, and the men that put her in danger, and probably her fiancé, were burning in hell.

I made it to the harbor in less than fifteen minutes.

My face stung from the chill and the wind, but it didn't matter.

There were a ton of people milling around, but no urgency.

No one seemed panicked or like they were doing anything important.

I could see the yacht off in the distance, but it looked perfectly normal from the shore.

No one knew my girl was in trouble.

I quickly looked around for something that could get me out to that yacht. Everything was huge and slow, meant for luxury sailing.

How could so many people have this much fucking money and no taste for adventure?

The longer it took to find something that could get me to that yacht quickly, the more frantic I was becoming. I was ten seconds from diving into that icy water and swimming when I saw a giant lime-green monstrosity. The lime green boat had yellow eyes and jagged teeth painted on the front, and across the side were the words *the beast*.

It was huge, gaudy, and would stick out like a sore thumb. But it would fucking move.

It looked like another fucking tourist trap that was put away for the season, probably only at the harbor to be cleaned or serviced.

It would have to do.

I looked around to make sure no one was watching me, and aside from a little five-year-old kid hanging onto his mom's arm while she spoke to somebody else, no one gave a damn.

I pressed my fingers to my lips to tell the kid to be quiet as I snuck down to the boardwalk next to *the beast* and quickly unhooked it from the pier.

Then it only took me a few minutes to hotwire the speedboat, and I was in business.

The twin jet engines were extremely loud, but as I got to the helm and started maneuvering the boat out of its resting spot, no one really even looked over. Just the same kid was watching. The mom did look over once and shoot me a dirty look as she let go of the child's hands and covered her ears.

Really, was there no security?

Did rich New Yorkers just think people didn't have the audacity to steal boats, or that they were somehow above common theft?

Had they never seen a pirate movie?

I was going to use their ignorance to my advantage.

I pushed the engine as hard as I could until I was about a hundred yards out, and then I cut it completely. If the assailants knew that I was coming, I would lose my edge. I used the momentum from the engine and carefully maneuvered *the beast* to coast alongside the edge of the yacht.

The closest I could get was six feet away. That would have to be enough.

As carefully and quietly as I could, I stood on the edge of *the beast*, balancing with the waves as I waited for the boat to line up with the ladder on the side of the yacht.

I could hear the assailants screaming on the deck.

Some nonsense about big oil destroying the planet for everybody, blah blah blah, hug a tree, blah blah blah.

They may have had a point, but their point no longer mattered the second they put my girl in danger.

Once Charlotte was in the crosshairs, they were dead men.

I didn't give a fuck what they wanted.

The only thing I wanted was to see their life drain from their eyes. And that was the thing about me. I usually got whatever the fuck I wanted. I took it by force if I had to. This would be no exception.

As soon as the ladder was lined up enough, I jumped, caught the first rung, and my fingers slipped.

I managed to catch myself on the sides of the ladder using my feet to stop my descent. Thankfully, my clumsy moment was relatively silent, and no one looked over the side of the ship. I carefully climbed up and went to the lowest deck I could access. It was the main deck, but it was empty.

That was perfect. I could hear the people above me, all held on the smaller sun deck. It was smart, since it was a smaller area with fewer places people could hide.

Too bad it wouldn't be enough to save them.

Hunter was still bleeding out below, so that was where I needed to go.

Once I got him at least stable, then I would take his weapons as well as mine, sneak around the ship, and start taking motherfuckers out.

Hunter was easy enough to find. I just found the first

stairway down, and when I got to the bottom level, he was the only soul I saw.

He had managed to move himself, so he was leaning against a doorway, the trail of blood telling me exactly how far he had managed to crawl before giving up. It wasn't very far, but I suppose with two gunshot wounds, it was somewhat impressive.

Without a word, I ripped off the pieces of his shirt that covered his wounds and started assessing the damage.

"You know, out of all the people aboard this ship, I was pretty sure I wasn't on the list of people you wanted to get naked," Hunter said.

"You are definitely not on that list. Sadly, you are on the list of people on the ship that I don't want to die, so shut the fuck up while I figure out what to do with you."

At least the shots had missed his arteries and vital organs, so it really was just a blood loss issue. I took his shirt and ripped it into long strips, balling up some of it to press against the wounds, making him bite into his own forearm to muffle a yell.

"Don't be a bitch. If they figure out I'm here because of you, I will shoot you again myself. This time, I'll make sure it sticks," I said as I wrapped a few of the strips around his chest to secure the padding.

"You would, would you? You fucking dick."

"Yes, I would," I said, testing the bindings. "Now, where are they keeping the hostages?"

I knew where they were, but I needed to keep Hunter thinking for another moment. Maybe he had more information.

"Top deck. Fastest way up is through that stairway. I don't know which way they're facing, but that stairway will lead you to a door that is blocked by some catering tables."

"Okay, I'm going to go handle this situation. And once we get help, I'll make sure someone comes down and gets you and will get you properly patched up."

Hunter nodded for a second, and his eyes closed as he leaned his head against the wall. "Oh, and Reid?"

"Yeah?" I asked, turning back to look at him.

"You so fucking owe me for this. The bar tab is on you forever."

"I don't fucking owe you for doing a half-ass job. You're here to protect Charlotte, and you're down here just lying around doing nothing while she's up there. Do you think two little tiny pieces of lead change that? Bitch, please."

When he flipped me off, I knew that he'd be fine for at least a little bit, and I went to go get my girl back.

The second I got to the main deck, I could hear them screaming again.

I snuck up to the sun deck, thankful that they actually had most of the hostages facing me, so the assailants had their backs to me.

There were four men. Each of them was dressed in solid black, with black ski masks and holding Glocks, and two were holding AK-47s.

They were all facing the hostages, with their leader pacing back and forth. While his men were demanding that all the women surrender their jewelry and were roughing up the other men for their expensive watches and wallets, he was demanding those with cellphones initiate wire transfers into a shady offshore account.

So clearly, not a typical smash and grab robber. These men were hoping for a high seven figure payout.

I needed to make a plan.

There was no way for me to sneak around and take out the assailants one by one. There was no way for me to easily kill more than one of them without risking hostage lives.

If I really thought about it, I didn't give a fuck about the hostage lives.

I only cared about one.

It took me a moment to spot her.

She was standing at the front of the crowd. The sniveling prince was on one side of her. And her friend from the quartet, Ginnie, on the other.

At least she was alive.

All I needed was the right moment.

The leader strutted in front of them. "You people need to understand exactly how serious we are," he said, holding up his Glock.

He turned toward the center of the crowd and took aim at Charlotte's fiancé.

A small part of me was tempted just to let him shoot the smarmy bastard and take the moment of chaos as my opportunity to get in there and start disarming men.

It would mean one dead hostage, but over a hundred saved.

Including my girl.

Except that pathetic little bitch grabbed Charlotte and used her as a human shield just as the man opened fire.

I then watched the woman I love take a bullet and crumple to the deck.

CHAPTER 30

REID

*W*ithout thinking, without making a plan, just acting on pure instinct—the one thing that I was trained to never do—I lifted the pistol in my hand and shot the nearest assailant in the back of the head.

That was immediately followed by a single shot to the other men, all but the leader.

"Put down your weapon now," he screamed, pointing his gun at me.

His hands shook.

He didn't have the balls to shoot a man.

An unarmed woman, sure, but not someone coming at him.

I would have bet anything in that moment.

This wasn't the man who had shot Hunter. One of his now-dead minions had done that.

The pistol I was holding was out of bullets, and I had forgotten to grab Hunter's gun. Instead of reloading my gun, in case he somehow grew a pair in the split second that would have taken, I grabbed my standard USMC utility knife from the side pocket on my holster, flicked it open, never taking my eyes off my target, and threw it.

Knife throwing was not something I had been particularly skilled in, in the past, but it didn't stop my blade from burying itself into the leader's throat.

I ran to him first, stripping him of his AK-47 as well as several knives, his Glock, and a rope.

It would have been easy and cost me nothing to shoot him in the head, but he didn't deserve a quick death.

I turned my back on him, letting him choke on his own blood while I tried to move to Charlotte.

"Back the fuck up," I shouted at everyone crowding around her. "Get off of her now."

They didn't move.

Each one of these rich pricks thought that the threat was gone.

They had no idea who the threat really was.

I tried to push my way through the crowd when a woman wrapped her manicured claw-like hand around my bicep and tried to pull me away.

"That was really brave. I wish there was a way I could repay you," she said in a breathy voice. It was supposed to sound sexy, and at one time I would have taken her up on the thinly veiled offer and had her bent over the railing in moments.

I did not have time for that shit, and I had no interest in the over-plucked sack of silicone.

I forcibly pushed her away so hard that she tripped on her ridiculous shoes and fell flat on her flat ass.

Her male companion screamed and then tried to get into my face, saying that was assault and they were going to sue, and did I know who the fuck they were.

I didn't know, I didn't care.

As far as I was concerned, she was an obstacle between me and what was mine.

I grabbed the cheap piece-of-shit, high-point semi-automatic handgun that I had pulled off the assailant and stuck it in his face.

"Back the fuck off," I said between gritted teeth and watched as the blood drained from his face. He stumbled back and fell over her still prone form.

I lifted the piece-of-shit pistol straight into the air, angling it over the open ocean, and fired three shots, getting everyone's attention.

"Move away from the injured girl now," I demanded and watched as everyone stared at me, eyes wide and mouths open.

Slowly, they backed away.

The only one who wasn't fucking smart enough to move was her goddamned fiancé.

"Oh, Charlotte, my love." He was weeping over her like he gave a fuck about her.

"You too," I said, pointing the gun straight at his face.

"She's going to be my wife."

"No," I said. "She's not."

"Yes, we..." His words trailed off as he looked at me and recognized me.

"Over my dead body." I shoved him away, and someone was smart enough to grab him before he could come back and get shot in the face.

I didn't care what it took.

As long as I lived, he would never fucking lay another goddamned finger on my girl again.

Finally, I was at Charlotte's side.

She had two wounds that were bleeding far too quickly, her beautiful pale blue dress now soaked in her dark red blood.

One shot was in her stomach, the other a little higher in her ribs. Reaching under her, I couldn't feel exit wounds. But that didn't make me feel better.

She was losing so much blood, her face was already pale.

Her beautiful, natural pink lips were almost as white as death. I ripped a few layers of the soft material on her skirt, balled it up, and put pressure on the wounds.

She made a painful groaning sound, and her eyes flickered open.

"I know, baby," I said. "I know it hurts, and I'm sorry. But I have to put pressure."

She didn't say anything.

She just nodded.

One hand slowly came up to touch my cheek.

Her fingers were ice cold.

She needed a doctor, and she needed one now.

"Is there a doctor on board?"

A man raised his hand. "I'm a dermatologist."

"Is there a real doctor on board?"

No one raised their hand. Of course there wasn't a single medical professional here. Working on anything other than world domination was beneath most of the people here.

God forbid any of these people ever did something useful with their lives.

I held the pressure on her wound as tightly as I dared while fishing my cell phone out of one of my pockets.

Immediately, I called 911. When the dispatch answered, I didn't let them get through their little speech. I just started shouting into the line.

"This is Sergeant Reid Taylor, US Marine. I'm on the Fortune, a luxury cruising yacht about two miles from New York harbor. There was an attack. Two people are down. One civilian with two GSWs, bleeding out quickly. I have another Marine down with two gunshot wounds. He is

stable. I need emergency medical choppers here immediately."

The dispatcher started to say something in a dismissive tone,
like this was a prank call.

"I need emergency EMT choppers to this yacht immediately."

"Then, sir, can you bring the yacht into the harbor, and we
can have an ambulance meet you at…"

"No," I demanded into the phone. "I have a civilian who will
not make it to the harbor. I need emergency medical services in a
fucking helicopter on their way to me five minutes ago!"

Charlotte's hand fell from my jaw, and her eyes slid shut.

"No, no, baby," I said in a much softer but just as urgent tone.
"I need you to open up those beautiful brown eyes for me. Come
on, baby, stay with me. Be my good girl and open those eyes."

Her eyes flickered open. They were heavy-lidded and glazed
over, but they were open for right now, and that would have to
be enough.

The dispatcher tried telling me again that I needed to get the
ship into the harbor.

I hung up on them, giving up.

Instead, I called someone I hadn't talked to in a long time,
and I prayed they still had the same fucking number.

"Hello?" the familiar voice answered, and I breathed a sigh of
relief.

He may be working for the coast guard now, but once a
Marine, always a Marine.

"Daniels," I barked. "Are you still with the Coast Guard in
New York?"

"Yeah. Hey, Reid. I haven't heard from you in a while. Can I
call you back after I'm off shift?"

"No, goddamn it! I'm on a yacht called the Fortune."

"About two miles off of the harbor," he finished for me.
"Right, yeah, I have their manifest. What's going on?"

"There was a gun attack on the boat. I need medical choppers to me now."

"I don't know if I can authorize—"

"Shut the fuck up and listen. Hunter is down. I have a civilian with two GSWs, one to the chest and one to the gut."

"I'll have two choppers en route to you, and I will be there in two minutes. Clear the sun deck. That is where they will have to land one at a time," he said, and the line immediately dropped.

I looked back down at Charlotte.

Her eyes were closed again, and my heart froze.

Immediately, I reached up and placed my fingers gently on her neck.

Her pulse was faint, and her breath was shallow.

Visions started to flicker before my eyes.

First of the life we could have had.

What it would have been like coming home to her after every mission, making love to her every night, and fucking her hard every time she mouthed off to me.

Watching her play her cello every single chance I got, whether it was for a packed concert hall or she was alone in our home playing just for me.

Then another vision flashed before my eyes that made my heart hurt, and an unfamiliar stinging tickled behind my eyes and on my nose.

Charlotte looked lovely in a white dress and walked down an aisle of rose petals lit only by candlelight as she moved toward me, ready to say the vows that would bind her to me, just me, for the rest of our lives. Her eyes were filled with tears of happiness, and her smile was bright and so full of life.

Then the vision shifted to another future. One where she was still dressed in white, but she wasn't walking. She was lying completely still, her hands placed on top of a small bouquet of flowers while mourners walked past her one-by-one to pay their respects.

That would not be her future. I forbade it.

It wasn't long before I heard the familiar sounds of the medical rescue helicopter.

I looked around, ensuring Charlotte and I were far enough on the side to not be in their way, but close enough that I could get her on board with minimal movement.

I picked her up, cradling her delicate body in my arms, holding her to my chest with one hand wrapped around her, still putting pressure on the wound in her stomach while the wound in her chest was pressed against mine as firmly as I could without causing too much pain.

The last thing I wanted to do was hurt her more.

This was all my fault.

She was on the brink, and it was because of me.

The first chopper landed, two EMTs rushed out, and I laid her out on the floor gently, letting them check her out.

"Have you been putting pressure on these wounds the entire time?"

"About two minutes after she was shot. There are no exit wounds, so I was putting pressure on them, trying to slow the bleeding."

The first EMT nodded and then spoke to the radio on his shoulder. I couldn't make out what he was saying over the engines and the wind being whipped by the blades.

"Then you probably saved her life," the second EMT said. "There's nothing more we can do until we get her to the hospital. We have emergency services waiting on the roof at New York Presbyterian."

I looked up as the second chopper arrived, ready to pick up Hunter. Hunter's eyes first went to the helicopters in relief. Then he saw me holding Charlotte, and the blood drained from his face.

"Okay, the other one is clearly stable. Let's get her on the first chopper, and he can take the second," the first EMT yelled.

"Do you want us to take her?" the second one asked.

"No, I'll hold her. I'm going with her." I scooped her back into my arms, pressing her chest to mine and putting my hand back on the wound on her stomach.

She groaned in pain as I got her situated.

I kissed her forehead as I murmured against her cheek, "Stay with me, baby. Don't leave me, princess."

CHAPTER 31

REID

My clothes became drenched with her blood as her pulse grew fainter.

"Come on, princess," I begged. "Stay strong for me. Be my good girl and stay with me. You are mine, my brave girl, my strong girl. Show the world how strong you are. Can you do that for me?"

Her hand came up and closed around my finger, just holding on to me.

She wasn't squeezing very tight, but she was showing me that she was still with me even if she didn't have the strength to open her eyes.

Then I did something I swore I would never do again.

But for Charlotte, I would break any vow.

I closed my eyes, and I started to pray.

I didn't know what God may have been listening to me or if I had done so much wrong in my life that I wasn't worth listening to at all.

But I had to try.

Surely, if there was a creator, they would save this woman.

Not because she was wealthy and privileged, but because she was sweet and kind, and her living was the only thing that would stop me from burning the entire world to ash.

So for her and the sake of every other damned soul in this world, I prayed.

I vowed to do anything.

I would protect her with everything I had.

I would marry her, provide for her.

There would not be a single thing in this or any life that she wanted that I wouldn't give her.

Dear Lord, who art in heaven, hallowed be thy name, save this girl.

This is a brilliant, strong woman who has lived life at the whim of others. She deserves more. She deserves people who will fight for her, instead of those who use her and who refuse to let her share her gifts with the world. She deserves to share her light, to learn what it means to be free, and to make choices for herself.

Please, lord, let her live, and let her choose me.

My head was bowed, my eyes closed, and my words were silent, but I had to believe they were reaching whoever it was that needed to hear them.

At this point, I didn't give a fuck if I had to sell my soul to Satan himself to save this woman.

My prayers turned angry.

How dare God let this happen to Charlotte.

Of all the women in the world, why did he have to let this happen to mine?

I went from pleading for her life to threatening God himself in my head, promising to find a way to make him pay if she didn't live.

It must have been less than five minutes before we were land-ing, and I carried Charlotte out of the helicopter and through the first hallway. The doctors met us in the middle of the second hallway, bursting through a set of double doors with a stretcher.

Immediately, I laid her down and let them examine her while they started to run toward an operating room.

I ran with them as I gave the details I had.

Everything: her heart rate, where the wounds were, how long they'd been like that, and approximately how much blood she lost. I even had her blood type and list of allergies memorized. She was allergic to a few medicines, nothing that seemed pertinent to what they would have to do, but I didn't want to run any risks. I held her hand as we ran, not wanting to let go while she still had the strength to reach for me.

Outside the operating room, one of the doctors looked up at me with kind eyes and said, "Honey, we've got it from here. I need you to stay back here and let us do our job. Someone will come get you as soon as there is news about your wife."

My wife.

Not yet, but soon.

"Don't make me leave her."

"You aren't leaving her. You are letting the professionals do their job. You slowed her bleeding and got her to us fast enough that I am sure you saved her life. We will do everything we can to bring her back to you."

The doctor spoke with such authority, I had to believe she would save Charlotte.

"Thank you," I said and dropped to my knees. I felt exhausted as the adrenaline suddenly left my body.

The kind of exhaustion you only feel after a long, stressful mission.

I found an empty chair and stayed where I was in that hall, covered in Charlotte's blood as I watched her disappear behind the next set of double doors.

There was nowhere to go, nothing I could do until I knew she would live.

This was the worst part: not knowing and not being able to control what happened.

It felt like if I was in that room, if I was in control, I could make sure she lived.

The hard truth was she needed someone who wasn't me. Someone else had to save her. Her life was in someone else's hands, and I didn't have the skills to be the one to save her.

I wasn't there to protect her.

After a moment, a nurse came by to make sure none of the blood on me was mine and tried to point me to a waiting room when I heard my name.

"Reid, where is she?" Hunter's voice came echoing down the hall. He was on a stretcher but trying to get off while two large male nurses tried to restrain him.

"Lie down and let the medics take care of you," I ordered.

"No, I failed you. Where is she?" His eyes trailed over my body, and I knew he saw how bad she was by how much of her blood I was wearing.

"She is being taken care of. Let them take care of you." I tried to get Hunter to lie back.

"No, she has to be okay first. I was supposed to keep her safe. I failed." Hunter was damn near delirious as the nurses tried to force him to stay in the bed.

"Sir, please calm down."

"Hunter," I yelled, making him stop and look at me. "She will be fine. Charlotte may look like a tiny little thing, but she is strong. You did right by her. You called me and I got back up there in time to save her life."

"But I should have…"

"Rest, Marine. You did your job. Now let the medical team do theirs before they tie you down."

"They did tie him down. Asshole pulled a knife and cut himself free," one of the nurses said under his breath.

Sure enough, the frayed ends of the woven nylon straps were hanging from the sides of the stretcher.

"I'm fine. I don't need medical treatment. It's just a scratch."

"Sit down, shut up, and let the nice doctors look at you," I barked.

"I'm fine. It's going to take more than one little —"

I cut off his words with one swift jab just below where he was shot, and he made a wheezing sound before falling back on the bed.

"There you go, boys. The patient should comply now."

"Thanks," the bigger one said, nodding. The other looked at me with a scowl, then twisted his lips before shrugging it off and moving his patient back behind the same double doors Charlotte had disappeared behind.

"Tell him to come find me once you have him patched up," I called after them. I saw one nod before the doors swung shut.

I sat back in the same uncomfortable plastic and metal chair beside those double doors.

Until I knew if Charlotte was going to be okay, or until they moved her, this was my post.

Leaning my head against the wall, I took a few deep breaths, ignoring the sterile smell of the hospital, the coldness of the blood that still soaked my shirt, and the itchiness of the few places where it had dried.

I ignored the chatter of the nurses and the beeping of heart rate monitors from various rooms.

I blocked out everything for a moment and tried to focus on Charlotte.

There wasn't any type of God I could pray to anymore. All I could do was plead in my head over and over, telling Charlotte to be my strong girl. To be my brave girl, to be my good girl.

Call it prayer, call it manifestation. I didn't care.

All I knew was that if there was any energy left in my body, I would give it to her to help her fight. All while making promises that this would be the last fight she would ever face on her own.

If anything like this ever happened again, I would be by her side the entire time. I wanted to face every obstacle and every challenge with her. She deserved at least that much.

"We demand your best surgeon and there must be a plastic surgeon in the room. There must be no scars."

"Mummy, it hurts!" whined Charlotte's former fiancé as they wheeled him into the emergency room.

"Oh, darling. You were so brave." The women then turned to address the mysteriously present paparazzi. "My son is a hero. He saved a thousand people tonight from a gang of gun-wielding thugs."

Several flashes went off as photos were taken.

Romney barked, "Get those cameras out of my face. What is taking so long. I need a doctor. I'm bleeding to death."

Then Mary Astrid appeared at his side. With a strained laugh, she patted his shoulder. "What he means to say is he is here to check on the welfare of his beloved bride, Charlotte Manwarring, whom he bravely tried to save by stepping in front of a bullet."

Romney lowered his head in dramatic fashion as he gripped his arm. "Unfortunately, my mortal flesh was not able to stop it from hitting her."

I didn't give a fucking damn if he wanted to steal the glory.

But there was no goddamn way, I was going to let that bastard claim my girl as his beloved bride.

Fortunately, the paparazzi had already shifted their attention down the hall as Lucian, his son Luc, and daughter Olivia rushed into the hospital with Lucian bellowing at the top of his lungs, asking for a status on his daughter's well-being.

If I'd learned anything in the military, half the strategy behind battle tactics... was timing.

Marching over to Charlotte's former fiancé, I grabbed Romney by the shirt front, lifted him out of his wheelchair, and punched him squarely in the face.

CHAPTER 32

CHARLOTTE

A steady, high-pitched beeping was the first thing I heard as I started to wake up.

My entire body ached, and I didn't want to open my eyes.

I wanted to let the drowsiness take me back under.

My head was swimming, and even though I was lying in an uncomfortable bed with rough sheets, all I wanted to do was fall back into unconsciousness.

Then I felt a warm, rough hand gripping my fingers. I ran my thumb up and down the familiar skin, trying to use that as my anchor to come back to reality.

"Are you awake, princess?" a deep, familiar voice asked me. It took me a second to place the voice, but it instantly made me feel safe, wanted, and at peace.

I opened my mouth to answer him, but my throat was too dry.

"Come on, beautiful, open up those gorgeous eyes for me. Let me see them so I know you're okay."

The light was blinding and sent sharp jabs of pain through my head, but for him, I would endure it.

It took several moments for my eyes to focus, and I could see Reid clearly sitting at the side of my bed, holding my hand.

He looked different.

His jaw, which was usually clean-shaven, had a thick cover of stubble. More than a five o'clock shadow, like he hadn't shaved in a few days.

I kind of liked it.

What I didn't like were his bloodshot eyes and the exhausted way his body slumped in the chair next to the bed.

"What—" I tried to ask what had happened, but the dryness in my throat made it impossible.

I struggled to sit up, but he gently touched my shoulder and held me to the bed.

Reaching over me, he grabbed the little remote for the bed and pressed the red button at the top to call the nurse, then pressed one of the arrows that slowly raised the bed so I was in a sitting position. The movement hurt a lot, but it was much better than trying to sit up on my own.

I tried to speak again, but Reid gave me a soft smile and shook his head.

"How is the patient doing?" A loud and far too cheerful voice came from the doorway. A large woman wearing dark teal scrubs and Uggs walked into the room.

"She is awake, but she can't speak. Why can't she speak? She wasn't hit anywhere near her vocal cords. What did those over-paid quacks do to her?" Reid stood taller with every angry word.

My brain was still fuzzy, and he reminded me of a colossal grizzly bear, face all covered in fur as he made himself bigger to scare the nurse away from his injured mate.

The nurse shoved him aside like she had dealt with men like him her whole life and was no longer intimidated. "Mr. Taylor—"

"It's Sergeant," he growled like the big bear he was, and I had to suppress a giggle.

"Fine." The nurse looked at me and rolled her eyes, and I pressed my lips together. A single laugh escaped, and I winced at the pain in my stomach and chest as my head started spinning again.

"Sergeant Taylor," she started again. "We have been over this. If you don't get out of my way, I will have security come up here and tase you again, and this time, you won't be able to charm your way past the night nurse to get back in this room. Now move."

Reid stared her down for a long minute, then relented by stepping back.

She stared him down for another moment, watching as he moved across the room and stood against the wall, arms crossed.

He looked so good like that, like he was watching over me, with his thick arms and piercing blue eyes seeing everything.

I couldn't help how my eyes trailed down his body, and I knew he knew exactly what I was doing. I remembered what he looked like without all the clothes.

From the tattoos over his chest that I hadn't gotten a chance to fully explore yet, to his toned abs, to his massive dick and the way the metal of his piercings felt inside me.

The heart rate monitor next to me started beeping faster, and he gave me a knowing smirk and a wink, making my heart literally skip a beat.

"Hey." The nurse snapped her fingers in front of my face, pulling my attention back to her. "You need to behave, too, or I will kick him out."

I looked down, the tops of my cheeks heating in a blush, but I couldn't help it.

The nurse checked my bandages, as well as the IV in my arm

and the various liquids hooked up to it. Then she ran through my vitals and listened to my breathing.

"You are very lucky. Your man over there saved your life. You lost a lot of blood, and they almost lost you on the table." The nurse was talking, and I was catching maybe every fourth or fifth word. "The bullets didn't hit anything vital, but man, did they do a number on you."

My head was spinning again, and I reached up to press my fingers against my temple.

"Dizzy?" the nurse asked.

I tried to speak again, but my throat was raw.

"That is probably from the pain meds. Here." She handed me a little white stick with a red button on top. "This is for your morphine pump. Press it when you need it. It will make you dizzy. You have anti-nausea meds already in your IV, so that shouldn't be an issue. Try not to press it too often. It won't let you OD, but the more you take, the worse the withdrawals. It's probably best for the next twenty-four hours to sleep as much as you can. Your body has been through a lot. You need to heal."

I nodded again, understanding what she meant.

The pain was there, but I wanted to be a little clearer to talk to Reid and find out what happened before I let the morphine lull me back to sleep.

"He said you can't talk? Is your throat sore or dry?"

"Dry," I mouthed.

"Yeah, that is to be expected. The IV keeps the rest of you hydrated, but that cotton mouth can be intense. The doctor has cleared you for clear liquids, so I have some ice water. You can also eat ice chips, and if you want later, we will get you some bone broth. Here you go, sweetie." This time, she grabbed a large white Styrofoam cup on the rolling bedside table, took the paper cover off the top of the straw, and held it to my lips.

The water was the best thing I had ever tasted.

Cold, crisp, and refreshing. The nurse let me take a few small sips before taking it away.

"Better?"

"Yes, thank you," I said.

My throat was still sore, and my voice sounded grainy to my own ears, but I could speak.

"Good, only small sips. I'll leave you and your man alone for now, but no funny business. The doctors will be in soon. And if I have to come running in here because he is doing something he shouldn't, I will ban him from this room."

"Good luck with that," Reid muttered under his breath.

"Thank you," I said before she and Reid could get into another argument or stare down.

I had no doubt that she would get him out of this room, and I knew he would find a way back in, but I was tired and didn't want to wait for him to break back in. I just wanted him with me now.

Reid didn't move until the nurse was gone, and then he closed the door behind her before returning to his seat at my side.

"Does it hurt, princess?"

"Yes." There was no way I could lie to him.

"Do you need to hit the button?" He looked around for it, and I lifted my hand to show him I had it.

"Not yet. Can you tell me what happened?"

"The asshole you are never going to marry used you as a human shield." His eyes darkened as he spoke. There was real hatred there.

"He organized the whole thing."

The anger in Reid's face grew. A dark red crawled up his neck while his jaw clenched so hard I was worried about his teeth breaking. "What?"

"Romney was complaining that they weren't following the

script, and they said something about his wire transfer not clear-ing. And I thought we were safe because they were just actors, but then they shot Hunt— oh my God, is Hunter okay? What am I saying? Of course, he isn't okay. I saw him... Reid, I am so sorry."

My monitors started beeping rapidly again, and Reid grabbed my hand and held it tight, running his thumb over my knuckles to soothe me.

"Shh, princess, it's okay. Hunter is fine. He played dead so the men wouldn't take his phone, and he texted me the second he could. He was patched up while you were in surgery."

"Really?"

"Yeah, that bouquet over there with the daisies and the little bear, that one is from him. An apology for letting you down."

"He didn't—"

"He did." The tone in Reid's voice was enough to make me drop it for now, but I made a mental note to talk to Hunter later and tell him he had nothing to apologize for.

"He's okay." Tears of relief started to spill down my cheeks.

"Be careful. You cry for another man, and I might get jealous."

He was teasing, but it reminded me of him storming off that morning.

"Reid, I need to tell you something." My voice started going hoarse again, and he grabbed the cup, letting me take a few long pulls of the icy water.

"Slow down, princess. Take it easy. I'm not going anywhere. And I need to tell you something first." He took a deep breath, and I braced myself for whatever he was about to throw my way. "Charlotte Maeve Manwarring, I love you. I will never let you out of my sight again for as long as we live."

"Reid." More tears sprang to my eyes.

"Shh, don't say anything, baby."

"I still need to tell you, that morning, before the charity event, after our… night together. As soon as you left, I called Luc. I told him I was going to tell Father I refused to marry the baron. That it was time I started making my own decisions."

"What are you saying, Charlotte?"

"I'm saying I love you too, and I don't ever want to be with anyone else."

"Oh, thank fuck." Reid surged to his feet, leaned over me, and sealed his lips to mine.

At first his touch was gentle, not wanting to hurt me.

My hands went to his arms and then up to his shoulders, and my fingers, all except the one with the blood oxygen monitor on it, laced through his hair and pulled him tighter to me. The kiss heated up, and I melted into it, loving the way he explored my mouth with his tongue and seemed to claim me at the same time.

He kissed me like he owned me, and I loved it. I craved it.

His kiss reminded me how good it had felt when his lips explored my body, how amazing it had felt when he'd kissed me as he pushed inside my body, invading me for the first time. I wanted him, only him. And he wanted me.

My heart rate monitor sped up again, and as he pulled away from me, I tried to pull him back.

The movement caused a jolt of pain through my body, and I bit back a cry.

"Press the button, princess. I will be here when you wake up, and we will figure everything out."

I nodded and reached for the button I'd left at my side. Reid reached for the remote to lay my bed back down. He placed a kiss on my palm as the bed went flat, and as the drugs worked their way into my body, my eyelids closed.

One final thought echoed through my head.

"How am I going to tell my family? My father is going to lose his mind."

CHAPTER 33

CHARLOTTE

"*H*ow many forbids is that?" Olivia asked.

She was perched on the edge of my hospital bed, snacking on a little bag of pretzels she'd picked up from the vending machine down the hall because, according to Olivia, a show like this needed salty snacks.

"Fifteen, I think," I answered, reaching for one of the mini pretzels in her bag.

"Seventeen," Luc corrected. His eyes were closed as he sat back in the chair next to my bed, his feet propped up at the foot of my bed.

"Are you sure?" Olivia asked. "I counted fifteen, too."

"Positive. You missed two of them while you were texting Marksen. By the way, is he going to try to make it to the rest of the show or..." He let the question hang as we both turned to listen to our father on speaker phone start another round of 'absolutely not' and 'over my dead body' and calling all of his children worthless and ungrateful.

After I had woken up the second time, I was starting to feel more like myself.

Reid was still by my side, holding my hand as the doctors came in and gave me a rundown of everything that had happened during the surgeries to remove the bullets and what was going to be required to get me back on my feet.

Unfortunately, I had lost so much blood that they wanted to keep me inpatient for at least a week to make sure that there were no other complications and that the gunshot wounds would heal completely.

I managed to convince the doctor to lower the dosage of morphine when I pressed the button, making it enough to manage the pain, but not so much that I couldn't think straight.

As soon as the doctor had left my room, Luc came in, first staring down Reid with a look of manly competition and unspoken threats.

Reid met the stare and then sat back with his arms crossed over his chest, daring Luc to say something.

Luc narrowed his eyes and then focused on me. "Can we talk privately?" he asked.

His shoulders were pushed back, and for a moment I thought he was talking to Reid, asking him to step out in the hall, but he was looking at me.

Asking my permission to speak with him.

It was the first time he had ever asked my permission for anything.

It took some convincing, but with Luc swearing he wouldn't leave the room until Reid got back, we managed to convince Reid that he needed to go home, take a shower, shave, and then come back.

I also wanted to suggest a nap, so he could get a little rest in his own bed, but I knew he wouldn't hear of it. He had left me alone once and look what happened. It wasn't his fault, but convincing him of that was proving to be rather difficult.

Once he was gone, Luc deflated in front of me.

For once, my big brother didn't look like the younger version of my father.

He looked tired and stressed. I had never seen him look like anything other than distantly cold and strong, unless he was looking at his wife.

I motioned to the chair Reid had just given up, and Luc slumped into it, resting his elbows on his knees and his head in his hand.

"Are you okay?" I asked.

"Am I okay? No, Charlotte, I'm not okay. I'm confused. And I feel like I failed you."

"You didn't fail me," I said, reaching over to pat his shoulder. "Tell me why you think you failed me, and I will tell you why you're wrong."

"I thought marrying Zeigler was what you wanted. I went along with it without checking with you. I'm your big brother, I should have known."

"You did that because I didn't tell you otherwise. I had always gone along with Father's plans before. This was the first time I had ever chosen something for myself. If the announcement had been made a few weeks ago, I might have wanted it. Or at least, I wouldn't have wanted anything more than to make Father happy."

Luc nodded, then stopped for a second, took a deep breath, and let it out, his shoulders sagging. "Then I learn the man we were going to entrust with your future actually staged the entire dangerous fucking stunt to somehow win the motherfucking scandal rag media cycle. It was all a fucking PR stunt by that stupid bastard cunt asshole."

Olivia and I exchanged a look as we smothered smiles. Although we of course shared his anger and outrage, my serious, business-like brother was amusing when he swore unabated.

Olivia then chimed in, "Don't forget cheap. If he had just paid the men the two-hundred and fifty thousand he had promised, none of this may have happened."

Tossing her a look for goading on our brother, I patted his hand. "I'm right here. A little banged up and a little worse for wear. But I will be fine."

"And then I find out that you have something going on with your guard. I don't even know what to think about that. It just seems so... unlikely."

I frowned as I hugged the blanket up closer to my chest, somehow already missing the warmth of Reid's presence.

Bracing for the worst, I asked, "What do you mean?"

"Reid is just so..."

"Poor? Working class?" I asked, wondering if Luc really thought so little of me.

"No, I was going to say blunt. He's rough and in your face, completely uncultured. He's just so Texas and such a Marine. You are soft-spoken, gentle, refined, and I'm having a hard time seeing it."

I nodded, thinking about what exactly Luc was objecting to, and if I looked at it from his point of view, I could see what he meant.

He and Amelia came from the same background and had similar interests.

Their coming together may have been a little unorthodox, but their goals were aligned.

They strengthened each other.

The same could have been said about Olivia and Marksen.

They came from the same background, they knew the same people, and they'd also had a rather unorthodox meet cute. She and Marksen made the perfect pairing. They pushed each other to work harder toward their own goals. They knew how to help each other.

If Reid needed help with a mission, I would be so out of my

depth that it wasn't even funny. Reid wouldn't know where to start if I needed help with a dinner party or music.

"I think," I paused, trying to figure out exactly how to put my feelings into words, "I think I don't know who I am."

"How many pain meds are you on?" he asked with a rueful smile, making me laugh.

I placed my hand on my stomach, trying to stop the laugh from jostling my wounds too badly. It hurt, but it was kind of worth it.

"No, I mean my entire life, I have done what I was told, not what I wanted. I have let our father groom me to be what he envisioned. The only time I have ever stood up for myself or fought for anything was for my cello, and even then, it wasn't to play professionally or follow my dreams. It was to be able to volunteer at charity events. I fought for a compromise."

"And you're saying you don't like that?"

"I don't like that for my entire life. Other people have made my choices for me. You are following our father's footsteps, but you're not letting him dictate your life. You are making your own decisions when it comes to the family empire. Olivia has completely disregarded what Father wanted and forged her own path, trying to make him proud. I just played the good little princess, and it's not what I want anymore. I don't think it ever was."

"Then what do you want?" The question wasn't said with malice or sarcasm.

He was genuinely asking, and I was at a loss.

It was such a simple question, something that I should have been able to answer, but I just didn't know.

"You know, I never really gave it much thought because it never even occurred to me to fight for what I want. I don't know when, but at some point, I stopped considering my own desires because being told I couldn't have them hurt too much."

"Okay," Luc said sitting back in the chair. "You don't need to know everything right now. But tell me one thing. One thing that you know is incredibly important to you and you are not willing to compromise on."

"Reid." His name flew through my lips before I even had a chance to consider it. And I didn't regret it.

"Reid? I asked you what the most important thing is in your entire life, the one thing you refuse to compromise on anymore, and it isn't chasing your dreams of being a professional cellist. It isn't your own apartment, or your own space to discover your passions? It's your foul-mouthed, uncouth bodyguard?"

"If someone had given you the same opportunity after you met Amelia, would your answer have been anything other than her?"

The truth blazed from his eyes.

I had hit my mark.

Because I knew he loved her more than anything.

Luc may not willingly admit it, but he would give up everything for that woman.

And I didn't know if it was reciprocated with quite the intensity that I felt, but that's how I felt about Reid. I wanted to be with him, more than I wanted anything.

"You know Father is not going to approve of this."

"You didn't ask me what I wanted that Father would approve of. You asked me what I wanted. This is what I want. Reid is who I want."

"To be honest, I don't know if I approve of this. What would that life even look like for you?"

I closed my eyes and tried to picture it.

Living middle class, selling my Hermes bags just because they were a ridiculous luxury. I had a few limited edition ones that would easily start a bidding war through auction houses. Christy's Auction House would salivate at my jewelry collection.

A few pieces I'd bought myself, but most of it was inherited and vintage.

I would spend my mornings practicing my cello, maybe even working for the Philharmonic or another orchestra. I wasn't quite sure yet. Several groups had tried to recruit me over the years. My music teacher always told me I would have the pick of positions, first chairs, and the most prestigious orchestras in the world.

In the evenings, I would come home to Reid's one-bedroom apartment and figure out how to make him dinner. There was a lot that I would have to learn, how to cook, how to clean, how to take care of myself instead of being taken care of. I knew how to set a table for eighteen, but I didn't know how to make a simple dinner for two. The thought should have scared me, but it made me feel excited.

There was so much the world had to offer, and I was going to get to experience real life.

It would be tough, but with Ginnie's help, I was sure I would be able to adapt.

Fueled by the pain meds, my mind wandered to what that could look like.

Coming home in the evening, fixing a meal for my husband, having it on the table when he walked through the door, and scolding him for tracking mud in on his big boots. At least until I was pregnant. I didn't even know where that thought came from, but the idea of giving Reid children made me warm and fuzzy inside.

That was the first time the idea of being a mother felt like anything more than an obligation, and instead felt like an adventure, one that I wanted to embark on, not just an inevitability.

"Well, we haven't talked about it. I know he loves me, but I don't know what he is or isn't looking for yet. So I will probably get a place on my own. I could sell some things to afford rent or maybe a down payment. I'm sure I could find work and make modest rent payments."

Homing in on my expectations made my heart ache, but before I let everything out in the open with Luc, I needed to make sure Reid and I were on the same page.

I wasn't going to have my brother demonize Reid because I'd misunderstood something.

"There is no way he's letting you get a place of your own," Luc interrupted my thoughts. "Especially not having come so close to losing you. Assume you will be living with Reid off of the money he makes and what he can provide for you. It's not the life that you're used to. How are you going to cope with that?"

"With grace and incredible, though less expensive, style," I said, giving him a wink.

"That's my girl," a chipper voice came from the doorway, and Ginnie walked in, holding a large arrangement of colorful flowers. They were beautiful and a stark contrast to the other bouquets that were all white. Nothing but a sea of white roses and lilies.

"Who are you?" Luc asked, looking Ginnie up and down.

"I am the other musician who was lucky enough not to be standing next to a massive dick, who ironically probably had a tiny dick, during the attack."

Luc's mouth opened and closed a few times. Then he looked at me in confusion.

"Luc, this is Ginnie. She and I play together. Ginnie, this is my brother."

"Nice to meet you," Luc said, getting to his feet and offering his hand for her to shake.

Instead, Ginnie handed him the bouquet of flowers and told him to find somewhere to put them as she looked around the room at all of the gifts from well-wishers and distant family.

"Put them somewhere I can see them, please," I asked Luc, who took the bouquet and gave me a single nod before trying to figure out what to do.

Ginnie quickly stole his seat. "So I can't stay long. I got another gig pretty soon, but I wanted to come and check up on you and see how you were doing and if there were any developments about that one thing that we talked about?"

"There have been a few developments," I confirmed. "But nothing has been absolutely decided yet."

"Ginnie, can you please help me convince my sister that there is no glamor in being a starving artist? And that she won't be able to survive New York City without the lifestyle she was born into," Luc said from across the room.

"I'll survive in the same way every other woman does. I will work. There are jobs I can get. I can try to work my cello, and I don't care if I have to bag groceries. I will figure out something—"

"You don't know how to buy groceries, let alone bag them. People who lose the kind of wealth we have generally don't live happier lives in a lower economic class."

"No, I suppose people who lose wealth are often miserable. But I wouldn't be losing anything. I am willing to give up the wealth and choose a different kind of happiness."

"Are you sure?" Luc asked.

Ginnie held my hand with an amused smile on her lips as she watched the back and forth between me and Luc.

"Of course she's sure," Olivia said, traipsing into the room. "Look at that glow. It's not all just the morphine. She's in love."

My cheeks heated at the comment, but I couldn't help the smile that graced my lips. She was right.

"She'll be fine," Ginnie said patting the back of my hand. "Giving up a life of wealth and convenience is not easy. But if it's for the right reasons, then it can make life so much sweeter.

Personally, I would rather live like a pauper and have my freedom than be surrounded by wealth but in a cage."

"And how would you know?" Luc asked, not unkindly.

"Ginnie Kristiansen." She smiled, reaching out her hand for Luc to shake. "Of the Nantucket Kristiansens."

"The one who ran away to some satanic cult?" Olivia's eyes widened in confusion.

"Yes, except it was a heavy metal band. But my family considers it to be the same thing." Ginnie gave Olivia a wink.

I laughed at the bewildered look on Luc's face as he took her hand and shook it.

"Well, you should have bought her a can opener for the baked beans and Spaghettios she'll be eating, instead of these flowers," remarked Luc.

I looked between them. "What are Spaghettios?"

CHAPTER 34

REID

I had been summoned.

Lucian Manwarring stood in front of a massive black marble fireplace inside what was arguably a majestic two-story library.

He didn't turn as I entered. "Help yourself to the whisky."

With a nod, I crossed to the credenza in the corner. Although displayed in an elegant, cut crystal decanter, I had no doubt the amber liquid would be a rather sublime, twenty-year aged Manwarring Single Barrel.

Just because I was battling with the enemy, didn't mean I couldn't enjoy myself during the exchange.

After I poured my drink, Lucian finally turned to face me.

He stretched out his arm and gestured to the gilt, lion-clawed table between two high-backed leather chairs with his drink hand. "Do you play?"

On the table was a sterling silver and gold chess set, the pieces carved to resemble actual kings and knights. No doubt an authentic replica of the famous medieval set which depicted a 9th

Century battle between the Ottoman Turks and the Carolingians.

Of course the man couldn't have a simple black and white marble set.

I smirked. "No."

He took a sip of his whisky as he rolled a pawn between his fingers. "Really, a military man like you?"

I stood over the table and moved a king's pawn forward.

He raised an eyebrow. "The King's Gambit opening. Luck?"

I settled into one of the plush seats. "I'm a Marine. We don't believe in luck."

He took the seat opposite as he moved his pawn to my knight. "Thought you said you didn't know how to play chess."

"You asked if I played, not if I knew how."

The corner of his mouth lifted as he watched me castle my king with the kingside rook.

He placed the tip of his finger on his queen. "My daughter is not going to marry you."

I caressed the side of my queen with my thumb. "With all due respect, I haven't asked her yet."

Lucian's brow lowered. "What the hell is that supposed to mean?"

I leaned forward close to the board. "It means that *when* I ask her, *her* answer will be *her* choice."

That wasn't strictly true.

I had no intention of allowing her to tell me no, but her father didn't need to know that.

Lucian leaned back as he laughed. "I'd say, for a bodyguard, you have balls speaking to me like that, but then we both know you're no ordinary bodyguard."

My hand stilled. A tactical mistake would be to talk. So I listened.

Lucian filled the tense silence. "It seems I have one of the infamous Taylors of Texas on my payroll."

I had never exactly hidden that I was from a rich oil family. I just never advertised it. My father and I had never seen eye-to-eye. He had expected me to take the reins of the family empire after graduating college. The day he learned I had enlisted in the Marines instead was the last day he spoke to me.

It was also the last day I took a withdrawal from my multi-million-dollar trust fund.

I wasn't opposed to touching the money. I just didn't need it. I preferred to live by the money I made through my own effort, not the hard work of my ancestors.

I leaned back and rubbed my index finger over my lower lip as I studied him. "A man is not defined by his family."

"That may be true in Texas where you patriotic boys believe in Manifest Destiny and the myth of the solitary man, but not here in New York. Here family, heritage, traditions are everything."

The corner of my mouth lifted as I used my queen to take his pawn. "So what? Now that you know I'm filthy rich, I'm suddenly the ideal son-in-law for your daughter?"

He slid his king across the board to take my bishop. "Not even close." Lucian then leaned back and took a sip of his drink. "To be clear. I don't like you, Reid."

I raised my drink in a mock toast. "In that at least, we are in agreement."

He rattled the ice in his drink. "I don't suppose you'd accept a check to just disappear?"

I stared at the prism of orange and crimson sparks from the fire through the crystal cubes in my own glass. "What do you think?"

An oppressive quiet settled over the room.

We each made several rapid moves. He took my rook. I took his bishop.

Neither of us gained an advantage over the board.

"You won't make her happy. You know that right? Charlotte needs structure, tempered with refinement and culture, not some uncouth, gun-toting gorilla. What she needs is a proper marriage to the right man, with the right connections, from the right family. The type of marriage only I can arrange."

I raised an eyebrow as I moved my other rook out of harm's way. "Really? Because I thought what she needed was love and the support of someone who believes in her and her talent."

His fingers wrapped around the head of a knight as he twirled the piece between his thumb and forefinger. "Was that your angle? Prey on my daughter's need for validation from her cold-hearted, bastard of a father. I didn't think taking advantage of a woman's vulnerabilities was your style, Reid."

In a bold move, I shifted my king to take his queen. "If your daughter was susceptible to such tactics, you have only yourself to blame."

It figured this man considered a desire to be accepted and loved a vulnerability. It was a basic human need to strive to belong, to be a part of something. Whether it was family, religion, a career, we all wanted to feel as though we mattered.

The wonderful thing about Charlotte was how her need was expressed through music, a noble endeavor to bring beauty and light into a dark and uncertain world.

The drive to entertain, enlighten, and soothe our fellow man was one of the most, quintessentially human of all. It was a goddamn miracle that growing up in this man's frigid shadow, she had somehow held onto that ability.

It was one of the things I loved about her the most.

How essentially her vulnerabilities were actually her greatest strengths. With an upbringing like hers, she should have been a spoiled, jaded bitch. And yet she was kind, sweet, and giving.

I couldn't wait to see what she was capable of accomplishing with the right sort of love and support behind her.

His gaze narrowed as it fell on his captured queen in my hand. "Are you questioning my parenting in my own home?"

"Not at all, sir."

Lucian relaxed.

With my forearms on the table, I leaned forward and continued. "There's no question about it. I'm calling you a piece of shit father who valued money over your daughter's affection."

"I should kill you for saying that to me."

I raised an eyebrow. "You could try. Then again, a man like you doesn't build a billion-dollar empire from nothing by surrounding yourself with yes-men. Family may be a means to an end with you, but the straightforward truth still counts for something."

He intertwined his fingers as he stared intently at me over the board. "You want straightforward? I don't give a damn about your money. You're not good enough for my daughter. And you're not good enough for this family. Marriage is about strengthening positions and securing the future for the next generation. All a marriage to you would bring is money. I have plenty of that, and I have no interest in filthy oil or acres of wasteland in Texas."

"Connections like the Zeiglers?"

He adjusted his seat. "I'll admit that was a... miscalculation."

"A miscalculation. You almost married your daughter off to a violent, inbred sociopath."

Lucian steepled his fingers and pointed at me. "Says you. He says differently. According to Romney, you framed him for the boat heist in an effort to get him out of the way so you could steal Charlotte from him."

"She was never his. Charlotte was—and will always be—mine."

"That is yet to be determined."

I shifted my knight forward. "Checkmate." Rising, I drained my glass and slammed it on the table. "I don't expect us to be like family or even friends, but I suggest you don't make me an enemy. Try to come between your daughter and me, and it will be war between us."

After saying all I intended, I turned my back on him and crossed to the threshold.

Lucian called out, "Does Charlotte know about your millions?"

I shifted my head to the right but didn't turn. Again, I remained silent.

He continued, "I only ask, because I'm told she has built up quite the domestic fantasy about a hand-to-mouth existence with her down-to-earth, blue-collar man. How do you think she'll take it when she learns you're one of the heirs to a billion-dollar fortune?"

My jaw clenched as I curled my fingers into a fist.

Fuck.

It turned out I wasn't the only one who knew how to strike at a vulnerability.

CHAPTER 35

CHARLOTTE

*M*y father was meeting with Reid.

I wasn't just nervous. I was terrified at what my father was going to tell him.

Would he bribe Reid with some exorbitant sum to leave me alone?

Every single moment my mind was filled with scenarios of Reid walking in to tell me it was over.

That my father had paid him some ridiculous amount of money to never see me again.

Or worse, what if my father bribed him, and he left without even saying goodbye?

Every time I thought about what my life would look like if Reid left me, my face would get hot. It became hard to breathe, and my heart rate monitor blared, making the nurse have to rush in to make sure I wasn't suddenly dying.

I didn't want to believe Reid would do that, but when you took someone working class and waved a check with a lot of zeros in front of them, it had to be tempting.

Or what if my father told him things that weren't true?

What if my father told Reid that he couldn't make me happy and that he couldn't provide for me?

What if he managed to convince Reid that I would never be anything more than a spoiled heiress?

"Girl, what are you doing?" The nurse came in again, rolling her eyes as she punched a few buttons on the machine next to my bed to make it stop beeping. "Are you borrowing trouble? It looks like you're borrowing trouble."

"I don't know what that means," I admitted, forcing myself to take long, slow breaths and calm down.

"It means you are worrying about something that you have no control over, that hasn't even happened yet. You look like you were sitting there with nothing better to do, so you're running through scenarios in your head of the horrible things that might happen. You are borrowing trouble from a reality that may not even exist."

"That's exactly what I was doing." I gave her what I hoped was a sheepish smile.

"Well, stop that. I got other people to look after. I can't keep coming in here every couple of minutes." Her words were stern, but she offered a sweet smile to let me know she wasn't really angry.

"Is she okay?" A deep voice came from the doorway, and the machine started beeping again.

"No," the nurse snapped at Reid. "Something has this poor little girl stressed, and I'm positive it has to do with you. So fix it before I have to come in here again."

She stormed out of the room, mumbling something about rounds.

"Look, I know what my father said to you. Well, I don't know, but I can make an educated guess, and before you make up your mind, I need you to hear me out," I said as I sat up and swung my legs over the edge of the mattress.

"Charlotte—" Reid rushed to the bed and eased me back.

"No, let me talk. I need to get this out. I need you to hear me. Can you promise me that you'll listen before you say anything and that you'll let me say my piece?"

"I'll listen, but only if you stay in bed."

"I don't want to stay in bed. I've stayed in bed for days. I need to move, and the doctor said I needed to get up and walk, so let me just walk around my room."

I was only half-lying. The doctors did say they wanted me up and walking around, but not for another two or three days. There was just too much nervous energy for me to sit still.

It was as if I had been sitting still my entire life, and I was sick of it.

"Charlotte, are you sure you're not pushing yourself too fast?"

"No, let me do this. I need to say what I need to say, and I can't be just lying there when I say it."

My stomach was hollow, and my throat dry, but it didn't matter.

I had to get this out before he said he was leaving me, or before I chickened out and missed my chance to live a life I could be proud of.

"Okay." Reid moved the blankets off my legs and offered his arm to help me stand.

A wave of dizziness slammed into me, and I had to grip Reid's arms to stop myself from falling over.

"Are you sure you want to do this, princess?"

"I need to do this," I said, meaning more than just the vertical movement. "Just give me a minute."

I leaned against him, and his arms wrapped around me and held me to his warm chest. The scent of spices and bergamot filled my senses, and I just stayed in his arms for a moment, letting his touch soothe me, letting his embrace take away my fear.

This man said he loved me, and I believed him.

He would protect me and keep me safe, and in return, I would be his partner.

I would shoulder half of his burdens, and we would share in each other's successes.

Once I was steady on my feet, I pushed back just enough that I could look into his eyes.

"I know my father probably offered you a lot of money and told you what a burden I would be. I can't offer you the money that he did. I don't have it. There's nothing in my name if you take me. I come with nothing. But I love you, and I know you call me a princess, and there's so much I need to learn to do, but I can do it. I'll learn how to cook. I'll get a job. I'm sure I could wait tables or work customer service somewhere. I'll even bag groceries if that's what it takes."

"Charlotte," he interrupted me, and I put my hand on his chest, silently asking him to listen.

"No, I need you to hear me. I need you to hear that I love you, and I won't be a burden. I know you can't afford the massive house that my father can, and that's fine. I don't need that. I don't need expensive jewelry. I don't need designer bags or anything like that. The only thing in my life I need is you and my cello. I can bring in some money with the Philharmonic, and if that's not enough, I will get another job. I can... handle it. I want to do this. I want to build a life with you. A real life, not some romantic, princess fantasy." I was rambling, but I couldn't stop.

I needed him to know I meant every word.

"Charlotte," he said again, and I expected to see regret in his eyes or something that told me he had already made the choice to leave me, and he was just here as a courtesy.

Instead, I found mischief. His eyes sparkled with humor as his lips twisted into his signature cocky smirk.

"What?" I asked. "Did you already take the money? Is it too late?"

"You're right. Your father offered me money."

"Did you take it?"

His eyes turned cold as he loomed over me, his hand moving to my throat.

Not choking me, there wasn't even any pressure, just the reminder that he could.

He would never hurt me, but I knew he liked showing me that he was in charge.

My heart was pounding as his thumb rested on my pulse point.

"That is the last time you insult my integrity. I love you, you are mine. Only mine, always mine, nothing will come in between us, especially not something as common and insignificant as money."

"You say that now, but what happens if—"

"Nothing will happen. And you don't have to work if you don't want to, baby. Princess, I can take care of you."

"I know you can, and I'm saying that I don't need everything that my father provided. That I don't need—"

Reid cut off my words with a consuming kiss, slamming his mouth over mine, devouring my lips, his hands roaming down my body, and that stupid machine started blaring again.

He reached over and hit the large red button himself, silencing the high-pitched beeping that would call my nurse.

I wasn't aware that was a thing we were allowed to do.

"I listened to you, Charlotte. I listened to your concerns. Now I need you to listen to mine, okay?"

My stomach was in knots, and I was still convinced that he was going to tell me it was over.

"Money will never be a problem for us."

"I know, because we don't need it. Well, we need it, but we don't—"

He cut off my further ramblings. "Princess, I'm a ridiculously wealthy man."

CHAPTER 36

REID

"So you lied to me?" She wasn't yelling, but there was definitely a tone.

"What did I just say about insulting my integrity?" I loomed over her, not wanting to jostle her wounds, but needing to make my point.

"How am I supposed to react when you insult my intelligence?" she bit back.

This version of her, my princess turning into a queen, was sexy as fuck.

There was a fire in her eyes as her shoulders pressed back, lifting those gorgeous tits barely covered by the thin layer of fabric.

Even in a hospital gown with no makeup, she was the most beautiful woman I'd ever laid eyes on.

"Watch yourself, princess," I growled. "I never lied to you. I just didn't tell you my net worth."

"No, you lied. Why would someone so wealthy live in such a tiny apartment?"

"Because not all of us need a ten-million-dollar mansion filled with useless shit to feel good about ourselves."

"If you have all this money, why are you working for my family?"

"Because I'm in security. I have the training. I have the skills, and until I laid eyes on you, I thought it would be an easy fucking gig."

"But if you're rich, why do you need any gigs at all?" she shot back.

She was pressing her fucking luck.

"Because unlike most people with my net worth, I don't like sitting on my ass all day playing at being useful. I make myself useful and I give myself goals. And I don't have to explain a damn thing to you."

"You do! You owe me explanations. Where did you get this massive net worth?"

"Princess, just because you're in the hospital doesn't mean that I won't take you over my knee right now and paddle that sweet little ass. You know I'll do it, and then you know I'll make you like it." My words came out a husky growl that made her breath quicken, and that fucking machine behind her started beeping again.

"You wouldn't," she gasped.

The last thing I wanted was for that nurse to come back in here, so I silenced the machine by ripping the cord out of the wall.

"You want to reconsider how you're talking to me, princess?"

"You tell me you love me, but then you don't tell me anything about yourself. I prepared myself to give up everything for you. I was looking forward to a simple lifestyle. I actually Googled how to clip coupons last night. I don't understand what's happening."

Her hands went to her forehead as she swayed on her feet.

I swept her up into my arms and gently placed her back in bed.

She didn't fight me as I covered her legs with the blanket.

"I didn't tell you anything before because you didn't ask, and it was none of your business before. I was going to tell you before you ran from my apartment so fucking fast the other morning. I didn't think you gave a shit."

"I was trying to figure out how to tell my father I wasn't going to marry Zeigler. I was working up the nerve to stand up for myself, and I didn't want to tell you in case I chickened out." She was just shy of screaming at me. Then her voice broke into a sob. "I didn't want you to be disappointed in me."

"Then ask me now." I crossed my arms over my chest and sat back in the chair next to her bed. "Ask me what you want to know."

"If you're so wealthy, why do you live in a tiny apartment?" she asked again, hung up on that little apartment.

"Because I don't need much. Until recently, I never really even thought about staying in one place long-term. I have a few apartments in different countries about the same size, and I'm hardly ever in any of them."

"Why?"

"Be more specific." I sat back, not letting her off the hook. She knew what she wanted, and she could ask.

"If you're as wealthy as you say you are, why do you work?"

"Because I hate feeling useless. I need something to do to occupy my time, and I fucking hate golf," I answered honestly and shrugged my shoulders. It was the truth. I needed a sense of accomplishment, and golf was a fucking waste of time.

"There are other jobs you could have taken that don't put your life at risk."

"But that's the fun part," I said, giving her a rueful smile. "Sitting at a desk shuffling papers and playing Monopoly with other people's lives doesn't make me feel accomplished. It makes me feel like a giant asshole who spent too much money on a suit that was probably made by children, being paid pennies just so another rich asshole can pocket the profit."

"I still don't understand."

"What don't you understand, princess? Tell me and I will answer any questions for you."

"How do you have so much money? Did you topple a small country?"

She was trying to be funny, but in my years serving the Marines, I'd actually toppled several countries. But that wasn't what she was asking, and I was not about to volunteer that information.

"It's family money."

"Family money? Are you a secret Rockefeller?"

"No, I'm a Taylor, of the Texan Taylors." I wasn't surprised when she kept giving me a blank look. So I added just a little more to help her connect the dots. "As in Taylor Oil, Taylor Ranch, Taylor Meat Packing."

"Your family owns cows?" she asked, her nose scrunching in the most adorable way I had ever seen.

"My brother owns a ranch that has a little over a hundred thousand acres and about fifty thousand head of cattle. My family also owns a meat distribution plant, and we are providers of the finest beef in North America. Although last I talked to him, he was also looking at expanding into Argentina as well as a few other places globally. Apparently, even in New Zealand. He's convinced he can make mutton have a comeback in North America."

"Okay…"

"But that's not what you asked. You asked how I have money. My grandfather had a little over three hundred acres when they struck oil. That made my family very, very wealthy.

When he died, he left the ranch to my brother, and I got the oil rights."

"So you are an oil baron?"

"If this was 1904, I would be called an oil baron. We prefer tycoons now," I said, mostly joking.

"But I don't understand. If you're so wealthy, how come we've never met before? You should be running in the same social circles as my father and brother, not working for them."

"When I was eighteen..." I took a deep breath, knowing that she needed to know this story but hating to tell it. I had never really told anyone this story. In fact, she was the only one, other than Hunter, who knew the truth of where I came from.

Most people assumed I was just some backwater country boy who joined the Marines so I didn't starve to death. I actually preferred that to be what people thought.

"When I was eighteen," I started again, "my father and I got into a fight. Because I didn't want to take over running the Taylor empire. It's sitting behind a desk in two-thousand-dollar cowboy boots that have never seen a day of mud in their life. It's endless shareholder meetings and pushing papers, signing checks, and just bullshit. That's not what I wanted to do, and my father threatened to cut me off."

"What did you want to do?"

"I wanted to be a cowboy. I wanted to be out working the land with the hired hands, but my father wouldn't hear of it. I couldn't spend my life like your brother does. Don't get me wrong, I respect Luc. I know in his way, he is a warrior as much as I am. But he's a man of talk, a man of planning, and I'm a man of action."

"So what happened?"

"What happened was my father got me accepted into the top colleges in the country. I had my pick, but the idea of sitting at a desk or a lecture hall listening to people talk made me want to scream. I couldn't do it. I couldn't let that be my life. So instead, on my eighteenth birthday, a month before I graduated high school, I took my GED test, and I enlisted in the Marines."

"Do you ever regret it?"

"Never once," I said honestly. "Not even when my father cut me off."

"But I thought you said—"

"My grandfather set up individual trusts for me and my brother. So he is the one who left me the oil rights and left my brother the entire ranching side of the business. Technically, he actually got the larger share, but he earned it. He stayed, and he runs that ranch far better than I ever could."

"When you say ranch, do you mean like the Yellowstone?"

Of course, she would compare it to the fucking Yellowstone. Maybe when I got her back home and settled into her new life, I would admit that I loved that show and we could watch it together.

"Yes and no," I said, trying really hard not to laugh. "Yes, there's cows and a lot of beautiful land, but it's not fictional, and to the best of my knowledge we have never branded a single one of our hired hands. They tend to get a little too wily when it comes to human rights violations."

She rolled her eyes at me and gave me a sweet smile, but there was still something behind those eyes, something she was unsure of.

"Charlotte, princess, look at me."

Her beautiful Bambi-brown eyes looked up at me, and I could see she was conflicted.

"Are you upset that I have money?" I asked.

"I... I... I don't know."

"Don't lie to me." My heart ached, and my stomach flipped, and I realized that my wealth might actually be a problem.

"I'm not lying," she said.

"Do you somehow love me less because I can provide for you?"

"No, I just don't know what to think."

"What does that even mean?" I stood and paced from the foot of her bed to the wall with its windowsill covered in white flowers.

"It means this is a lot. I prepared myself for a life that was going to be different, away from the hypocrisy, intrigue, and loose ethics of high society. I was going to learn how to freaking bake bread and buy an alarm clock. But now I don't know."

I cupped her cheek. God, she was adorable. "You can still bake bread and buy an alarm clock."

Her lower lip pushed out in a pout. "It's not the same. I just... I'm tired, and I'm confused, and I don't know what to believe, and I still feel like you lied to me, and I just..."

"Let me tell you what is important." I laced my fingers in her soft hair, tightening them just enough until she felt the pull.

I knew my girl. She liked it when she knew I was in control. She liked just a hint of pain with her pleasure.

"You are mine. That is what's important. You're mine to love, to protect, to provide for. I have the means to provide any life that you could ever want. You will want for nothing."

"At what cost?" she asked, sticking out her chin in defiance.

My cock stirred, and I wanted to remind her what happened to bad girls. "Excuse me?"

"I want for nothing now, but it cost my freedom. Are you going to put me in some gilded cage as well and forbid me from having my own goals?"

Letting go of her hair, I stalked across the room, closed her door and locked it. "You were warned. You will not insult my integrity again, little girl."

I didn't want to hurt her.

I didn't even really want to spank her.

253

Not when she was still so frail. But I couldn't let a slight like that slide.

If I did, I wouldn't be the man that she wanted.

My girl craved a firm hand, and that's what I was going to give her.

I stood next to her bed with one hand flat on her pillow, just barely allowing my thumb to touch her cheek as I leaned over and spoke just loud enough I knew she could hear me. "Do you want a chance to apologize, babygirl? Or are you going to take your punishment?"

"I don't have anything to apologize for."

My other hand moved under her blankets to her ankle and squeezed. Not enough to hurt her, just so she knew exactly where my hand was. "Are you sure about that?"

"I don't think it's unreasonable to want answers." Her voice broke.

"Oh it's not. I even told you I'd answer any question you have, but that last one wasn't a question, was it? It was an accusation. You think that I'm the type of man who would leave you chained up in some gilded cage. After everything?"

My hand moved from her ankle to her inner thigh, pushing her legs apart.

"Every other man has."

"I am not every other man in your life." I pushed my hand up between her thighs and felt her wet pussy.

"I…" Her voice was trembling.

"No, it's too late for apologies now, princess. Let me tell you exactly how this is going to work. You are mine. Body and soul. That means when you're out of this hospital bed, we are going to march to the nearest church, and you are going to be a good girl and say I do."

She gasped as I slid one finger into her tight little cunt.

"If you're a bad girl, then I'm going to bend you over the kitchen counter and fuck you until I break you."

"Reid." My name on her lips sounded more like a prayer than a plea.

"As far as what you do in between those times, you only have to follow a few rules. You will never be somewhere that I don't think is safe. You will never let another man touch you. And you will never go a single day without sharing your gift with the world. I don't care if you do charity events or if you work for a world-class orchestra. Your music deserves to be heard by the world."

I pushed harder on her clit, ramping her up and making her back bend a little, and if she wasn't such a brat, I would have let her come.

I probably would have lifted the hospital gown and licked her until she screamed my name, letting every single person in the hospital know what was going on in this room.

But that would have been a reward. I didn't reward bad behavior.

I pulled my hand away from her just before she reached her climax, and she let out a pained groan.

"Any other questions, princess?" I asked, licking my fingers clean.

CHAPTER 37

CHARLOTTE

I sat straight up in bed, my heart hammering in my chest and the rapid beeping of my monitor at my side.

My room was dark and peaceful.

The only sound was the storm raging outside.

That must have been what woke me.

I took a few deep breaths, calming my heart rate, and the machine stopped beeping all on its own.

The rain pelted the windows, and a flash of lightning lit up my room.

It's just a storm. No reason to worry.

I lay back down on the thin mattress, resting my head on the pillow Olivia had brought me because, according to her, thin hospital pillows were the devil's invention.

Thunder rolled through the air again, a loud crack of pressure.

I closed my eyes, willing sleep to come.

Another flash of lightening and another crack of thunder, but there was something else.

A different noise like a shuffling, and then the creak of my door opening.

Probably a nurse coming to take more blood or check on the monitor.

Or Reid coming back in.

He had been by my side constantly, even when I asked for some time to think, he'd propped his feet on my bed and said I had all the room I needed for thought.

It took some convincing, but eventually, he'd left to shower and change. Still, I knew he wouldn't stay away long, preferring to sleep in the chair next to my bed.

I sat up, prepared to greet whoever had come into my room when a black canvas bag was forced over my head. The monitor started screeching as I clawed at the hands holding the bag tight around my neck.

"Shut that thing off," a gruff and slightly accented voice said, before my IV was ripped out and the sensors taken off my body.

Hands grabbed at my arms and legs and hauled me off the bed.

I fought with everything I had, kicking and punching out, but it wasn't enough.

My bare feet hit solid muscle, and soon I was put in some kind of chair and strapped down.

"Reid!" I screamed, silenced only when something slammed across my face. Blood filled my mouth as my body jerked, flooding me with pain from my gunshot wounds.

"That is the last time you ever fucking say his name," a cold British voice sneered. "You will learn your place, one way or another."

My head swam. It took me a second to realize we were moving. The chair I was in was being rolled out of the hospital.

"Where are you taking me?" My words were slurred, my

stomach ached, and something hot and thick ran down my arm from where the IV had been ripped from my vein.

"Where you belong," that voice said.

I knew that voice, but I couldn't place it.

My eyelids were heavy, my ears were ringing, and I had to fight to stay awake.

"Is she really worth all this trouble?" one of the voices asked.

"No, but her father's fortune is," the familiar British voice answered. "We need to hurry. This is the first time she has been without her bodyguard. He is probably on his way back."

"The dumb bitch opened her legs, and now he thinks he has a claim to her."

"It doesn't matter. I'm not afraid of a rent-a-cop."

I laughed at their hubris.

"What was that?" the man with the gruffer voice said and ripped the hood off my face, taking several strands of my hair with it.

I winced, but really, between the gunshot wounds, the pain meds leaving my body, and where they'd ripped out my IV, it was just a drop in the bucket.

"Find something funny, bitch?"

There were three of them, all wearing head to toe black, with ski masks pulled over their faces. Two of them were large hulking men, with broad shoulders, clearly hired to kidnap me, and the third was tall, but with a much more slender frame.

Romney, the man who couldn't take fuck off for an answer.

I glared at Romney in a way I knew would make Reid proud.

I needed to be strong like him and I needed to make him proud of me.

"He isn't a rent-a-cop. He's a Marine, and I'm his girl. Which means you are all dead men walking. Didn't Romney tell you he doesn't have the money to pay you?"

"That is enough out of you." Romney backhanded me again, and I almost fell over in my chair.

The old Charlotte would have cried, screamed, or worse, cowered.

The new me got pissed.

"You will learn your place, one way or another." Romney lifted his hand, ready to strike me again.

The zip ties securing me to the wheelchair dug into my wrists, not allowing me to fight back or protect myself. So, instead, I spat in his face, sending drops of bloody spittle over his exposed mouth and eyes.

He recoiled. He had no idea what I was capable of. I had no idea what I was capable of, but we were about to find out together.

"You're going to pay for that," he growled.

"Fuck you," I fired back, before working up enough blood and phlegm to spit at him again.

The elevator stopped just in time, and one of the other men yanked the chair, pulling me backward. The halls were wide, with concrete floors and walls with what looked like industrial lighting every few yards. They were unfortunately deserted.

This part of the hospital was clearly not meant for the general public.

How was Reid supposed to find me if he didn't know about these tunnels?

I looked down at my arm. The gash from the IV dripped blood onto the rubber wheel. The wheel then left a trail of blood I could only hope started near my room, but the trail was turning faint as the wound clotted.

As carefully as possible, I moved my arm down, getting the zip tie to lie across the open wound, and pressed.

It hurt more than I'd expected, but that didn't matter, not when the blood flowed again.

Pushing my lips together so I didn't make a sound, I pressed harder and soon the line on the concrete was nearly solid.

Not perfect, but it would be easy enough for Reid to follow as long as he got to me soon.

God, I hoped he got to me in time.

I was going to be strong for him. I would never give up on him, but I didn't know how much longer I could fight off the rising darkness.

They whipped me around, triggering vomit-inducing vertigo as they ran down another long corridor, ending in a set of double doors leading outside to a loading bay.

Through the glass doors I could see a white, windowless van waiting in the pouring rain.

"No!" I screamed and struggled against the zip ties.

"Stop struggling, bitch. I should have drugged you like Mary suggested."

Mary? Mary who?

The second I was pushed through the double doors, freezing rain pelted my exposed skin, like icy bee stings. The frigid air burned my lungs, but I pushed past it and screamed, "Help!"

"Go ahead, darling," Romney taunted as he yanked my hair back so rainwater went into my mouth and nose. It was raining so hard, I couldn't even open my eyes against the onslaught. "No one is going to hear you."

I tried to scream again, but instead, I choked and struggled to cough up the water in my lungs without breathing in more.

He laughed as he tightened his grip on my hair and leaned down to whisper in my ear, "You are mine now, and there isn't a thing you can do about it. Your father will honor that marriage contract or face the scandal of having his precious daughter outed as a whore."

"I'll never marry you, you dickhead," I choked out as lightning flashed across the sky again, followed by another deafening boom of thunder.

The other men had already reached the van and held open the back doors, waiting for Romney to roll me the rest of the way.

Then two hollow-sounding pops cut through the air.

CHAPTER 38

REID

*T*his shit was never going to happen again.

Charlotte was soaked through, blood still dripping down one of her arms.

The sight nearly knocked me to my knees. I would never let this happen again.

When I walked into her hospital room, I realized she must have just been taken.

The blood on the floor was still wet, leaving a blood-smeared wheelchair trail.

The nurses had been on a shift change, so they had no idea where she'd been taken.

The head nurse taking over rounds hadn't yet made it to her room.

I told her to stay where she was and lock down the rest of the floor while I followed the bloody path leading to a well-hidden service elevator.

The second I was in the elevator, I pulled my gun, not wanting to scare the nurses and then get slowed down by security.

I didn't know where they had taken my girl, but I knew I had to get her back before they left the building.

Once they managed to get her to a second location, the chances of me finding her alive were slim to none.

I would find her, but the sooner I found her, the better.

Protecting Charlotte was my responsibility, and nothing was going to stop me from that.

There was a small puddle of her blood on the elevator floor, with two separate sets of tracks. That meant not only were the tracks heading into the elevator, but there would be tracks on whatever floor she got off on.

I started by hitting the button for the first floor, thinking that was the most obvious.

When the doors opened, there was nothing on the smooth tiles other than a little bit of dirt and grime, so at least I knew that that floor hadn't just been cleaned.

I considered heading to the roof, knowing there was a possibility of her attacker taking her by helicopter. But first, I wanted to check the basement level.

Something in my gut told me she was on the ground, not in the air.

I hit the button for B1 and checked my gun as I waited. I knew it was clean. I knew it was fully loaded, but I had to do something other than stare at the pool of my girl's blood on the floor.

When the elevator doors slid open on the first basement level, I saw the trail of blood leading out. This was where they had taken her. I wanted to run after her, shouting for her, but I knew better.

There was too much I didn't know. I didn't know how many men had her. I didn't know if they were armed or what condition she was in.

I had to be smart about this.

Moving as swiftly as I was able, I crept down the corridors, keeping close to the wall, my gun aimed at the floor directly in front of me. I saw a black canvas bag that had a few strands of her beautiful hair left in it. Whoever had put it on her had ripped it off, clearly not caring if she knew their identity.

My heart froze in my chest as a cold sensation crawled up my spine. The only reason an attacker would remove a blindfold from their victim was if it didn't matter if the victim knew who had attacked them.

They weren't trying to hide their identity, so they were either stupid, or they intended to kill her.

I moved faster, needing to get to her now.

I followed the trail around a corner, and that was when I saw them.

Three assailants, all wearing ski masks. It looked like at least two were armed with a single pistol each, and probably a few that were hidden. The third man, a much slimmer man, didn't have anything other than the audacity to hit my woman.

I saw them through the glass double doors. The two larger men ran through the rain to get to the truck. The skinny one stopped and ripped her hair back, holding her under the torrential downpour of freezing rain.

The son of a bitch was essentially waterboarding my girl, watching her choke as she tried to breathe, tied down to a fucking wheelchair. There was a sick smile on his face that I could just see in the mask. He liked it. He liked watching her suffer.

I knew exactly where he was planning on taking her and why he didn't give a fuck if she knew who he was. He was going to take her and force her to marry him so he could drag her out of this country and keep her from my grasp.

They picked the wrong motherfucker to mess with.

With a fire raging through my veins, I marched through the

double doors, lifted my pistol, and fired. One shot in the shoulder of one of the assailants, the other into the van.

I just needed them gone, and it worked the second they realized what had happened. Both men were in the van, the doors closed, the tires squealing, and the back end of the van fishtailing as they left.

All that was left was Zeigler, standing between me and my woman.

I aimed my gun at him, ready to place a bullet between his eyes.

"What do you think you're doing? Do you know who I am?" he screamed. I had to admit, for a man wearing a mask, that was a really fucking stupid question.

I pulled off his ski mask, making sure to grip his hair and yank a chunk of it out. A little retribution for my girl. Then I punched him square in the jaw hard enough that I knew he would be out for at least a few hours.

And if, in those few hours, he happened to drown in a 4-inch puddle of rainwater, well, that was just an act of God, now wasn't it?

He didn't matter, but protecting my girl from him did.

Slicing through the zip ties that held her down as quickly as I could, I bundled her up in my arms, not realizing I hadn't been able to breathe for the last several seconds.

It wasn't until I held her, and I knew she was safe, that my body allowed oxygen to enter my lungs.

I didn't know how it had gotten like this so fast, but I couldn't breathe without her.

"Reid." Her voice sounded so small, so frail. How could I not have been here to protect her? How could I have let her be in a position where she was so vulnerable?

She threw her arms around me. "I'm so sorry. I tried to fight them. I tried to be strong and make you proud."

"Shh, princess. I got you. I am so proud of you, babygirl." I kissed her forehead before cutting the ties on her ankles. "I'm sorry. I'm so fucking sorry."

Her brow furrowed as she clung to my wet shirt. "What for?"

"For not anticipating this tactic. I thought Zeigler was a neutralized threat."

She sniffed as she buried her face against my neck. "This isn't going to end. There will always be another threat as long as my father doesn't approve of us."

I picked her up and cradled her in my arms as I carried her inside, tightening my grip as she trembled. "I know. That's why we are going to go take care of this right now."

Her father wanted her married.

So that was what he was going to get—just not to the man he picked.

I carried her into the hospital, and two nurses immediately saw us and started trailing after us, asking what had happened.

"Your security sucks. That's what happened," I growled out as I pushed past them.

I wasn't going to her room, not yet. She would be back safe in her bed with me by her side, protecting her, in a moment. First, we were going to take care of this.

"Where are we going?"

"We're going to give your father what he wants."

CHAPTER 39

REID

"hat?"

"Charlotte Maeve Manwarring, I'm not going to ask you the question I should be asking you, because I'm not giving you a choice. You are mine. You've already said you were mine, and I am never letting you go." I didn't look down at her. I kept my eyes up, following the signs for the hospital chapel.

"I don't want you to ever let me go."

"Good. So we are going to the chapel now, and we are making it legal."

"Yes," she whispered, as if I had actually asked her a question instead of issuing a simple fact.

"Good. I will give you the wedding you deserve once you have healed. You can spend a ridiculous amount of money on a dress, flowers, invitations, anything you want. But this, the legal side, is being handled tonight. I don't want that asshole, or any other assholes that your father can find, to think he can claim what is mine."

"Okay."

I didn't know why I'd expected her to fight me. Maybe it was because I thought that she would realize that money or not, she was far too good for me, but I was not about to look a gift horse in the mouth.

"Wait, she needs her arm bandaged." One of the nurses chased after me.

"Then grab the shit you need and meet us in the chapel. You can wrap her up there."

I didn't say anything else. I just held Charlotte to my chest, feeling her heartbeat against my skin as her fingers tangled in my hair, massaging the back of my neck, a small way for her to show her affection and approval.

God, I was going to love to find all the ways that she showed affection, all the small little ticks she had, annoyances, what made her happy, what made her sad, and what pissed her off beyond all belief. I was going to spend the rest of my life exploring every facet of this beautiful creature in my arms and protecting her with my life.

She was my mission now.

The chapel was completely empty when we got there. A small button on the side of the altar had a little wooden placard that said *press for assistance*.

I slammed my hand down on that button several times until a small door opened in the back of the room.

"Can I help you?" a man wearing a black button-down shirt asked, stepping out of the room.

"Yeah, you ordained?" I asked, cutting off the pleasantries.

My girl was cold and uncomfortable. I needed to get this handled before I could fix that. Safety might come before comfort, but as far as I was concerned, they were both important when it came to my girl.

"I am. Can I help you with something?" He looked me up and

down as he took a step back, no doubt getting ready to call security.

"We need to be married. Now."

"That's not usually how—"

"I'm not looking for usual. There is nothing about this situation, or this woman, that is usual. The fact of the matter is—we need to be married for her safety. This is a matter of urgency. We need to be married immediately."

The priest looked at us both for a moment, then focused on Charlotte. She looked so small in my arms, her eyes a little bloodshot and tired, her hair dripping on the carpet and streaks of blood on her arm and staining part of her patterned hospital gown.

"Ma'am, are you okay?" the priest asked. The way he disregarded me would usually get under my skin, and it did a little, but I knew he was trying to check on her well-being. I couldn't fault him for that.

"She's fine."

"I'd like to hear it from her." The priest wasn't giving an inch.

"I will be fantastic as soon as I'm this man's wife," she said, giving him a bright smile.

One of the nurses started wiping the blood from her arm.

He still looked unsure. So, I tried something new for me: the diplomatic approach.

"We need to be married tonight. To show our gratitude for making this happen, we would be willing to make a $250,000 donation to fund the new pediatric oncology center." I plastered an unnatural smile on my lips that just felt wrong.

"I doubt that you have—"

The priest was cut off when one of the nurses ran to him and whispered in his ear, probably telling him who the bloody, damp, and still-stunning creature in my arms was.

"Well, okay then." The priest motioned us over to the altar.

The second I sat her down, two of the nurses surrounded her, wrapped her arm, and quickly put a dry gown over her soaking wet one.

As soon as we were done here, I planned on taking her up to her room and making sure she was dry and comfortable, but this had to be done now.

The priest uttered a few words about love, marriage, honor, and commitment, and I didn't hear a word of it. Instead, I was staring at those gorgeous brown eyes looking up at me like I was her everything. And it just seemed so fitting because that was exactly what she was. She was my everything.

When she said, "I do," my heart stopped for a moment, and a soothing warmth came over my body.

I realized with a start that I was happy. Not content, not entertained, amused, or even satisfied. I was actually happy. I didn't think I'd ever felt that before.

It made sense that Charlotte was the one who had given me that feeling. That she was the one who made me feel complete. I didn't have to travel the world anymore to find something to do. I was going to build a home and start a real life with this woman.

Once the priest said, "You may kiss the bride," I leaned down, sealing my lips over hers, and she was holding me as tightly as I was holding her.

After the ceremony, I picked her back up again and brought her back to her hospital bed. The nurses asked that I step out for just a moment so that they could clean her up and get her into dry clothes. I wanted to do that by myself, but they needed to insert a new IV and check her over for any other injuries.

I stepped out of the room and stood guard at the door, not letting anyone else in, and dialed her father.

Lucian answered on the first ring. "Reid. You change your mind about my offer?"

I smirked as I looked over my shoulder at my wife, curled up under the covers of her hospital bed. "Not exactly."

There was a long pause, then a sigh. "Something you want to tell me?"

"Just wanted to call and say hi… dad."

"Charlotte married you? When?"

"Just now."

"What? Some half-ass wedding in a cheap hospital chapel. I have news for you—*son*—God doesn't have any rights in a New York court."

"Maybe not, but we both know perception is everything. How would it look if the Irish Catholic Manwarrings didn't recognize a union sanctioned by God?"

"You're a real son-of-a-bitch, Reid," he growled.

"I'll take that as a warm welcome to the family." Chuckling, I hung up, sliding the phone into my back pocket as the nurses came out and let me in to see my wife.

CHAPTER 40

CHARLOTTE

"*A*re you sure?" Luc asked in his perfectly tailored suit, offering his arm for me to take. "This is your last chance to pull a runaway bride."

I tapped my chin, careful not to touch my pinkish nude lipstick, and pretended to consider it.

There was no way I was leaving this building without a ring on my finger, and Luc knew it. That didn't mean I couldn't have a little fun.

"Well, the roads are covered in ice, and even the streetlamps are out. It might just be safer to cancel. Oh wait! I'm already married."

The storm of the century raged outside.

Something about a freak blizzard on its way to blanket the city in a winter wonderland from hell.

It made sense. My father was one of the most powerful men in the city.

He acted as if he were God himself.

He did say that I would marry 'the help,' when hell froze over.

According to the weather man, we were well on our way.

The storm had picked up faster than we'd expected. Not even half of our last-minute guests were able to make it, but Reid and I refused to put off the ceremony.

We wanted to have a proper wedding no one would question before he brought me home to the new brownstone he'd bought for us.

Neither of us were willing to wait another day to start our life together.

Mother nature be damned.

"Well, as long as you have a good reason." Luc winked, ready to walk me down the aisle "Are you ready to be Mrs. Taylor?"

"I'm already Mrs. Taylor, but let's go tell the world."

I took his arm, and he guided me to the aisle between the rows of seats at the Lincoln Center for the Performing Arts main stage.

When the storm picked up and the power went out an hour ago, I thought for sure we would have to cancel the ceremony, but Reid had refused.

He'd said he would fix it with a bit of help from my family and friends.

They'd lined the aisle with candles of all shapes and sizes. The stage was lit with a few hundred candles in the front corners and along the center, giving the room an almost ethereal glow.

Then the music started.

At first, a single cello, then another, and a few violins. It took me a moment to recognize the tune *Perfect* by Ed Sheeran.

It was breathtaking in its simplicity and so very touching. Ginnie played and other friends from different orchestras and ensembles I had played with over the years joined her.

I wasn't even on the stage yet, standing in front of the man I loved, and I was already having to hold back tears of joy.

When I was still in the hospital, I told Reid I didn't want to wait too long to have our formal wedding.

He'd agreed, and the next day, he had Olivia, Amelia, and Ginnie in the hospital room, helping me make plans while he and Luc went ring shopping.

Olivia even had designers bring dresses to the hospital room for fittings, which was really convenient since I wasn't supposed to spend too much time on my feet.

I had only been released this afternoon and told to take it easy, and I would… tomorrow.

The officiant wasn't a priest.

They could only do weddings in a church, and there was no way to get this all ready in time, so the director of the New York Philharmonic agreed to marry us if I agreed to join as first cello after I recovered.

Apparently, he had been ordained before in order to marry some other friends of his.

The entire thing was perfect.

No, it was better than perfect.

It was magical and more than I could have ever hoped for. I wore a vintage dress Amelia found when none of the stuffy haute couture designers felt right. She'd even organized a small team of seamstresses to come in and alter the dress to fit me with its beautiful art deco beadwork and long elegant train. It was so exquisite, soft and feminine, and just stunning.

Olivia took care of the business end, making sure to invite everyone I would want in a private, intimate ceremony.

Despite the weather, she even managed to get Reid's brother and his family flown out.

I never thought my wedding would be filled with people I knew and cared about. I always assumed it would be more of a business networking event for my father and whomever he married me off to.

This was so much better.

I just wished my father was here.

Despite her protests, Olivia did deliver an invitation to our father, but he still chose not to come. I knew his refusal was coming, but that didn't mean it hurt any less.

Fortunately for me, my brother was there to give me away.

When Luc handed me off to Reid, he kissed my cheek, then shook Reid's hand before leaning in and whispering something in Reid's ear.

"You don't have anything to worry about," Reid told Luc, clapping him on the arm before Luc turned to sit with everyone else in the audience.

Our vows were short and simple.

We did not promise to honor or obey. We didn't even say in sickness or in health. Instead, we promised to love and support each other's dreams and passions. We promised to listen to each other and encourage one another to find our passions together.

Reid had listened to me.

He'd had the vows changed, so I was free to make decisions in my life.

I was his, always his, only his.

But I was no longer forced to live my life in a gilded cage, watching as everyone else around me lived their life and mine just passed me by.

Reid gave me the freedom I needed to make my own choices, while still choosing him.

He slid a perfect two-carat princess cut diamond on my finger, elegant but not too flashy. Just big enough to sparkle but small enough I could wear it while I played cello without it being a hindrance.

A single tear slid down my cheek as I looked into his eyes, knowing he saw me.

Not my name, not who I was raised to be, but me.

All of me.

Then on his finger, I slid a titanium band.

It was like him: strong, to the point, and unbreakable.

Reid Taylor had burst into my life as a domineering shadow I did not want, but now he was my protector, my savior, and my love.

EPILOGUE

LUCIAN MANWARRING, SR.

I stood in the shadows of the balcony.

Muddy slush from the sleet outside dripped off my wool overcoat and pooled at my feet, ruining the expensive Persian carpet. Not that I gave a damn.

Off to the right of the stage below, in the wings, I caught a flash of white.

My daughter Charlotte, dressed in a simple, yet elegant wedding gown, twirled as someone took her photo on their phone.

My son, Luc, appeared and offered his arm.

He would be walking her down the makeshift aisle.

Not me.

My children thought me cruel and unfeeling.

They weren't wrong.

But they were wrong regarding my motivation to stay away.

My relationship with my children was... complicated.

Especially with Charlotte.

I was going to hell for so many fucking reasons, but the

primary one, was that deep down, I had always resented my own daughter.

No, resented was too refined of a word. Hated.

Every time I looked at her sweet, smiling face, all I could see was the light dying in my beloved wife's eyes.

My wife and I had truly loved one another. From the moment I laid eyes on her at that debutante ball, I knew, with a frightening clarity, that she was the only woman I wanted to spend the rest of my life with. It was a once in a lifetime moment.

It was why we married so impossibly young.

I couldn't bear the thought of her not being mine.

So when the doctors had come to me with a choice between my daughter and my wife—I chose the woman I loved.

I was, and still am, a pragmatic businessman. I ran the numbers in my head. We could always have more children, but there would only be one her. Perhaps I could be forgiven for the heat-of-the-moment decision then—but not for the fact that I still didn't regret it.

That is the true stain on my soul.

If I had the chance to do it over again, I'd make the same decision without hesitation.

Only a heartless monster would look upon the lovely, talented, kind woman my daughter had become and believe such a thing.

Sometimes, I think I died the day my wife did, and by some strange occurrence, the shell of my body just continued to go through the motions of living.

The relentless demand of empire building allowed me to hide behind an icy wall, built brick by brick, through an unending march of meetings, contract negotiations, legal maneuverings, and long business trips.

That was the secret curse of almost limitless resources and money.

It bought distance.

Unlike most people, I wasn't forced to face my conflicted feelings toward my children.

They were raised by nannies and tutors, followed by a succession of boarding schools.

Part of an opposing army, doomed to never breach the wall.

To never close the distance.

And that was why I was now lurking in the darkness, like a fiend of the theatre, unable to show my face.

I didn't deserve to share in this happy moment.

And while I may not approve of the son-of-a-bitch she was marrying, he was at least one of the Texas Taylors. Truth was, even though none of my children married the way I'd planned, they had, at least, each married lucratively—if not strategically.

It was the strategic element that now caused problems for me.

Business was war. A man could build an empire on his own, but strategic alliances were what maintained it. Otherwise, any business was vulnerable.

With Luc cutting Manwarring ties with the Irish mob, we were losing both a crucial ally and money resource, but more importantly—we had now made a dangerous enemy.

As the crowd below cheered and Charlotte kissed her chosen groom, I left.

I had work to do.

* * *

I TURNED my collar up against the freezing rain and lifted my arm to signal to my waiting driver.

Just then, a beauty in a crimson silk gown completely unsuitable to the weather slipped on the ice nearby and collided against me.

My arm encircled her waist to steady her as my fingertips grazed the exposed skin of her lower back.

Without thinking, I instinctively opened my overcoat, pulled her against my chest, and wrapped the warm, soft wool around her bare shoulders.

Laughing, she pushed her golden-brown hair away from her eyes and looked up at me. "I'm sorry, I... oh—" Her smile faded. "It's you."

To be continued...

Unwillingly His

Gilded Decadence Series, Book Five

THE GILDED DECADENCE SERIES

Ruthlessly His

Gilded Decadence Series, Book One

His family dared to challenge mine, so I am going to ruin them... starting with stealing his bride.

Only a cold-hearted villain would destroy an innocent bride's special day over a business deal gone bad...

Which is why I choose this precise moment to disrupt New York High Society's most anticipated wedding of the season.

As I am Luc Manwarring, II, billionaire heir to one of the most powerful families in the country, no one is brave enough to stop me.

My revenge plan is deceptively simple: humiliate the groom, then blackmail the bride's family into coercing the bride into marrying me instead.

My ruthless calculations do not anticipate my reluctant bride having so much fight and fire in her.

At every opportunity, she resists my dominance and control, even going so far as trying to escape my dark plans for her.

She is only supposed to be a means to an end, an unwilling player in my game of revenge.

But the more she challenges me, the more I begin to wonder... who is playing who?

Savagely His

Gilded Decadence Series, Book Two

He dared to steal my bride, so it's only fair I respond by kidnapping his innocent sister.

Only a monster with no morals would kidnap a woman from her brother's wedding...

Which was precisely what I've become, a monster bent on revenge.

After all, as the billionaire Marksen DuBois, renowned for being a jilted groom, my reputation and business were in tatters.

There was nothing more dangerous than a man possessing power, boundless resources, and a vendetta.

I would torment him with increasingly degrading photos of his precious sister as I held her captive and under my complete control.

She'd have no option but to yield to my every command if she wished to shield herself and her family from further disgrace.

She was just a captured pawn to be dominated, exploited, and discarded.

Yet the more ensnared we become in my twisted game of revenge, the more my suspicions grow.

As she fiercely counters my every move, I begin to question whether I'm the true pawn... ensnared by my queen.

Brutally His

Gilded Decadence Series, Book Three

From our very first fiery encounter, I was tempted to fire my beautiful new assistant.

Right after I punished her for that defiant slap she delivered in response to my undeniably inappropriate kiss.

As Harrison Astrid, New York's formidable District Attorney, distractions were a luxury I couldn't afford.

Forming a shaky alliance with the Manwarrings and the Dubois, I was ensnared in a dangerous cat-and-mouse game.

As I strive to thwart my mother's cunning manipulations and her deadly alliance with the Irish mob.

Yet, every time I cross paths with my assistant, our mutual animosity surges into a near-savage need to control and dominate her.

I am a man who demands obedience, especially from subordinates.

Her stubbornness fuels my urge to assert my dominance, my need to show her I'm not just her boss—I'm her master.

Unfortunately the fiancé I'm to accept to play high society's charade, complicates things.

So I rein in my desire and resist the attraction between us.

Until the Irish mob targets my pretty little assistant... targets what's mine.

Now there isn't a force on earth that will keep me from tearing the city apart to find her.

Reluctantly His

Gilded Decadence Series, Book Four

First rule of being a bodyguard, don't f*ck the woman you're protecting.

And I want to break that rule so damn bad I can practically taste her.

She's innocent, sheltered, and spoiled.

As Reid Taylor, former Army sergeant and head of security for the Manwarrings, the last thing I should be doing is babysitting my boss's little sister.

I definitely shouldn't be fantasizing about pinning her down, spreading her thighs and...

It should help that she fights my protection at every turn.

Disobeying my rules. Running away from me. Talking back with that sexy, smart mouth of hers.

But it doesn't. It just makes me want her more.

I want to bend her over and claim her, hard and rough, until she begs for mercy.

That is a dangerous line I cannot cross.

She is an heiress, the precious daughter of one of the most powerful, multi-billionaire families in New York.

And I'm just her bodyguard, an employee. It would be the ultimate societal taboo.

But now her family is forcing her into an arranged marriage, and I'm not sure I'll be able to contain my rising rage at the idea of another man touching her.

Unwillingly His

Gilded Decadence Series, Book Five

The moment she slapped me, I knew I'd chosen the right bride.

To be fair, I had just stolen her entire inheritance.

As Lucian Manwarring, billionaire patriarch of the powerful Manwarring family, my word is law.

She's a beautiful and innocent heiress, raised to be the perfect society trophy wife.

Although far too young for me, that won't stop me from claiming her as my new prized possession.

What I hadn't planned on was her open defiance of me.

Far from submissive and obedient; she is stubborn, outspoken and headstrong.

She tries to escape my control and fights my plan to force her down the aisle.

I am not accustomed to being disobeyed.

While finding it mildly amusing at first, it is past time she accepts her fate.

She will be my bride even if I have to ruthlessly dominate and punish her to get what I want.

ABOUT ZOE BLAKE

Zoe Blake is the USA Today Bestselling Author of the romantic suspense saga *The Cavalieri Billionaire Legacy* inspired by her own heritage as well as her obsession with jewelry, travel, and the salacious gossip of history's most infamous families.

She delights in writing Dark Romance books filled with overly possessive billionaires, taboo scenes, and unexpected twists. She usually spends her ill-gotten gains on martinis, travels, and red lipstick. Since she can barely boil water, she's lucky enough to be married to a sexy Chef.

ALSO BY ZOE BLAKE

CAVALIERI BILLIONAIRE LEGACY

A Dark Enemies to Lovers Romance

Scandals of the Father

Cavalieri Billionaire Legacy, Book One

Being attracted to her wasn't wrong... but acting on it would be.

As the patriarch of the powerful and wealthy Cavalieri family, my choices came with consequences for everyone around me.

The roots of my ancestral, billionaire-dollar winery stretch deep into the rich, Italian soil, as does our legacy for ruthlessness and scandal.

It wasn't the fact she was half my age that made her off limits.

Nothing was off limits for me.

A wounded bird, caught in a trap not of her own making, she posed no risk to me.

My obsessive desire to possess her was the real problem.

For both of us.

But now that I've seen her, tasted her lips, I can't let her go.

Whether she likes it or not, she needs my protection.

I'm doing this for her own good, yet, she fights me at every turn.

Refusing the luxury I offer, desperately trying to escape my grasp.

I need to teach her to obey before the dark rumors of my past reach her.

Ruin her.

She cannot find out what I've done, not before I make her mine.

Sins of the Son

Cavalieri Billionaire Legacy, Book Two

She's hated me for years... now it's past time to give her a reason to.

When you are a son, and one of the heirs, to the legacy of the Cavalieri name, you need to be more vicious than your enemies.

And sometimes, the lines get blurred.

Years ago, they tried to use her as a pawn in a revenge scheme against me.

Even though I cared about her, I let them treat her as if she were nothing.

I was too arrogant and self-involved to protect her then.

But I'm here now. Ready to risk my life tracking down every single one of them.

They'll pay for what they've done as surely as I'll pay for my sins against her.

Too bad it won't be enough for her to let go of her hatred of me,

To get her to stop fighting me.

Because whether she likes it or not, I have the power, wealth, and connections to keep her by my side

And every intention of ruthlessly using all three to make her mine.

Secrets of the Brother

Cavalieri Billionaire Legacy, Book Three

We were not meant to be together... then a dark twist of fate stepped in, and we're the ones who will pay for it.

As the eldest son and heir of the Cavalieri name, I inherit a great deal more than a billion dollar empire.

I receive a legacy of secrets, lies, and scandal.

After enduring a childhood filled with malicious rumors about my father, I have fallen prey to his very same sin.

I married a woman I didn't love out of a false sense of family honor.

Now she has died under mysterious circumstances.

And I am left to play the widowed groom.

For no one can know the truth about my wife…

Especially her sister.

The only way to protect her from danger is to keep her close, and yet, her very nearness tortures me.

She is my sister in name only, but I have no right to desire her.

Not after what I have done.

It's too much to hope she would understand that it was all for her.

It's always been about her.

Only her.

I am, after all, my father's son.

And there is nothing on this earth more ruthless than a Cavalieri man in love.

Seduction of the Patriarch

Cavalieri Billionaire Legacy, Book Four

With a single gunshot, she brings the violent secrets of my buried past into the present.

She may not have pulled the trigger, but she still has blood on her hands.

And I know some very creative ways to make her pay for it.

I am as ruthless as my Cavalieri ancestors, who forged our powerful family legacy.

But no fortune is built without spilling blood.

I earn a reputation as a dangerous man to cross… and make enemies along the way.

So to protect those I love, I hand over the mantle of patriarch to my brother and move to northern Italy.

For years, I stay in the shadows…

Then a vengeful mafia syndicate attacks my family.

Now nothing will prevent me from seeking vengeance on those responsible.

And I don't give a damn who I hurt in the process... including her.

Whether it takes seduction, punishment, or both, I intend to manipulate her as a means to an end.

Yet, the more my little kitten shows her claws, the more I want to make her purr.

My plan is to coerce her into helping me topple the mafia syndicate, and then retreat into the shadows.

But if she keeps fighting me... I might just have to take her with me.

Scorn of the Betrothed

Cavalieri Billionaire Legacy, Book Five

A union forged in vengeance, bound by hate... and beneath it all, a twisted game of desire and deception.

In the heart of the Cavalieri family, I am the son destined for a loveless marriage.

The true legacy of my family, my birthright ties me to a woman I despise.

The daughter of the mafia boss who nearly ended my family.

She is my future wife, and I am her unwelcome groom.

The looming wedding is a beacon of hope for our families.

A promise of peace in a world fraught with danger and deception.

We were meant to be the bridge between two powerful legacies.

The only thing we share is a mutual hatred.

She is a prisoner to her families' ambitions, desperate for a way out.

My duty is to guard her, to ensure she doesn't escape her gilded cage.

But every moment spent with her, every spark of anger, adds fuel to the growing fire of desire between us.

We're trapped in a dangerous duel of passion and fury.

The more I try to tame her, the more she ignites me.

Hatred and desire become blurred.

Our impending marriage becomes a twisted game.

But as the wedding draws near, my suspicions grow.

My bride is not who she claims to be.

IVANOV CRIME FAMILY TRILOGY

A Dark Mafia Romance

Savage Vow

Ivanov Crime Family, Book One

Gregor & Samara's story

I took her innocence as payment.

She was far too young and naïve to be betrothed to a monster like me.

I would bring only pain and darkness into her sheltered world.

That's why she ran.

I should've just let her go…

She never asked to marry into a powerful Russian mafia family.

None of this was her choice.

Unfortunately for her, I don't care.

I own her… and after three years of searching… I've found her.

My runaway bride was about to learn disobedience has consequences…
punishing ones.

Having her in my arms and under my control had become an obsession.

Nothing was going to keep me from claiming her before the eyes of
God and man.

She's finally mine… and I'm never letting her go.

Vicious Oath

Ivanov Crime Family, Book One

Damien & Yelena's story

When I give an order, I expect it to be obeyed.

She's too smart for her own good, and it's going to get her killed.

Against my better judgement, I put her under the protection of my powerful Russian mafia family.

So imagine my anger when the little minx ran.

For three long years I've been on her trail, always one step behind.

Finding and claiming her had become an obsession.

It was getting harder to rein in my driving need to possess her… to own her.

But now the chase is over.

I've found her.

Soon she will be mine.

And I plan to make it official, even if I have to drag her kicking and screaming to the altar.

This time… there will be no escape from me.

Betrayed Honor

Ivanov Crime Family, Book One

Mikhail & Nadia's story

Her innocence was going to get her killed.

That was if I didn't get to her first.

She's the protected little sister of the powerful Ivanov Russian mafia family - the very definition of forbidden.

It's always been my job, as their Head of Security, to watch over her but never to touch.

That ends today.

She disobeyed me and put herself in danger.

It was time to take her in hand.

I'm the only one who can save her and I will fight anyone who tries to stop me, including her brothers.

Honor and loyalty be damned.

She's mine now.

RUTHLESS OBSESSION SERIES

A Dark Mafia Romance

Sweet Cruelty

Ruthless Obsession Series, Book One

Dimitri & Emma's story

It was an innocent mistake.

She knocked on the wrong door.

Mine.

If I were a better man, I would've just let her go.

But I'm not.

I'm a cruel bastard.

I ruthlessly claimed her virtue for my own.

It should have been enough.

But it wasn't.

I needed more.

Craved it.

She became my obsession.

Her sweetness and purity taunted my dark soul.

The need to possess her nearly drove me mad.

A Russian arms dealer had no business pursuing a naive librarian student.

She didn't belong in my world.

I would bring her only pain.

But it was too late…

She was mine and I was keeping her.

Sweet Depravity

Ruthless Obsession Series, Book Two

Vaska & Mary's story

The moment she opened those gorgeous red lips to tell me no, she was mine.

I was a powerful Russian arms dealer and she was an innocent schoolteacher.

If she had a choice, she'd run as far away from me as possible.

Unfortunately for her, I wasn't giving her one.

I wasn't just going to take her; I was going to take over her entire world.

Where she lived.

What she ate.

Where she worked.

All would be under my control.

Call it obsession.

Call it depravity.

I don't give a damn… as long as you call her mine.

Sweet Savagery

Ruthless Obsession Series, Book Three

Ivan & Dylan's Story

I was a savage bent on claiming her as punishment for her family's mistakes.

As a powerful Russian Arms dealer, no one steals from me and gets away with it.

She was an innocent pawn in a dangerous game.

She had no idea the package her uncle sent her from Russia contained my stolen money.

If I were a good man, I would let her return the money and leave.

If I were a gentleman, I might even let her keep some of it just for frightening her.

As I stared down at the beautiful living doll stretched out before me like a virgin sacrifice,

I thanked God for every sin and misdeed that had blackened my cold heart.

I was not a good man.

I sure as hell wasn't a gentleman… and I had no intention of letting her go.

She was mine now.

And no one takes what's mine.

Sweet Brutality

Ruthless Obsession Series, Book Four

Maxim & Carinna's story

The more she fights me, the more I want her.

It's that beautiful, sassy mouth of hers.

It makes me want to push her to her knees and dominate her, like the brutal savage I am.

As a Russian Arms dealer, I should not be ruthlessly pursuing an innocent college student like her, but that would not stop me.

A twist of fate may have brought us together, but it is my twisted obsession that will hold her captive as my own treasured possession.

She is mine now.

I dare you to try and take her from me.

Sweet Ferocity

Ruthless Obsession Series, Book Five

Luka & Katie's Story

I was a mafia mercenary only hired to find her, but now I'm going to keep her.

She is a Russian mafia princess, kidnapped to be used as a pawn in a dangerous territory war.

Saving her was my job. Keeping her safe had become my obsession.

Every move she makes, I am in the shadows, watching.

I was like a feral animal: cruel, violent, and selfishly out for my own needs. Until her.

Now, I will make her mine by any means necessary.

I am her protector, but no one is going to protect her from me.

Sweet Intensity

Ruthless Obsession Series, Book Six

Antonius & Brynn's Story

She couldn't possibly have known the danger she would be in the moment she innocently accepted the job.

She was too young for a man my age, barely in her twenties. Far too pure and untouched.

Too bad that wasn't going to stop me.

The moment I laid eyes on her, I claimed her.

She would be mine… by any means necessary.

I owned the most elite Gambling Club in Chicago, which was a secret front for my true business as a powerful crime boss for the Russian Mafia.

And she was a fragile little bird, who had just flown straight into my open jaws.

Naïve and sweet, she was a tasty morsel I couldn't resist biting.

My intense drive to dominate and control her had become an obsession.

I would ruthlessly use my superior strength and connections to take over her life.

The harder she resisted, the more feral and savage I would become.

She needed to understand… she was mine now.

Mine.

Sweet Severity

Ruthless Obsession Series, Book Seven

Macarius & Phoebe's Story

Had she crashed into any other man's car, she could have walked away—but she hit mine.

Upon seeing the bruises on her wrist, I struggled to contain my rage.

Despite her objections, I refused to allow her to leave.

Whoever hurt this innocent beauty would pay dearly.

As a Russian Mafia crime boss who owns Chicago's most elite gambling club, I have very creative and painful methods of exacting revenge.

She seems too young and naive to be out on her own in such a dangerous world.

Needing a nanny, I decided to claim her for the role.

She might resist my severe, domineering discipline, but I won't give her a choice in the matter.

She needs a protector, and I'd be damned if it were anyone but me.

Resisting the urge to claim her will test all my restraint.

It's a battle I'm bound to lose.

With each day, my obsession and jealousy intensify.

It's only a matter of time before my control snaps…and I make her mine.

Mine.

Sweet Animosity

Ruthless Obsession, Book Eight

Varlaam & Amber's Story

I never asked for an assistant, and if I had, I sure as hell wouldn't have chosen her.

With her sharp tongue and lack of discipline, what she needs is a firm hand, not a job.

The more she tests my limits, the more tempted I am to bend her over my knee.

As a Russian Mafia boss and owner of Chicago's most elite gambling club, I can't afford distractions from her antics.

Or her secrets.

For I suspect, my innocent new assistant is hiding something.

And I know just how to get to the truth.

It's high time she understands who holds the power in our relationship.

To ensure I get what I desire, I'll keep her close, controlling her every move.

Except I am no longer after information—I want her mind, body and soul.

She underestimated the stakes of our dangerous game and now owes a heavy price.

As payment I will take her freedom.

She's mine now.

Mine.

ABOUT ALTA HENSLEY

Alta Hensley is a USA TODAY Bestselling author of hot, dark and dirty romance. She is also an Amazon Top 10 bestselling author. Being a multi-published author in the romance genre, Alta is known for her dark, gritty alpha heroes, captivating love stories, hot eroticism, and engaging tales of the constant struggle between dominance and submission.

She lives in Astoria, Oregon with her husband, two daughters, and an Australian Shepherd. When she isn't walking the coastline, and drinking beer in her favorite breweries, she is writing about villains who always get their love story and happily ever after.

ALSO BY ALTA HENSLEY

HEATHENS HOLLOW SERIES

A Dark Stalker Billionaire Romance

Heathens

She invited the darkness in, so she'll have no one else to blame when I come for her.

The Hunt.

It is a sinister game of submission. She'll run. I'll chase.

And when I catch her, it will be savage. Untamed. Primal.

I will be the beast from her darkest fantasies.

I should be protecting her, but instead I've been watching her. Stalking her.

She's innocent. Forbidden. The daughter of my best friend.

But she chose this.

And even if she made a mistake, even if she wants to run, to escape, it's far too late.

She's mine now.

GODS AMONG MEN SERIES

A Dark Billionaire Romance

Villains Are Made

I know how villains are made.

I've watched their secrets rise from the ashes and emerge from the shadows.

As part of a family tree with roots so twisted, I'm strangled by their vine.

Imprisoned in a world of decadence and sin, I've seen Gods among men.

And he is one of them.

He is the villain.

He is the enemy who demands to be the lover.

He is the monster who has shown me pleasure but gives so much pain.

But something has changed…

He's different.

Darker.

Wildly possessive as his obsession with me grows to an inferno that can't be controlled.

Yes… he is the villain.

And he is the end of my beginning.

Monsters Are Hidden

The problem with secrets is they create powerful monsters.

And even more dangerous enemies.

He's the keeper of all his family's secrets, the watcher of all.

He knows what I've done, what I've risked… the deadly choice I made.

The tangled vines of his mighty family tree are strangling me.

There is no escape.

I am locked away, captive to his twisted obsession and demands.

If I run, my hell will never end.

If I stay, he will devour me.

My only choice is to dare the monster to come out into the light,
before his darkness destroys us both.

Yes… he is the monster in hiding.
And he is the end of my beginning.

Vipers Are Forbidden

It's impossible to enter a pit full of snakes and not get bit.

Until you meet me, that is.

My venom is far more toxic than the four men who have declared me
their enemy.

They seek vengeance and launch a twisted game of give and take.

I'll play in their dark world, because it's where I thrive.

I'll dance with their debauchery, for I surely know the steps.

But then I discover just how wrong I am. Their four, not only matches,
but beats, my one.

With each wicked move they make, they become my obsession.

I crave them until they consume all thought.

The temptation to give them everything they desire becomes too much.

I'm entering their world, and there is no light to guide my way. My
blindness full of lust will be my defeat.

Yes… I am the viper and am forbidden.

But they are the end of my beginning.

SPIKED ROSES BILLIONAIRE'S CLUB SERIES

A Dark Billionaires Romance

Bastards & Whiskey

I sit amongst the Presidents, Royalty, the Captains of Industry, and the wealthiest men in the world.

We own Spiked Roses—an exclusive, membership only establishment in New Orleans where money or lineage is the only way in. It is for the gentlemen who own everything and never hear the word no.

Sipping on whiskey, smoking cigars, and conducting multi-million dollar deals in our own personal playground of indulgence, there isn't anything I can't have… and that includes HER. I can also have HER if I want.

And I want.

Villains & Vodka

My life is one long fevered dream, balancing between being killed or killing.

The name Harley Crow is one to be feared.

I am an assassin.

A killer.

The villain.

I own it. I choose this life. Hell, I crave it. I hunger for it. The smell of fear makes me hard and is the very reason the blood runs through my veins.

Until I meet her…

Marlowe Masters.

Her darkness matches my own.

In my twisted world of dancing along the jagged edge of the blade…

She changes everything.

No weapon can protect me from the kind of death she will ultimately deliver.

Scoundrels & Scotch

I'll stop at nothing to own her.

I'm a collector of dolls.

All kinds of dolls.

So beautiful and sexy, they become my art.

So perfect and flawless, my art galleries are flooded by the wealthy to gaze upon my possessions with envy.

So fragile and delicate, I keep them tucked away for safety.

The dark and torrid tales of Drayton's Dolls run rampant through the rich and famous, and all but a few are true.

Normally I share my dolls for others to play with or watch on display.

But not my special doll.

No, not her.

Ivy is the most precious doll of all.

She's mine. All mine.

Devils & Rye

Forbidden fruit tastes the sweetest.

It had been years since I had seen her.

Years since I last saw those eyes with pure, raw innocence.

So much time had passed since I lusted after what I knew I should resist.

But she was so right.

And I was so wrong.

To claim her as mine was breaking the rules. Boundaries should not be broken. But temptation weakens my resolve.

With the pull of my dark desires…

I know that I can't hide from my sinful thoughts—and actions—forever.

Beasts & Bourbon

My royal blood flows black with twisted secrets.

I am a beast who wears a crown.

Heir to a modern kingdom cloaked in corruption and depravities.

The time has come to claim my princess.

An innocent hidden away from my dark world.

Till now.

Her initiation will require sacrifice and submission.

There is no escaping the chains which bind her to me.

Surrendering to my torment, as well as my protection, is her only path to survival.

In the end…

She will be forever mine.

Sinners & Gin

My power is absolute. My rules are law.

Structure.

Obedience.

Discipline.

I am in charge, and what I say goes. Black and white with no gray.

No one dares break the rules in my dark and twisted world… until her. Until she makes me cross my own jagged lines.

She's untouched. Perfection. Pure.

Forbidden.

She tests my limits in all ways.

There is only one option left.

I will claim her as mine no matter how many rules are broken.

THANK YOU

Stormy Night Publications would like to thank you for your interest in our books.

If you liked this book (or even if you didn't), we would really appreciate you leaving a review on the site where you purchased it. Reviews provide useful feedback for us and our authors, and this feedback (both positive comments and constructive criticism) allows us to work even harder to make sure we provide the content our customers want to read.

Made in the USA
Middletown, DE
13 June 2024

55706673R00181